# Sherlock Holmes:
## The Affair at Mayerling Lodge

# Sherlock Holmes:
## The Affair at Mayerling Lodge

John Lawrence

*Belanger Books*
2023

**Sherlock Holmes: The Affair at Mayerling Lodge**
© 2023 by Belanger Books
© 2023 by John Lawrence

*Print and Digital Edition © 2023 by Belanger Books, LLC All Rights Reserved. No part of this book may be used or reproduced in any manner whatsoever without written permission except in case of brief quotations embodied in critical articles or reviews.*

*This book is a work of fiction. Names, characters, businesses, organizations, places, events, and incidents either are the product of the author's imagination or are used fictitiously. Any resemblance to actual persons, living or dead, events, or locales is entirely coincidental.*

For information contact:
**Belanger Books, LLC**
61 Theresa Ct.
Manchester, NH 03103

derrick@belangerbooks.com
www.belangerbooks.com

Cover and Design by Brian Belanger
*www.belangerbooks.com and www.redbubble.com/people/zhahadun*

# Table of Contents

Preface ............................................................................................. 9
Preface by the Editor ....................................................................... 11
Main Characters ............................................................................. 13
Introduction .................................................................................... 15
Chapter 1: The Prime Minister Comes Calling ................................ 18
Chapter 2: An Audience with the Emperor ...................................... 31
Chapter 3: The Fiacre Bratfisch ....................................................... 40
Chapter 4: Dinner at the Hofburg Palace ......................................... 44
Chapter 5: The Tragedy ................................................................... 52
Chapter 6: The Locked Room ......................................................... 56
Chapter 7: A Gruesome Examination .............................................. 64
Chapter 8: Seeds of Doubt .............................................................. 83
Chapter 9: A Curious Angle ............................................................ 94
Chapter 10: The Second Bullet ...................................................... 101
Chapter 11: A Visit to Mizzi Kaspar .............................................. 107
Chapter 12: The Go-Between ........................................................ 121
Chapter 13: The Hungarian Question ............................................ 137
Chapter 14: A Terse Interview with Hoyos .................................... 150
Chapter 15: Disposing of Mary Vetsera ........................................ 155
Chapter 16: The Crown Princess' Account ................................... 159
Chapter 17: The Sealed Box .......................................................... 167
Chapter 18: The Case Thus Far ..................................................... 178
Chapter 19: A Warning from President Taaffe .............................. 184
Chapter 20: Albrecht, Duke of Teschen ........................................ 190

Chapter 21: The Missing Witness ...................................................... 198
Chapter 22: Holmes Makes a Diagnosis ........................................... 201
Chapter 23: An Unanticipated Arrival ............................................... 205
Chapter 24: A Summons is Issued ..................................................... 215
Chapter 25: Holmes Explains............................................................. 240
Chapter 26: A Shocking Appearance ................................................. 254
Chapter 27: The Confession............................................................... 264
Chapter 28: The Aftermath ................................................................ 268
For Further Reference: A Selected Bibliography .............................. 284

# Preface

## By Ronald Grigor Suny

University of Michigan

### The Family Firm

"The Affair at Mayerling Lodge" centers on a mystery that has bewildered historians for over 134 years. Integral to the tale that Dr Watson tells is the precarious state of the Hapsburgs at the end of the 19th century, and so some historical background is helpful to help readers understand the emperors, archdukes, baronesses, countesses and other members of the royal family and the Empire they ruled.

A great state made up of diverse peoples with disjointed histories, the Hapsburg Empire was cobbled together by conjugal empire-building -- marriages of Princes and Princesses -- from the sixteenth century into the early twentieth. What held the scattered lands of the Habsburgs together was the dynastic principle: legitimacy conferred by rights of the ruler enforced by force when necessary. Sovereignty was conveyed from above, not by the people, perhaps by God, more often by inertia and tradition. For almost 400 years, the empire managed to cultivate devotion, or at least acquiescence, from its subjects, but by the late nineteenth century, when this story takes place, nationalists maintained that the Empire ruled by Franz Joseph had become anachronistic and doomed to decline and collapse.

The trend towards nationalism was affecting far more than the Hapsburgs, but in the last decades of the nineteenth century, the imperial families of eastern Europe – the Romanovs in Russia, the Ottomans in the Balkans, Anatolia, and the Middle East, and the Hapsburgs perched precariously between them – were not ready to give up or give in to rising nationalism. They worked hard to keep up the glittering facade. Palaces, smartly uniformed soldiers, and the pomp of imperial ceremonies were designed to awe the common folk, to keep them at a distance and off the streets.

In this context, the concerns of Emperor Franz Joseph and his advisors about the emergence of reformist sentiments within the Hofburg palace were understandable. If the ruling family faltered, the damage could be irreparable. Franz Joseph had enough troubles with his Hungarian subjects and the Slavs in the peripheries of his empire. But he also had to deal with his irascible wife, the Empress Elisabeth, herself the subject of several contemporary films, and his son Crown Prince Rudolf, the heir to the throne. Since clear, indisputable dynastic succession was the guarantee of imperial legitimacy, the Emperor had reason for grave concern should Rudolf, who as yet had produced no son, challenge the Empire that his family had spent centuries building and defending. The tragedy that unfolded at Mayerling Lodge therefore was not an isolated event, but a telling moment in a series of historical developments that would culminate with the outbreak of World War I and the subsequent unraveling of the Hapsburg Empire.

# Preface by the Editor

For nearly a century and a half, what actually occurred at the Mayerling hunting lodge just outside Vienna on the morning of 30 January 1889 has been one of the great unsolved mysteries involving the royal families of the nineteenth century. Since the shocking discoveries, there has been no end to the speculation about what transpired in that locked bedroom. The aftermath of the tragedy shook the Austrian Empire, setting in motion geopolitical and military forces that ultimately shredded longstanding alliances among European nations and their leaders. The fracturing of those tenuous diplomatic and personal relationships helped lay the groundwork for unparalleled tragedy in the early 20$^{th}$ century.

In 1992, more than a century after the horrible events occurred, the son and heir of the last Emperor of Austria, Karl I, addressed the still-unresolved mystery concerning these long-ago events.

"As long as I live, the secret of Mayerling will not be completely solved," declared Archduke Otto, hinting that an undisclosed "secret" did, in fact, exist. Yet thirty years later, after additional decades of speculation, investigation and even exhumation, definitive answers continue to elude all those who have delved into the mystery.

Those hoping for a definitive explanation of the case were ecstatic to learn in 2015 that several letters and papers in the original hand of one of the victims in the drama, Baroness Mary Vetsera, remarkably had been discovered in a leather-bound folder, still sealed with the insignia of Crown Prince Rudolf. The folder had been locked in a safe deposit box in the private Schoeller bank in Vienna and might easily have gone undiscovered for another century. However, when the contents of the folder were read, the papers offered few facts or insights that might help to resolve the unanswered questions.

That discovery was the most significant development in the Mayerling case in over a century, until archivists at Cox and Company in London discovered, shortly after the outbreak of the Great COVID Pandemic in early 2020, the manuscript that follows. After an exhaustive clearance process in London, Vienna and Budapest, its authenticity has been confirmed and permission was finally granted by the respective governments to allow its publication.

The manuscript was written by Dr John H. Watson, the well-known chronicler of the cases of Sherlock Holmes, the famed British detective. Watson wrote this account in the midst of the First World War, nearly three decades after the events it describes had occurred. Concerned about the impact of these revelations during the Great War and its troubled aftermath, he declined to publish the account during his lifetime and left strict instructions that it remain unpublished until long after all those mentioned in the story were long gone.

The editor and publishers have agreed that now, over a century after it was written, the time is appropriate to share Dr Watson's account with the public. Presented herein for the first time, therefore, is an account of the hitherto unacknowledged role of the world's greatest consulting detective in the unraveling of Europe's greatest enduring mystery, "The Affair at Mayerling Lodge."

I am grateful to my friend, the distinguished historian Professor Ronald Grigor Suny of the University of Michigan, who has written the Foreword to this book, and to Germanic scholar Daniel M. Lawrence, whose expert advice has greatly contributed to my own efforts as editor of this extraordinary document.

John Lawrence, Editor

# Main Characters

**Franz Joseph** (1830-1916), Emperor of Austria and King of Hungary

**Elisabeth** (1837-1898), Empress of Austria and Queen of Hungary

**Rudolf** (1858-1889), Crown Prince of Austria, Prince Royal of Hungary and Bohemia

**Stéphanie** (1864-1945), Crown Princess of Austria, Hungary and Bohemia

**Mary Alexandrine Freiin von Vetsera** (1871-1889), Baroness and mistress of Rudolf

**Marie Louise Larisch von Moennich** (1858-1940), Countess and cousin to Rudolf

**Mizzi Kaspar** (1864-1907), actress and mistress of Rudolf

**Albrecht Friedrich Rudolf Dominik** (1817-1895), Duke of Teschen, Field Marshall in the Armies of Austria-Hungary and Germany, Inspector General of the Austrian Army

**Karl Ludwig Josef Maria** (1833-1896), an Archduke of Austria, brother of Franz Joseph

**Count Joseph of Hoyos-Sprinzenstein** (1839-1899), Rudolf's friend and hunting companion

**Prince Philipp Maria August Raphael of Saxe-Coburg and Gotha** (1844-1921)

**Hermann Freiherrn von Widerhofer** (1832-1901), personal physician to the Crown Prince

**Johann Loschek** (1845-1932), valet to Rudolf

**Josef Bratfisch** (1847-1892), fiacre (carriage driver) to Rudolf and virtuoso whistler

**Archduke Johann Salvator of Tuscany, Prince of Austria, Prince of Hungary, Bohemia and Tuscany** (1852-1890), cousin to Crown Prince Rudolf

# Introduction

## By John Watson, M.D.

The death of the aged Emperor of Austria Franz Joseph on the 21$^{st}$ of last month [*Editor*: November, 1916] – at the advanced age of 86 – and the shocking assassination of Austrian Prime Minister Karl Count Stürgkh one month earlier have persuaded me to reconsider my decision to refrain from writing down my account of the controversial incidents that occurred at the royal Mayerling hunting lodge nearly three decades ago. Unquestionably, the tragedy has remained one of the most confounding mysteries of the 19$^{th}$ century and questions about exactly what transpired during the night of 30 January 1889 have long remained the subject of wild speculation.

  Over the years, many devotees of my writings have remarked that the unresolved mystery was a case worthy of my friend Sherlock Holmes, the world's first (and deservedly most acclaimed) private consulting detective. As I had agreed upon with Holmes at the time the case occurred, I would bite my tongue upon hearing such comments and agree that this calamity represented a missed opportunity for the great sleuth of Baker Street. But in fact, Holmes and I were very much engaged in investigating the events at Mayerling lodge and indeed, the case was undoubtedly one of the most remarkable (and clandestine) of his illustrious career.

  Many of the faces and events remain as vivid in my mind today as they were at the time. Pouring through my notes and the newspaper clippings of the period has, at long last, convinced me to set down the details of this complex and consequential case whilst I still have the faculties to do so accurately. Indeed, this Great War [*Editor*: Watson refers here to what today we know as World War I] has created so much exhaustion, tragedy and loss; who amongst us can even be sure if the history of its origins, stretching back so many years to Mayerling, will be of any interest to readers of the future?

For reasons that will become all too evident as the details of this case are revealed, I have faithfully complied with requests to refrain from prematurely the intrigues that, even at the time, appeared to hold such grave implications for the future of peace across the continent. Nevertheless, I have spent some time over the past weeks engaged in the endeavour of writing down this complete account, with the intention that it will reside under seal in my private box at Cox and Company in London until such time as my executors agree the time is propitious for the world to learn what transpired all those years ago, and Holmes' role in the inquiry.

With the death of the Emperor, nearly all the principal figures in the story have departed this Earth save Holmes and myself; those still amongst the living have ensconced themselves in remote areas (some seeking anonymity through new identities) to escape any association with the events at Mayerling lodge. The fate of others remains tantalizingly unknown.

For many who pay insufficient attention to the details of international affairs, and I would include myself among those ranks, the rapid decline of the world into unparalleled war following the horrific events in Sarajevo on 28 June 1914 may seem to have been precipitated by the incomprehensible action of a solitary madman. But to those knowledgeable of the corrosion eating away at many of the royal houses of Europe, the catastrophe that took the life of the Archduke Franz Ferdinand (like the incident at Mayerling years earlier) was the outgrowth of several decades of intrigue upon intrigue, concluding in a rapid decline into a war so terrible as to dwarf all previous conflicts and hopefully militate against those wars still to come.

John H. Watson, M.D.<br>London, 23 December 1916<br>January, 1889

*The guests in their opulent finery, glittering jewels strung around their necks and dazzling on their long fingers, filled the large ballroom at the German embassy in Vienna. At one end of the ornate hall, a quartet of string musicians bowed their way through a half-completed version of Strauss' new Kaiser Waltz that the composer was preparing for Austrian Emperor Franz Joseph to present to his German counterpart Wilhelm II later that year. An elegant young woman, immediately recognized as the Austrian Crown Princess Stephanie, pressed her way through the dancing couples, her eyes darting about purposefully. Finally they located the person she was seeking, her husband, Crown Prince Rudolf, as he entered the ballroom in the company of a beautiful young woman.*

*Stephanie's pace quickened and she drew herself up to her husband, who seemed more annoyed than startled by her sudden appearance. "I wish to return to the palace immediately," she firmly declared loudly enough to draw the attention of several couples standing near the Crown Prince. "If you do not mind, please fetch me my cloak!"*

*A look of anger flashed across Rudolf's face. "Go to blazes with your silly cloak!" he seethed at his wife. As the startled guests looked on, the Crown Prince of Austria turned on his heels and disappeared into the whirling couples filling the dance floor....*

# Chapter 1: The Prime Minister Comes Calling

The Christmas season of 1888 had been marked by uncomfortably cold temperatures in London, leading most residents to spend as much time as possible in their sitting room enjoying the comfort of a blazing fireplace. Unfortunately, the bone-chilling unpleasantry was unaccompanied by snow that might have added some cheer to the holidays (at least until the soot from the chimneys and muck of the streets turned its brilliant white to a dismal black).

Several cases of significant interest had occupied my friend and fellow lodger, Mr Sherlock Holmes, the famed private consulting detective, during the preceding twelve months. The sinister plot to sabotage the holiday season of the haggis producers of Dundee, Scotland by poisoning the lamb's pluck on the farm of Limus McGregor is one I will doubtless record at a future date. The terrifying case of the Baskerville family's dreadful hound had been resolved just weeks before the harsh winter set in.

It was in the third week of the new year of 1889, shortly before my marriage to Mary Morstan was to take place and occasion my departure from the rooms I shared with Holmes at 221$^B$ Baker Street. The frigid weather, perhaps combined with the holiday spirit, evidently had discouraged most of London's criminals from undertaking the nefarious activities that typically drew the attention of the renowned detective. The resulting absence of cases had afforded me time to pack up clothing, several years of accumulated mementos, medical books and various other odds and ends in preparation for my impending departure. Holmes devoted the overcast days to puttering about with several noxious chemical experiments that drove Mrs Hudson, our housekeeper, and sometimes even myself, into the cold to seek refuge from the offensive odors of the sitting room that also served as his laboratory.

## Chapter 1: The Prime Minister Comes Calling

On this particular morning, the Bunsen burners mercifully had not yet been lit and we were finishing our second cup of coffee whilst perusing the newspapers. I occupied a well-used stuffed chair directly before the glowing hearth while Holmes sat closer to the window, allowing him to gaze out periodically onto Baker Street in hopes of identifying a prospective client who was contemplating ringing our bell.

I had allowed my thoughts to ramble, lulled into a grey haze by the warmth of the fire and the mellow orange glow of the coals in the hearth. Indeed, I had nearly drifted off into a mid-morning nap when I was startled awake by the vigorous sawing of Holmes on his violin. The familiar melody ceased and he dropped his instrument into his lap, regarding me with a sly smile.

"I agree, Watson! Bach's 5th Brandenburg concerto is certainly an inspired piece of music. I hope my humble rendition meets with your approval." The astonished look on my face caused his thin lips to curl into an involuntarily self-satisfied grin.

"By all that is holy, Holmes," I cried. "have you now added mindreading to your formidable list of talents? How could you possibly know what I was thinking? Why, I was barely awake enough to note it myself. You played this trick on me some years ago when I was musing about the futility of war and gave away my thoughts by touching my war wound, but this![1] I was not even moving a finger and yet you accurately broke into my thoughts with that infernal violin of yours, playing the very tune of which I was thinking!"

Holmes's wounded face told me I had overstepped in my critique of his mastery of the violin and I regretted my comment immediately.

"My deepest apologies, Holmes," I quickly proffered. "You startled me awake. Indeed, your mastery of Bach was quite impressive.

---

[1] Holmes performs this example of deduction in the short story, "The Resident Patient."

## Chapter 1: The Prime Minister Comes Calling

But how could you have known I was thinking of the concerto in D major?"

"Well, at least my feeble efforts were recognizable!" he said with a laugh. "Alright, I will tell you the progression of my thoughts, which consumed only a fraction of a second before I reached for my violin and bow.

"You will recall that we recently attended a splendid recital of the Marderosian string quartet at which Bach was the featured composer. This being the holiday season, the Brandenburg concertos unsurprisingly made an appearance on the program. As I sat here moments ago, disapprovingly noting your descent into a state of slumber at not quite half nine in the morning, I could not help but be drawn to your fingers as they tapped out a silent tune on the arms of your chair. I decided it would be challenging to attempt to determine what the melody might be and then to play it for you on the violin in an attempt to interrupt your reverie."

"Yes, but we attended the Bach concert nearly a week ago and yet you were able to relate the program to my finger tapping this morning! How could you possibly have drawn the conclusion that I was thinking of the 5th concerto?"

"Child's play, Watson, I assure you. The delightful opening bars of the 5th are quite distinct in the musical canon." He hummed the staccato notes.

*Dum dum dum dum*
*da-da-da-da-da-da-da-da*
*Dum dum dum da-da-da dum dum!*

"Forgive me, my dear friend, but contrary to your insistence, you most certainly *did* move your fingers quite rhythmically and they have disclosed your thoughts. The discrete tune you were tapping out so enthusiastically on the chair arm was as discernible to me as if you

## Chapter 1: The Prime Minister Comes Calling

were seated at Bach's own harpsichord and playing the concerto. Indeed, I decided to join your performance on the violin."

I looked at my hand reproachfully for having betrayed my private thoughts and shook my head in disbelief.

"Why, I suppose your next deductive miracle will be to predict the identity of the next client to arrive at our door." I regretted having made the prediction as soon as it had escaped my lips.

Holmes cast a look outside to Baker Street and turned back towards me. As if on cue, the downstairs bell rang, followed by the front door opening and closing noisily. There was the audible sound of murmuring voices in the vestibule and then the sound of heavy footsteps carefully lumbering up each of the 17 stairs to our rooms.

Our visitor had no sooner set foot on the landing than Holmes abruptly stood and called out loudly enough to be heard through the closed door,

"No need to knock, Prime Minister, please, come right in!" After a momentary pause, the door flew open and through it strode our distinguished visitor. Astonished as much by the accuracy of Holmes's prediction as by the great statesman who strode across the threshold, I sprang to my feet.

Robert Arthur Talbot Gascoyne-Cecil, 3rd Marquess of Salisbury, stood before us. Heavy-lidded eyes below a hairless pate surveyed the room with a serious and distinctly disapproving gaze. The nearly imperceptible flaring of his nostrils signaled that the stench of Holmes's chemistry experiments from the previous day had not yet dissipated as completely as one might have hoped prior to the arrival of guests.

He was a formidable figure, made all the more so by his heavy beard, somber mien and massive bulk, and it required several moments for him to catch his breath after the exertion of climbing up to the first story. He turned and shut the door behind him and returned his gaze to Holmes, who stood mutely regarding the eminent visitor.

*Chapter 1: The Prime Minister Comes Calling*

"I have been made aware of your deductive powers," he said without offering a salutation and pausing to catch his breath, "our common acquaintance at the Diogenes Club." His discrete reference could only have meant Holmes's older brother, Mycroft, a denizen of the aforementioned club and an invaluable (although generally unacknowledged) advisor to the British government for some time. I had not even been aware of his existence until the prior year, when we met during the matter of the Greek interpreter. Mycroft almost never ventured far from the exclusive London club and the company of its members, a highly confidential group of men of enormous wealth, standing and influence who were prohibited from speaking to each other within its walls.

Holmes motioned in my direction.

"May I present my good friend and the indefatigable chronicler of my work, Dr John Watson?" he said.

The Prime Minister indifferently acknowledged my introduction.

"The matter that brings me to your door is of the greatest consequence," he said, looking askance at me, "*and* confidentiality. I would prefer our conversation be limited to the two of us, if you do not mind," he said.

I opened my mouth to acquiesce to his reasonable request but I was cut off abruptly by Holmes.

"But I most definitely *do* mind," Holmes declared. "Perhaps I did not make myself clear," he added crisply. "I do not engage in consequential matters without the collaboration of my entirely trustworthy and supremely knowledgeable colleague. And I can only imagine that whatever has brought you to my rooms so early this morning must certainly be most consequential."

I admit Holmes's uncharacteristically gracious words led me to stand straighter than normally and to push out my chest a bit. Lord Salisbury stared back at the detective and then at me before evidently deciding not to contest the point.

*Chapter 1: The Prime Minister Comes Calling*

"It is just that it is so difficult to keep confidential matters secret," he said. "For example, how came you to know it was I at your door? My visit was meticulously planned to be utterly clandestine. Who violated that confidentiality and gave you advanced notice of my visit?" He looked accusingly in my direction, as though I had had the faintest notion of his impending arrival.

Holmes betrayed an almost undetectable smile and motioned for Lord Salisbury to take a seat by the fire. He pointed to the newspaper which lay on the floor near the chair into which he descended once again.

"The newspaper gave away your visit to my humble quarters, Your Grace," he responded, picking up the scattered pages from the carpet. "There are several stories this morning raising alarms about political developments on the Continent that might impact British interests. It is early morning, a very official looking carriage has arrived at my lodgings, a large man exits the cab and is admitted to my residence and immediately sent upstairs without being announced or accompanied by Mrs Hudson."

"How did you know that?" I asked.

"I have had enough experience to recognize the footsteps of our reliable Mrs Hudson as she escorts a visitor to my rooms," he replied. "If our guest was permitted to ascend the stairs alone, he must be either someone well known to me – very unlikely given the early hour – or someone whose prominence commands deference to his wishes, however unconventional. The heaviness of the steps established quite distinctly that the visitor was a man of, forgive me, considerable size.

"There was a remote chance the step might have been that of my brother Mycroft, but his visits to these lodgings have been infrequent and, at this hour of the morning, non-existent. Given this morning's troubling headlines, I deduced I was being visited by none other than the Marquess of Salisbury, Prime Minister and foreign secretary of Great Britain," he said to our visitor, "here to see me of matters both consequential and confidential."

*Chapter 1: The Prime Minister Comes Calling*

"Quite an impressive guess," the politician responded.

A dark cloud fluttered across Holmes's face and he gave a little start. "I never *guess*," he gently corrected our visitor. "May I offer you some coffee while you explain the reason for your visit?"

Lord Salisbury nodded in approval and Holmes handed him a cup of steaming coffee.

"You are quite right, Mr Holmes, I have come because I require your assistance on a matter of some considerable urgency and discretion." He cast another censorious glance at my notebook and pen, which commanded that I suspend my usual practice of taking notes.

"All of us at Whitehall are aware of your recent actions on behalf of the king of Bohemia, and we appreciate your discretion in keeping the matter out of the press."

"Of course, I cannot comment upon my past cases," Holmes declared, looking quickly but disapprovingly in my direction. "That is a task that seems to have been taken up with some enthusiasm by my unofficial biographer in the penny weeklies. However, yes, I can confirm my success in resolving a small matter in Bohemia that landed upon my doorstep last year." Although Holmes would offer no greater details about his services to the Grand Duke of Cassel-Felstein and his indiscrete involvement with the famed opera singer Irene Adler, I was already writing an account of this case. "A Scandal in Bohemia" was planned for publication once the troubled political waters had calmed.[2]

"I do not wish to pry into your private business, Mr Holmes," Salisbury assured. "However, I assure you, the matter on which I seek your advice and counsel is highly consequential to the security of all of Europe."

"I confess your words do intrigue me, Lord Salisbury," Holmes replied. "What precisely is it that you wish me to do?"

---

[2] Editor: The story would be published a year and a half after this current case, in June, 1891 in "The Strand" magazine.

*Chapter 1: The Prime Minister Comes Calling*

"You must go to Vienna immediately to meet with the Emperor Franz Joseph. He is about to make a most consequential visit to Hungary, a somewhat unstable portion of his domain, and wishes to consult with you prior to his departure about several serious threats looming against the Hapsburg dynasty."

Franz Joseph had ruled both Austria and Hungary, and several smaller European states, since the mid-century, having replaced an uncle who had abdicated following the revolutions that swept through Europe in 1848. In his forty years on the throne, he had proven a most conservative sovereign, resisting efforts from many quarters (including his wife, Elisabeth, and his son, the Crown Prince Rudolf) to embrace several modernizing, reformist measures. Agitation from several parts of the Empire, particularly Hungary, in favour of greater autonomy or even independence had done little to shake the Emperor's resolve or that of the band of elderly military officers and civilian advisors who dominated the royal court.

Holmes looked taken aback by the enormity of the charge.

"Surely that is a mission better suited to a trained diplomat from Whitehall," he responded, "or perhaps even the foreign minister," he added coyly. "My place of work is the crime scene, the laboratory and the police offices, not the palaces of Austrian royalty."

"The Emperor will not hear of it," Salisbury insisted. "He knows of your past services, your discretion, and your trustworthiness. He wishes to engage you in investigating whether saboteurs and traitors have infiltrated the Hofburg palace or the military. No one who formally represents the British government could possibly perform the work he envisions. The diplomatic risks are far too great."

"Surely there are detectives and police officials in Vienna," Holmes protested.

"The Emperor trusts no one within his own circle to provide him an unbiased assessment on such a delicate matter. Nor can he venture far from his most trusted circle."

## Chapter 1: The Prime Minister Comes Calling

Holmes considered the Prime Minister's words silently before speaking.

"What precisely is the task I am to undertake?" Holmes pressed.

"That can only be communicated to you by Franz Joseph himself," our guest responded. "But I can assure you that a dangerous instability is coursing through the royal houses of Europe, Holmes. The crowned heads are linked by an intricate web of marriages, alliances and rivalries. The intrigue has risen to a dangerous level and the entire continent has become a veritable powder keg awaiting a spark that could engender a conflation like nothing the world has ever seen."

"Why need we inject England into the sordid mess the Europeans have created for themselves?" I wondered, regretting my intervention in a conversation in which I was, at least by the Prime Minister, decidedly unwelcome.

"I share your aversion to involvement in foreign matters," he assured. "As reluctant as I am to pursuing complex international engagements, the modern age compels us to acknowledge our interdependence with the Europeans. Portions of our own Empire, after all, lie adjacent to one or more of these nations, and what transpires in Vienna or Berlin is likely to influence and impact our own security, if not today then invariably in the years to come. We have little choice but to engage with the Europeans."

"Very wise," I offered, drawing a sideways glance of disapproval from Holmes. "I must agree."

"The destabilization of the Austro-Hungarian Empire in particular would naturally raise the concern of any political leader concerned about maintaining peace in Europe. Your services, Mr Holmes, may well be all that stands between England and engagement in a catastrophe too horrible even to contemplate."

Holmes considered the weighty issues Lord Salisbury had raised. Lighting a long wooden match, he sucked several times on his churchwarden before blowing a puff of blue smoke in the direction of the fireplace.

## Chapter 1: The Prime Minister Comes Calling

"There are also personal considerations," Salisbury added. "Our own Queen is progenitor of most of the intermarriage schemes that stretch from Prussia to Austria, from Russia to Denmark. You are aware, I presume, that Archduke Rudolf, Franz Joseph's only son, is married to Princess Stephanie, daughter of King Leopold II of Belgium. She is a cousin to Her Majesty Queen Victoria."

"The study of heraldry is among my pastimes," Holmes sniffed. "Even a cursory familiarity with the subject assures a deep appreciation for the tangled connections of royal bloodlines. Why, just last year, I..." Holmes caught himself before he revealed his recent success in foiling a blackmail scheme against another notable member of a European royal family.

"Tug on any strand of that web, Mr Holmes and Dr Watson, and the whole of Europe may well unravel, with catastrophic results." His face took on grave expression. "And England will be unable to escape involvement.

"Do you know a great deal about the House of Hapsburg?" he inquired, referring to the dynasty that had dominated much of central Europe for six centuries.

"Their heraldry far better than their politics," Holmes replied indifferently.

The Prime Minister quickly noted that the Hapsburg line over the centuries had ruled not only Bohemia and Austria-Hungary, but Spain, Portugal and even Mexico (albeit only briefly and unhappily by Franz Joseph's younger brother, Maximilian, who had been executed by Mexican nationalists in 1867). Emperor Franz Joseph, an aging yet powerful monarch, and the rest of the Hapsburg royal family, had spawned men of varying competence and intelligence as well as women who had served as consorts to monarchs and other members of the continent's royal families. Speculation about a familial proclivity towards insanity was widespread.

"Europe is a festering cauldron of in-bred nationalists and egotists," Salisbury declared, "several of them as mad as a British

## Chapter 1: The Prime Minister Comes Calling

hatter, which is why I prefer that England have as little to do with all of them as possible." The Prime Minister's ambivalence to entanglements with the nation states of the continent was a well-known feature of his governing philosophy.

"And yet here you are, undoubtedly soliciting me to plunge head-first into that bubbling cauldron!" Holmes remarked. "May I ask why you evidently believe my services to Franz Joseph are of greater value than more conventional diplomatic approaches?"

"To be frank, you were most certainly not my first choice," he replied archly. "The Queen had attempted to engage Sir Augustus Paget – our ambassador in Vienna. But the Emperor insisted on Sherlock Holmes! It is your involvement, and yours alone, in which he has confidence. I assure you, his reasons escape me entirely.

"Fulfilling the request will require a relatively painless effort on your behalf. You may, of course, decline Her Majesty's entreaty," and here he paused to allow Holmes to contemplate the gravity of his words, although I suspect he appreciated the disinclination of Holmes to refuse any request from that great lady.

"I must advise you that the Queen believes that without your assistance, the simmering crisis in Vienna could escalate into something far more serious – perhaps even war."

"War?" I exclaimed with alarm. "That hardly sounds like a 'relatively painless' assignment for Holmes!"

*Chapter 1: The Prime Minister Comes Calling*

Emperor Franz Joseph of Austria-Hungary and Queen Victoria (1897)

    Salisbury once again ignored my comment.
    "Surely you must realize that in providing such invaluable aid to the Emperor, you would also aid in the gathering of intelligence about affairs on the Continent that would be of immense value to our own defence. You would gather 'all the details, however distressing they may be,' she put it to me." He handed Holmes a note on which the instructions had been written and waited expectantly. Holmes cursorily scanned the message and gazed into the fire. For a few tense moments, the clicking of the pipe on his teeth was the only sound in the room but for the occasional crackling and sizzling of the fire. He tucked the message into his pocket.
    "Your..." Salisbury hesitated. "*Our* mutual acquaintance at the Diogenes Club encouraged me to come to you directly with this proposition," he pressed. "Of course, if you wish to consult with him, I would certainly understand. But a decision must be forthcoming without procrastination as the situation grows more urgent by the day."
    "I typically have no hesitation declining an entreaty that comes from royalty," Holmes declared. His statement was undoubtedly true;

## Chapter 1: The Prime Minister Comes Calling

in the time we had shared quarters alone he had refused requests from no fewer than three kings, four princes, and several dukes and earls, as well as an archbishop or two. "But when *two* royal houses simultaneously request my services, I can find little justification for refusal."

I was thrilled he had reached this conclusion and even the stolid Salisbury could not contain himself, clapping his hands sharply as Holmes confirmed his engagement.

"Watson," he declared, "let us pack our trunks! We are off to Vienna in the morning."

Salisbury stood, a look of disapprobation on his large face, and waved his hand dismissively.

"No, sir," he insisted to Holmes, "I thought I had been quite explicit. Only *your* involvement is required."

"And I thought I had been quite clear, it will be the two of us or neither," Holmes replied as we rose in deference to the distinguished visitor. "I would not consider undertaking the case without the companionship and professional assistance of Dr Watson."

I was touched by Holmes's vote of confidence in my contribution to our partnership.

The stern look of disapproval from the minister left little doubt that he disliked being challenged by Holmes who, unlike hundreds of backbenchers in Parliament, refused to capitulate to his will. He regarded Holmes through eyes that had closed to a narrow slit.

"You have quite well-developed negotiating skills, Mr Holmes. Perhaps you should have taken up politics!"

"I prefer my role as a consulting detective," he replied with a sharp laugh. "I will leave politics to you."

# Chapter 2: An Audience with the Emperor

I spent the remainder of the day arranging for a medical colleague to see my scheduled patients during my brief absence. A more delicate endeavour was assuring my bride-to-be that the case was but a brief distraction and would in no way interfere with our scheduled nuptials. The sun was still low in the yellow London sky the following morning when Holmes and I boarded a cab to Victoria Station for the train to Dover. The roads were clear despite an overnight dusting of snow, and we reached the station with time to purchase several newspapers brimming with reports of developments unfolding on the Continent. We took note of one story referencing the growing tensions between Austria and Hungary and the speculation about a possible visit by the Emperor to Budapest to calm the growing agitation.

The ride to Dover was uneventful as was our ferry to Ostend on a mercifully calm Channel, which spared me the discomfort that would have led me to question the rather sizeable breakfast in which I had indulged. Soon we were mercifully once again on *terra firma*, ensconced in a comfortable compartment as our train whisked us through Brussels and then into Germany, through Cologne, Frankfurt and Nüremberg before crossing the Austrian border to Salzburg and finally into the Westbahnhof station in Vienna.

We had barely alighted from our train amid the bustle of a throng of weary travelers when we were approached by a military officer accompanied by a retinue of soldiers, all of whom sharply saluted us in a curt manner.

"Herr Holmes, I presume?" the officer questioned in English with a crisp accent, looking in my direction. "And Dr Watson as well?"

"I am Holmes," my friend confirmed, and this is indeed my companion and friend, Dr John Watson." With the efficiency for which

## Chapter 2: An Audience with the Emperor

the Germans are deservedly renowned, our bags were taken by the young soldiers while the officer motioned us towards the exit.

"I am Captain Hans Siegler, a member of the Emperor's guard, at your disposal" he explained as we walked with him. "I will take you to your hotel where you might wish to rest. Your presence at the palace has been requested at 13 o'clock this afternoon, if that would be convenient for you."

Outside the train station, an elegant coach of impressive size from the palace was awaiting us. An elaborate royal crest displaying the dual eagle heraldry of the Hapsburgs had been skillfully painted on the door in red and gold.

"This is Josef Bratfisch," explained the Captain, introducing the driver, who curtly bowed to both of us from his seat. "It is quite an honour to be fetched at the station by the exclusive fiacre for the Crown Prince Rudolf." At the mention of the familiar name, Bratfisch grinned, the ends of his long, waxed mustache turning upwards. "I regret to inform you, however, that he unfortunately does not speak any English," Captain Siegler advised.

*"Es ist mir eine Freude, Ihre Bekanntschaft zu machen, mein guter Mann,"* I interjected, plumbing the depths of the linguistic skills I had mastered years earlier as a medical student.[3] "Any physician must possess a passing knowledge of German, if only to keep up with the remarkable advances in neurology being made right here in Vienna."

Bratfisch's grin grew more pronounced with the exhibition of my halting German proficiency. We exchanged several superficial pleasantries in his native tongue as he drove us to the famed Rathausplatz hotel that was situated not far from the massive royal palace known as the Hofburg. The rooms that had been booked for us were extraordinarily luxurious and I desperately wished to avail myself of the extremely comfortable bed for a long sleep to compensate for a day and night of jostling on the train. But we only had time to unpack

---

[3] "It is a pleasure to make your acquaintance, my good man."

## Chapter 2: An Audience with the Emperor

and dress before the intrepid captain reappeared, knocking at the door to convey us to our meeting with the Emperor at the palace.

The magnificence of Vienna – which I had not previously visited -- was evident even on the short ride to the massive winter home of the Hapsburgs in the center of the city. As we approached the Hofburg, Bratfisch pointed out a massive new wing under construction to the north of the existing edifice, which reflected a confidence in the durability of the Emperor who lived within. We drove through the Swiss Gate entrance and found ourselves in an expansive courtyard in which colourfully uniformed guards with plumed hats awaited our arrival. We were briskly ushered into the building, whose magnificence certainly rivaled any of the great castles of our native land. An extraordinary collection of painted landscapes and portraits, tapestries and sculptures lined the corridors through which we passed. We strode under ceilings shining with gold leafing that accentuated the moldings and intricately carved ceilings, our boots clicking sharply on the highly polished mosaic and marble floors. After several minutes, we arrived at an elaborate door that was opened to reveal an impressive meeting room within the imperial apartments.

"I admit I am overwhelmed by the grandeur of this place," I confessed to Holmes, looking about the cavernous room.

*Chapter 2: An Audience with the Emperor*

The Hofburg Palace in Vienna, the winter residence of the Hapsburg emperors.

Holmes seemed preternaturally calm, however, awestruck by neither the sheer opulence of the palace nor the imminent meeting with an Emperor whose ancestors had exercised a domineering influence over the affairs of Central Europe since the days of the Holy Roman Empire.

"Quite remarkable," he drolly declared, casting an indifferent eye at the sumptuous décor, adding softly, "although I remain somewhat uncertain as to why are we here." We settled into chairs facing a large fireplace.

"Is it not sufficient that the Prime Minister of the United Kingdom, not to mention Her Majesty herself, implored us to make a journey of a thousand miles to meet with the Emperor of Austria-Hungary?" I responded. "Well, to be more accurate, implored *you*. As you will recall, Salisbury was quite ambivalent about my attendance."

Thus engaged in our conversation, we had not heard the door behind us open. The sound of military boot heels on the marble floor behind us alerted us that others had entered the room. We turned in our chairs and quickly rose to our feet in respect.

Before us, accompanied by a retinue of soldiers, stood the Emperor Franz Joseph. Far less corpulent than Salisbury, he was similarly bald but festooned with an array of whiskers that left only his chin exposed. Although typically portrayed in a military uniform, bedecked with medals and a red and white sash proclaiming his royal status, on this occasion he was dressed in a modest business suit that did little to conceal his royal bearing.

By his side was his wife, the Empress Elisabeth, a strikingly beautiful woman with long brown hair that fell braided behind her neck. Although I knew them to be of nearly the same age, the Emperor appeared considerably older. On both of their faces, there was

## Chapter 2: An Audience with the Emperor

unmistakable evidence of great stress and, I imagined, perhaps unhappiness as well.

"Your Excellency, I am Sherlock Holmes," my friend intoned, nodding slightly and employing a solemn voice I rarely heard even when addressing notable figures in London. "And may I present my friend and colleague, Dr John Watson. We are honoured by your summons to your resplendent home, and we are grateful to serve you and the Empress however we might be of assistance."

The Emperor and Empress offered tight smiles in response and he motioned for us to sit.

"You have done me a great service by traveling this great distance," Franz Joseph began in perfect English, settling into a chair.

"I understand you have been made aware of some small service I provided to your cousin last year," Holmes said.

"It was no 'small service,'" Franz Joseph corrected. "You preserved his name and therefore his dignity and his crown. There are no words that can be proffered to thank you sufficiently and no amount that can be paid in sufficient compensation."

"I took but a photograph of a certain young lady in payment," Holmes said, "and that was entirely ample."

Franz Joseph nodded in understanding.

"My distant cousin, your Queen, has assured me that I may speak with complete candor to you, Herr Holmes. This gives me great comfort.

"I am an old man and quite set in my ways. There are some amongst my friends and relatives who believe it is time for change in the way this country is governed. They espouse a modernization that I believe could destabilize not only the monarchy but our Empire itself.

"Among these reformers, it grieves me to tell you, is my son and heir Rudolf. He is still a young man, just 30, and I am hopeful that his views are still being formulated. But as of today, his vision of the future of the Empire remains quite at odds with my own. My concerns are shared by many of my most trusted associates and advisors, men

*Chapter 2: An Audience with the Emperor*

like the Minister-President Taaffe and the Field Marshal of the army, Archduke Albrecht. These men have been by my side for many years and have earned my trust. I have the greatest confidence in them. When you occupy a position such as mine, such loyalty is not merely appreciated but absolutely essential."

His voice grew somber. "Some of my confidents have suggested that I should be wary of my own son. I hear rumors about Rudolf conspiring against me -- his own father!"

He clenched his fists and tapped them onto the arms of the chair. Looking somber, he rose to his feet and walked towards the fire.

"It is true that Rudolf and I have had a troubled relationship for some time. I know he favours some of this so-called 'modernization' but as his father, I cannot believe he would take any action that would jeopardize the Austro-Hungarian Empire. As Emperor, however, I cannot ignore such serious allegations, regardless of who may be implicated.

"You can understand why the scrutiny of such charges cannot be entrusted to my own investigators! Some of them may be loyal to others in our government who do not share my confidence in my son's devotion to me. Indeed, I worry that some elements in Vienna may have become determined to keep him from inheriting the Hapsburg throne," adding gravely, "at any cost.

"Your Queen has been a close confidante to the Empress and has long expressed a special fondness for the Crown Prince and his wife, Stephanie. I know how it would grieve her should anything befall Rudolf that would preclude his ascension to the crown, whenever that time comes. While I question some of his judgments about the desirability or pace of reform, he is my son and I am determined he will replace me! It is my intention, at a gathering I have scheduled for tomorrow evening, to quash any discussion about displacing him as my successor. But before I do, I must know beyond question that he is loyal and trustworthy, Herr Holmes."

## Chapter 2: An Audience with the Emperor

A pained look had come over his face and that of the Empress Elisabeth.

"There are also some other troubling matters as well, of a more, shall we say, non-political nature," Franz Joseph added. "The sort of scandal with which you proved so helpful with my Bohemian cousin."

"Ah, personal indiscretions," Holmes responded knowingly.

The old man nodded his head in acknowledgement.

"As with idealistic dreams of 'reform,' such involvements are hardly unknown amongst young men of his age and station. He knows I strongly disapprove of his personal recklessness, which is nothing short of demeaning to the Princess Stephanie. Such flagrant conduct jeopardizes not only his marriage, about which he appears to care very little, but the future of the Hapsburg line as he is my only male heir."

"You delicately refer, may I presume, to the possibility of his producing future claimants to the throne?" Holmes asked as discretely as possible.

"Yes, Rudolf and Stephanie have a charming daughter, named Elisabeth after his mother and my Empress. But to this point, they have failed to produce a son: an heir. The dilemma over succession will not manifest itself for several decades, I would hope. Even so, I need not tell you how the absence of a clear line breeds conspiracies of the most dangerous sort."

"They are still young," I interjected. "From a medical standpoint…"

"I hold out little hope of a male heir," the Empress added. "Their marriage seems a farce, much to my despair. Rudolf certainly must take responsibility for his childish frolics. And now, there are rumors that Stephanie is consorting with a Polish count -- Potocki is his name. Indeed, she appears more interested in cavorting with him than in winning back the attentions of her husband."

Although the complexity of the familial drama of the Hapsburgs was becoming evident, there was no question in my mind that Holmes had already decided to accede to the Emperor's

## Chapter 2: An Audience with the Emperor

impassioned request, particularly given the appeal from our own monarch.

"It is of course essential that I have the opportunity for a frank conversation with the Crown Prince in order to determine how I may best be of service to you," Holmes said. "Perhaps he can offer a credible refutation of the accusations that have been leveled against his loyalty."

"I anticipated just such a request on your part, Herr Holmes," the Emperor responded. "You shall have that opportunity before tomorrow's gathering for our family and several members of the Army Council. It is being described as something of a departure party prior to the departure of the Empress and myself for Hungary. You will be given a private audience with Rudolf and are free to question him as you see fit. Meanwhile, I have kept your presence in Vienna s a well-guarded secret from all but the most high-ranking and loyal of my court."

"Tomorrow is bound to be busy, with preparations for what appears to be a crowded and elaborate affair, Your Highness," Holmes protested. "I wonder, might it not be possible to see him today?"

"Such a meeting would have been my preference as well, but I am afraid it is quite impossible," the Emperor responded. "He has gone off to the royal lodge at Mayerling on a short hunting trip with several friends. It has been his favourite destination since its construction two years ago. But he has promised to return in time for the dinner tomorrow evening and you will have abundant opportunity to conduct your interview. Leave no stone unturned, Mr Holmes! It is far better that suspicions and antagonisms be addressed now than allow them to fester."

The Emperor stood, signaling that our interview was at an end. The Empress rose with us and Franz Joseph came close to offer a final plea.

"Events may be moving swiftly, Herr Holmes," he advised. "Your presence alone might well be crucial to preventing events that could trigger the most devastating of consequences. And should the

*Chapter 2: An Audience with the Emperor*

worst actually transpire, your counsel will be invaluable in minimizing a level of damage I cannot even contemplate."

Holmes mulled over the Emperor's ambiguous ramblings before posing the very question I was preparing to ask.

"And what, may I ask, is, to use your own phrase, 'the worst that could transpire?'"

The Emperor placed his hand on Holmes shoulder and drew him close. Suddenly, he looked very old and beset by vexing challenges, unsure and perhaps even frightened.

"The worst?" he repeated. "I cannot even bring myself to say it."

# Chapter 3: The Fiacre Bratfisch

"What the deuce was that all about?" I exclaimed to Holmes. Our interview with the Emperor concluded, we made our way towards our waiting carriage. "I understand that the old man is overwrought by his diplomatic and personal problems, but it seems presumptuous to have summoned you here on such a thin tissue of facts!"

Holmes laid his hand on my forearm. "I agree the precise nature of the matter appears vague at the moment, but surely there is more roiling under the surface than the Emperor is prepared to admit. He has ruled with a firm hand for four decades, nearly as long as you and I have been alive! I will concede him the capacity to sense looming danger, and I am committed to assisting him. It is not only his head that could roll, Watson. All of Europe could collapse into internecine warfare should the Hapsburgs falter. Should that calamity occur, the narrow Channel that divides our own home from this continent will, I fear, provide painfully little protection for the British people.

"Let us devote some time to familiarizing ourselves with the intricacies of the Hapsburg court. I would think that after a few hours of study, we will have earned a respite in its museums and perhaps a concert hall before meeting Rufolf and attending the Emperor's dinner tomorrow."

"And perhaps a Viennese confection!" I suggested.

"Of course," Holmes added with a laugh. "The more whipped cream, the better!"

After Holmes and I had passed several hours poring through records at the royal archives, we spent the remainder of the day enjoying the sights of Vienna, a city of uncommon beauty filled with military statues, and stately buildings of intricate architecture. The magnificence of such edifices as the famed Opera House and the *Hofschauspielhaus*, or Court Theatre, I admit, rivaled any classical

## Chapter 3: The Fiacre Bratfisch

structure in London or Paris and testified to the enduring grandeur of the Hapsburg Empire. Even in the brisk temperature of January, one could imagine couples in the summertime strolling pausing past the fountains (that unfortunately had been emptied for the winter), seated under the colourful umbrellas that festooned the broad boulevards of the central city whilst enjoying a refreshing coffee and confection at one of the charming outdoor sidewalk cafés.

Our ramblings also exposed worrisome signs of division: a poster proclaiming political dissent pasted on a wall, a blaring newspaper headline accusing Franz Joseph's court of corruption, an impassioned and discontented speaker in a park. Despite the Emperor's heavy hand, the reasons for his unease were evident to Holmes and me by the end of our busy day exploring his capital. The evidence of divisions within the Empire and conspiracies against the Hapsburgs were surprisingly discernible.

Still, I remarked to Holmes that I still had seen and heard nothing that suggested anything particularly ominous: certainly nothing that might have warranted our long journey from London.

"Really?" he asked. "Did you not notice anything peculiar following our arrival at the train station?"

I thought back to our meeting with Captain Siegler and the previous day's activities but nothing struck me as especially noteworthy.

"No, I cannot say I noticed anything but the expected efficiency of Captain Siegler's meeting us and providing us quick transport to our hotel," I replied. "Am I missing something of significance?"

"Were you not struck by Mr Bratfisch's presence?" he asked.

"The carriage driver?" I wondered aloud. "What did they call him -- a 'fiacre'? It seemed terribly thoughtful to send Rudolf's personal man to fetch us. I took it as a sign of the Emperor's appreciation for our arduous journey. In any event, Bratfisch seemed a perfectly friendly but ordinary person. Why? Was his driving not up to your standards?"

## Chapter 3: The Fiacre Bratfisch

Holmes laughed at my remark.

"Did you hear the Captain describe him as 'loyal' to the Crown Prince. Does not 'loyal' strikes you as a rather peculiar term to use in describing a carriage driver? 'Skilled,' 'dependable,' even 'trusted' would not have caught my attention. But 'loyal'; the use of that particular adjective piqued my interest."

I admit I was mystified by the significance Holmes had wrung out of a seemingly inconsequential word.

"I must apologize, Holmes, but I must admit I fail to see the point. What do you find so intriguing about the use of the term 'loyal'?"

"Because it suggests a suspicion that someone very close to the Crown Prince might be *dis*loyal," Holmes said. "Perhaps there are doubts about others who have attempted to ingratiate themselves with the Prince. Or perhaps Bratfisch's responsibilities go beyond driving the Prince's carriage, including guarding him from adversaries and ensuring that the Prince's own secrets are kept safe from disclosure. Oh, yes, Watson, the use of the term 'loyal' is fraught with meaning, I am quite certain."

He must have seen in my eyes a hint of the skepticism with which I responded to this torrent of unwarranted speculation.

"I deduce you think I am inferring too much from a passing comment," he mused, "but it occurs to me that Rudolf may have learned of our summons to Vienna and desired to have his loyal driver keep an eye on our movements and an ear to our conversations. After all, it was his father, not he, who summoned us to Vienna. Indeed, the father's questions about his son's trustworthiness are the very reason for our being here."

"Well, if spying on us is the plan, the Crown Prince certainly picked the wrong man," I declared. "This man Bratfisch may be a competent driver, but he surely cannot serve as a very effective reporter on our conversations. He doesn't speak a word of English!"

Holmes assumed a look of amused surprise.

## Chapter 3: The Fiacre Bratfisch

"But you do not *know* that to be the case," he corrected me. "True, Captain Siegler informed us that the driver could not *speak* English, but many people are able to understand a language better than they can speak it themselves. And besides, we have only Siegler's word concerning Bratfisch's lack of fluency in our language. He may not know of the driver's proficiency or he, too, might have been deceiving us, hoping we would reveal valuable information through an indiscrete remark. People often conceal their facility in in other languages for just such reasons. Keep that in mind in Vienna, where intrigues run deep."

"But why is there a need to spy on *us*?" I asked.

"Now, that is precisely the question I asked myself when Bratfisch was described as 'loyal,'" Holmes answered. "Why, indeed."

# Chapter 4: Dinner at the Hofburg Palace

Disturbingly, however, we waited for several hours prior to the scheduled dinner for a summons to the palace to meet with the Crown Prince. Such a missive never arrived and Holmes' frustration was clearly growing as the time to depart for the dinner grew closer. Finally, Just before seven o'clock, we received a message in our room to come to the hotel's lobby where our ride to the Hofburg awaited us.

We expected to find the now-suspect (at least in my opinion!) Bratfisch but were approached by an unfamiliar man formally dressed as a carriage driver.

"Herr Holmes, Dr Watson?" he asked tentatively in heavily accented German.

"*Ja,*" I replied, deigning to make him feel at ease by the use of his own language, and he smiled broadly at my unmistakable accent.

"Ah, you speak German, a little bit?" he asked. "You can speak some English to me. I often drive the guests who are visiting from England." He paused to allow us to admire his fluency. "My name is Friedrich."

"You speak our language admirably!" Holmes responded, looking about. "We had been under the impression that Bratfisch would be serving as our chauffeur this evening."

I could tell that Holmes was alert to the possibility that the man was an imposter, possibly sent to divert us from attending the dinner. The maneuverings and rumors of Vienna were clearly running rampant with my imagination!

"Not tonight," he said. "Josef is the driver for his Highness, the Crown Prince, and has been attending him today at Mayerling, the hunting lodge."

*Chapter 4: Dinner at the Hofburg Palace*

"So will the Crown Prince not be attending the dinner?" Holmes asked, an edge of concern evident in his voice.

"Oh, Prince Rudolf will certainly return in time for the dinner!" he assured.

Holmes was sufficiently persuaded by the man's account and we clambered aboard the carriage for the brief drive to the expansive palace. Upon our arrival, we were led through halls redolent with fresh, magnificent bouquets that created a spring-like atmosphere in welcome contrast to the chilly winter temperature outside. Every corridor through which we were guided was filled with museum-quality artwork including innumerable family portraits and busts, magnificent tapestries, and glittering chandeliers. We entered the reception room filled with men dressed in elaborate uniforms and women resplendent in sparkling jewelry and gowns of silk and taffeta. A quartet of superbly skilled musicians provided a soothing background for the milling guests who held long-stemmed glasses of wine and champagne as waiters with trays filled with canapés and other hors d'oeuvres circulated silently. It seemed likely that Holmes and I were amongst the few guests not related to the royal family through birth, marriage or both (as was common amongst the royal families) or the innermost circle of advisors. By agreement with the Emperor, our presence was not to be announced so that we might observe the evening's discussions.

"Who knows what conspiracies may hatch if it is known that I have summoned the eminent Sherlock Holmes to attend the dinner?" the Emperor had noted.

From our anonymous perch at the edge of the room, we were able, thanks to our earlier research in the archives, to identify several of the prominent attendees. We quickly spied Archduke Karl Ludwig, the Emperor's younger brother, a portly man with reportedly gruff instincts. He was accompanied by Infanta Maria Theresa, a daughter of the king of Portugal, whom Karl Ludwig had married following the untimely deaths of his previous two spouses. Despite the family

## Chapter 4: Dinner at the Hofburg Palace

rivalries that frequently cleaved the royal houses of Europe, Karl Ludwig disdained the political obligations of the nobility and was content to allow the burdens of government to rest unchallenged on the shoulders of his older brother. He devoted himself instead to his religion and the promotion of the arts. Such ambivalence made it fortunate, therefore, that Rudolf's strategic placement in the line of succession assured that the Hapsburg Crown was unlikely to fall to the reluctant Karl Ludwig.

The Emperor's other brother Archduke Ludwig Viktor, unflatteringly known as "Luziwuzi," was neither expected at the dinner nor likely to be missed. Indeed, we had learned, his name was rarely mentioned in the royal household. A sallow-faced young man with a weak chin and watery eyes, Ludwig Viktor had been consigned against his will to a military career that he loathed. Numerous efforts by Empress Elisabeth to find a suitable wife for her son had been unequivocally rejected, and scandalous rumors had run rampant about his unconventional behavior. According to one such account, Luziwuzi was discovered in a notorious Vienese bathhouse dressed in women's clothing. Shortly afterwards, he had been permanently barred from entering any of the palaces.

Several of the other guests were quickly identifiable. The Archduke Albrecht Friedrich Rudolf Dominik, newly appointed a *Feldmarschall* in the army, was a grandson to an Emperor of the Holy Roman Empire and cousin to Franz Joseph's father. His own father, the Archduke Charles I, held the distinction of having defeated Napoleon I at Aspern in 1809. Now over 70 years of age, he was a man of considerable military achievements of his own. Through his service to the Emperor, Albrecht had become a wealthy owner of many substantial properties in Hungary, and for that reason was decidedly unsympathetic to growing calls among nationalists for greater autonomy in that portion of the Empire.

For three decades, he had served as the Inspector General of the army, a position from which he had recently been displaced by the

## Chapter 4: Dinner at the Hofburg Palace

appointment of the Crown Prince, a substitution that had displeased the old soldier. It was an open secret within the palace that the Albrecht viewed Rudolf with contempt, believing him ill-suited to a commanding position within the Austrian military and perhaps secretly sympathetic to Hungarian critics of the Emperor's iron-fisted control. That disdain was met with Rudolf's dislike for Albrecht, which was seconded by reformers who believed him too wedded to outdated tradition, leaving Austria's military antiquated and vulnerable to foreign attack or internal rebellion.

Shortly before the dinner was to begin, the arrival of the Emperor and Empress, together with the Crown Princess Stephanie, was announced and the reception room was filled with a respectful ovation. The resplendently dressed royal couple and their daughter-in-law entered the room and slowly made their way amongst the assembled invitees, often pausing to share a personal word. After several minutes on this mingling, a heavily bearded man of perhaps 45 or 50 approached the Emperor, who greeted him warmly. He leaned close to the Emperor's ear to whisper a confidential message.

The effect was alarming. Franz Joseph started noticeably and his face grew red as he engaged in a sharp exchange with the bearded man. Then, noticing that Holmes and I were nearby, he beckoned us to draw closer to him.

"This is Prince Philipp of Saxe-Coburg and Gotha, one of the gentlemen who has been with Rudolf at Mayerling lodge," Franz Joseph declared as the bearded guest bowed in greeting.

"Philipp is married to my own dear sister!" Stephanie added cheerfully, apparently oblivious to the Emperor's anguish. "Where is my husband?" she added, looking about the room.

"I am afraid Philipp brings disappointing news," the Emperor explained, looking at Holmes and myself. "It appears you will not have the opportunity to meet my son this evening."

We looked with interest to Prince Philipp.

## Chapter 4: Dinner at the Hofburg Palace

"Yes, that is true," he confirmed. "I regret having to report that Archduke Rudolf was taken ill earlier today and was unable to participate in the hunt that we had scheduled."

"Ill?" I asked. "I am a physician. It is nothing too serious, I would hope!"

"No, no," the Prince assured. "A sore throat and cold, nothing more! He has asked me to convey his deepest regrets to you, Your Majesties. He wishes to avoid the fatigue of travel and attending an official dinner and will instead remain tonight at Mayerling in hopes of rescheduling our hunt for the morning. He regrets he will be unable to visit with your majesties before your departure for Budapest."

"It would seem unlikely that he is terribly indisposed this evening if he is scheduling a hunt in the morning," Holmes interrupted.

Philipp looked curiously at Holmes.

"You are whom?" he inquired.

"A guest of mine, Philipp," the Emperor interceded, "the famed English detective Sherlock Holmes and his friends Dr. Watson. I have asked them to come to Vienna to meet with Rudolf on certain matters."

Philipp gave us a curt nod of the head.

"The name is familiar to me," he advised. Turning back to the Emperor, he described Rudolf's condition.

"It is but a minor indisposition," he insisted. "In fact, he begged that I return to Mayerling early tomorrow and report to him on the dinner."

An unmistakable scowl flashed across the Crown Princess' rather plain face.

"So he will remain at Mayerling tonight," she observed skeptically, her voice assuming a harsh tone. "And will he be there alone?"

"Count Hoyos has remained with him," Philipp declared, turning to my friend. "I refer to the Prince's close friend, the count of Hoyos-Sprinzenstein."

*Chapter 4: Dinner at the Hofburg Palace*

"A most respected diplomat!" the Emperor added approvingly. "He has served us most admirably as ambassador to America and France, and with great distinction."

The Crown Prince's wife made little effort to hide her annoyance.

"We are quite displeased," she declared, looking to the royal couple for confirmation. "He had promised our daughter Elisabeth that he would visit with her before her bedtime. I would have thought he would keep that promise, however ambivalent he might be about seeing me."

She gave each of us a tight smile and pressed a gloved hand to her forehead.

"I have developed quite a terrible headache and cannot remain," she explained, begging her parents-in-law to forgive her for missing the dinner. Without another word, she turned abruptly and walked out of the room.

Unsurprisingly, the atmosphere at the dinner became somewhat tense and the evening was abbreviated. None of the scheduled speeches were offered. Promptly at nine o'clock, the Emperor stood and, following brief words of gratitude to his guests for having attended, he left the room followed by his wife. Quickly, the guests gathered their coats and hats and departed into the chilly Vienna evening.

Holmes and I decided to take a walk through the nearly deserted streets of the center city back to the *Rathauspark*. As we silently passed the massive Parliament building, completed only a few years earlier, I could not contain myself any longer.

"Holmes, what do you make of the absence of the Crown Prince ?" I asked. "Why would he defy such a summons to the palace and arrange a frivolous hunting trip that could easily have been rescheduled? I can understand being inconvenienced by a sore throat but is that a reason to decline a request of the Emperor? Good Lord, the man is to be Emperor himself, perhaps in only a few years! And he had evidently promised his wife and daughter he would be in attendance."

### Chapter 4: Dinner at the Hofburg Palace

"I detest offering speculative conjecture, as you well know," he responded, "but the explanations suggest that neither national security nor his promise to his wife and child were foremost on Prince Rudolf's mind this evening. You noted the Princess' concern about her husband's companionship?"

"I imagine she was relieved to hear that Hoyos would be with him to assist should his illness worsen."

Holmes stifled a chuckle.

"I do not think the Princess was deceived as to who was providing the Prince with succor this evening," he said.

"You mean, she suspects the Prince's ... indiscretions?"

"Now *you* are the one sounding like a diplomat, Watson," he laughed. "Let us say the Prince's reputation as a rather indiscriminate Lothario substantially outweighs his mastery of statecraft. I think it is fair to conclude that tonight is neither the first nor the last time his family has been dismayed by his behavior. The only question is whether his lack of discipline carries with it greater consequences than an angry father, a disappointed daughter, and an irate wife."

We soon arrived at the hotel and after imbibing an outstanding brandy, I set about catching up on some of the sleep I had sacrificed during the arduous train journey. The day's activities had clearly worn me out, and my head was on my pillow by 11 o'clock. I do not believe I stirred until shortly after 8 the following morning when a vigorous pounding on my door unceremoniously awoke me. Hurriedly, I put on my dressing gown and flew to the vestibule.

"Coming, coming!" I cried, aggrieved at being disturbed at so early an hour. I had been hoping to sleep somewhat later so as to be refreshed when we would be conducting our delayed meeting with the Crown Prince following his return to Vienna in the early afternoon from Mayerling.

I threw open the door, expecting a messenger from the front desk but instead was confronted by Holmes who stood before me holding a piece of paper in his outstretched hand.

*Chapter 4: Dinner at the Hofburg Palace*

"Come, Watson! The game is afoot!" he declared urgently.

"Forgive me, Holmes, I did not remember that we had an appointment this morning," I said. "Where are we off to?"

"The royal Mayerling hunting lodge," Holmes declared.

"To consult with Crown Prince Rudolf?" I questioned, assuming the venue for our meeting had been changed during the night.

"I fear that such a conversation would be decidedly one sided," Holmes replied. "Rudolf is dead!"

# Chapter 5: The Tragedy

"Dead!" I cried, stumbling back dumbstruck as Holmes entered my room. "Surely not from the minor illness Prince Philipp described last evening? Why, the symptoms described were so insignificant that I suspected the complaint was little more than a ruse to avoid attending the dinner."

"This note from just arrived from Mayerling lodge," Holmes said. "You will recall that Hoyos remained there with the Crown Prince last evening. They were to be joined again by Philipp for a rescheduled hunt.

"Instead, we have been summoned to Mayerling by Philipp. Apparently he returned quite early this morning and was present when the bodies were discovered."

For a moment, I was unsure if I had heard Holmes correctly.

"Did you say 'bodies'?" I asked. "Someone else in addition to the Crown Prince has died?"

"Yes, Watson, and there is no time to lose. A carriage is awaiting us downstairs. We must travel without delay if we are to have an opportunity to examine all of the evidence before the police or anyone else bumbles their way about and ruins whatever hope we may still have of finding pertinent clues."

My head was reeling with the unfathomable news as I completed my toilet and dressed as quickly as possible. We rushed downstairs to the street where a carriage was waiting for us. In the early morning, the streets were clear and within minutes we were on the road to the forested preserve some 20 miles away. The noise from the wheels on the stone roadway assured our voices would not be overhead by the driver. As the city flew past us, I settled into my seat and learned over to Holmes.

"You said 'bodies,'" I reminded him.

## Chapter 5: The Tragedy

"So I did," Holmes replied. Quickly his eyes darting about the compartment searching for any means by which the driver could overhear our conversation. Once he had satisfied himself that our privacy was ensured, he leaned forward to speak in low tones.

"You will recall the Princess Stephanie's reaction last night to the news that her husband had chosen to remain at Mayerling."

"Yes," I responded, "she was disappointed that he would miss the dinner and even more importantly miss seeing their young daughter."

"Yes, but do you recall her sharp question to Prince Philipp about whether the Crown Prince would be spending the evening 'alone'?"

"Philipp assured her that Count Hoyos was remaining at Mayerling to keep the Crown Prince company," I said. "Do you think he is also dead?"

Holmes pursed his lips tightly.

"I think it was quite evident she suspected the Crown Prince was not planning to spend the night alone, and I do not refer to Hoyos' company."

"Well, we were not told of any other guest," I reminded him.

He shook his head at me in wonder. "Watson, you can be a hopeless naïf. Rudolf planned to spend the night with a woman."

"A woman?" I repeated warily.

"Yes, I am afraid a very young woman. Philipp's note informs me that the Baroness Mary Vetsera also has been found dead, and in the same bed as Rudolf!"

"A baroness! Good lord, the scandal!" I remarked. "How did such a tragedy occur?" I wondered. "Was it an assassination? A robbery? *Un crime du coeur?*"

"That is what we have been summoned to determine," Holmes explained. "At first appearances, there would seem to be a simple explanation. The bodies were found together with fatal gunshot wounds in both their heads."

## Chapter 5: The Tragedy

"An intruder, most likely," I hypothesized.

"The room was evidently locked, from the inside."

"Hmm, that would seem to complicate matters. Might the door not have been locked from the outside?"

"Perhaps. We shall have to see if the key can be found. Nevertheless, it is reported that the weapon used was found in the room."

"Abandoned by an attacker?"

"Actually, it has been identified with certainty as belonging to the Crown Prince," he said, scanning the message he had received. "And it was found in Rudolf's grasp, with his finger still on the trigger. Moreover, each victim had left a suicide note, unmistakably written in their own hand."

I stopped considering alternative explanations.

"Well, then, it would seem the conclusion of suicide makes perfect sense," I conceded, frankly regretting the absence of an impenetrably convoluted crime to solve.

"Yes," Holmes responded thoughtfully. "Perhaps *too* perfect."

"You mean you speculate there might be more to the tragedy than appears on its face?" I cried with a combination of excitement and horror. "What is your idea of what occurred?"

"You might as well direct me to rebuild the Tower Bridge without stones," he replied with annoyance. "You know I never speculate without facts, and we have precious few of them at the moment. But if the men at Mayerling follow my instructions to preserve the scene rather than trample all over it like our friends from Scotland Yard, we will soon determine if this tragedy is as straightforward as it might appear."

I allowed Holmes to contemplate the meager set of facts we had in hand without further interruption. The road ran out of the city and into the countryside where a light snowfall had left the fields covered with a pure white cloak that sparkled in the rising morning sun. Soon we began traversing a vast forested area that was left darkened by the

## Chapter 5: The Tragedy

tall trees on either side of the roadway. After several more minutes, we arrived at the imposing lodge that resembled a country estate.

A portion of the wooden exterior remained bare while most of the rest had been painted green while the window shutters were white. Wings of the building rose to various heights, some a single story, other two or three times that height. The tallest section was topped by a belltower. We pulled up to the main doorway and were met by several glum-faced men as we stepped from the cab. Immediately, we recognized Joseph Bratfisch, the Crown Prince's personal fiacre. The expression on his face, which could not have contrasted more thoroughly from that with which he had greeted us only a day earlier at the train station, reflected unspeakable sadness.

"Herr Holmes, Dr Watson," he said glumly, bowing in respect as we alighted. "*Welkommen bei Mayerling.*"

# Chapter 6: The Locked Room

A man of obvious aristocratic bearing strode towards us, with a number of others trailing after him, including our acquaintance from the prior evening's dinner, Prince Philipp. His full beard, mustache and thick hair were all of the same dark colour and he spoke in fluent English though with a clipped Germanic accent.

"You are Herr Sherlock Holmes?" he said. "The famous detective from London?"

"I am," Holmes responded, "but you have the better of me, sir."

"I am fully aware of your reputation," he said, ignoring Holmes's query. "And I assume this is Dr Watson, who has faithfully -- if melodramatically -- recorded your exploits." He looked indifferently in my direction.

"Quite so," Holmes answered as I nodded.

"I am the Count Joseph Hoyos-Sprinzenstein," he declared, thrusting his arm towards the entrance to the building. "Please, enter into the lodge." He stepped inside the doorway and bade us follow him. "I am the senior person here now that ..." His voice trailed off as he caught himself. "Forgive me. This is a very great tragedy for our country and our Emperor, and for me personally."

"I presume so," said Holmes. "I understand you were a close friend of Prince Rudolf and dined with him here only last night."

"That is all true," Hoyos replied, his voice growing thick with emotion. "A loss far greater loss than you could know."

Holmes paused for a discrete moment to allow the Count to gather himself.

"You will recall that we had the honour of meeting last evening at the Hofburg palace," said Prince Philipp interjected.

## Chapter 6: The Locked Room

"So we did, Your Excellency," Holmes said with a polite bow. "Your note reported that you had returned here, to the Mayerling lodge, early this morning."

"Yes, quite early," he corrected. "As I mentioned at the palace, the Crown Prince, Count Hoyos and I were to take part in the hunt that had been postponed yesterday due to Rudolf's indisposition. I arrived here about seven o'clock, just as the Count and others were proceeding to the Crown Prince's room. They informed me that they had found that the door was locked and he had failed to respond to several entreaties."

"I so deeply regret this most unfortunate occurrence," Holmes murmured. "But now, I am naturally anxious to examine the room and the victims," he said as we walked further into the entry hallway. "Time is of the essence in such matters. I am hopeful nothing has been disturbed."

"Nothing," Hoyos replied. "Everything remains just as it was discovered this morning. I must say the circumstances appear to leave little room for suspicion beyond what has already been ascertained."

"And that is what?" asked Holmes.

"Why, suicide, of course!" Hoyos responded. "A dreadful pact between the Archduke Rudolf and," he caught himself for a moment before finishing his sentence, "this ... young girl. If you wish, you may examine the Prince's body although an official post-mortem will take place upon the arrival of Dr Hermann von Wiederhofer, the Prince's physician, this afternoon."

"And the young lady?" Holmes asked.

Hoyos noticeably stiffened at the reference to the second victim.

"To be truthful, Herr Holmes, we were not even aware of her presence in the room for until after Rudolf's body had been discovered," said Hoyos. "It was not immediately evident upon entering the room that there was a second person alongside the Prince."

"You saw no evidence of blood?" Holmes pressed.

## Chapter 6: The Locked Room

"The bedclothes had been drawn up purposefully to cover her," explained Hoyos. "She was only a child. Such a tragedy!"

"That is certainly the case," replied Holmes, a slight hint of skepticism evident in his voice. "And who had the unhappy experience of discovering her body under the pile of bedclothes?"

Hoyos turned to a short man with mustaches and a goatee who bowed in an exaggerated fashion to Holmes. His face was a mask of sadness and his eyes were scarlet, evidently from weeping.

"This is Johann Loschek," Hoyos said.

The man looked up to Holmes, who towered a foot above him.

"Yes, your Excellency," he said in German, nervously making a little bow in our direction. "I am Loschek, the hall-keeper to my Prince." I quickly translated for Holmes.

"The Prince's valet," Hoyos explained. "It was Loschek who first raised the cry for help this morning."

"*Ja*, I knew something was very wrong! The door was locked and the Prince did not respond. I called for help! Then, in the room, I found her."

"Why don't you take me to the scene of this tragedy," said Holmes to the valet, "and then you can explain the series of events that led to this dreadful discovery?"

With Loschek in the lead, we walked through the corridors of the ornately furnished lodge. Heavy, dark wood with carved moldings and pilasters decorated the rooms into which we glanced as we passed by. The walls were replete with the heads and antlers of the unfortunate victims of earlier hunts. Interspersed with the trophies were the portraits of various dead Hapsburgs, all dressed in military uniforms and with a groaning collection of medals displayed on their chests. Enormous tapestries depicted scenes of battles and hunts. Weeping and grave-faced house staff watched as we moved through the weakly illuminated hallways, the intricate rugs of Ottoman origin muffling our footsteps.

## Chapter 6: The Locked Room

We soon found ourselves at a heavy wooden door, a portion of which had been splintered by powerful blows from a heavy hammer that rested against the wall. Hoyos put out a restraining arm before us before we could step into the room and spoke softly to Holmes and myself. His voice had lost some of the gruffness with which he had initially greeted us.

"Herr Holmes, I know I need not emphasize the need for the utmost discretion," he said. "I understand you will need to make a thorough examination, and we welcome your scrutiny. But I implore you to treat this matter in the greatest of confidence. Nothing about this situation can be disclosed before the Emperor has been notified. Frankly, I am unsure how I shall deliver this terrible news to him and the Empress. You can imagine how devastating it will be to learn your only son and heir has perished!"

"I have no interest in popularizing any of my cases," he said. "That is Dr Watson's province, and I am certain he will abide by the same confidentiality I am pledged to observe. He is, after all, a physician and bound by professional standards even more proscriptive than those applying to consulting detectives. My responsibilities, I should be clear, lie entirely with the Emperor who brought me to Austria albeit for a very different purpose than investigating the death of his son. He alone will determine the use of any information I distill from this investigation. I am sure you will abide by the same conditions, Herr Count."

Holmes stepped into the room followed by myself, Loschek and the Crown Prince's friends whom he asked to stand against the wall and not move until had conducted a cursory overview. We were no sooner inside the doorway than Holmes swung the shattered door shut, and it closed with a loud thud. We stood on a small pile of wood shards that had been torn from the door by the blows of the hammer. Impassively, Holmes's hooded eyes swept the chamber, which was of modest size and furnished with a small writing table and nightstands on either side of the wooden bed.

## Chapter 6: The Locked Room

Holmes ignored the appalling grisly human tragedy that lay sprawled only a few feet away. Instructing the rest of us to stand against the wall to avoid trampling any evidence, he fell onto his knees and withdrew from his coat pocket the large magnifying glass he frequently used when on a case. Given that we had traveled to Austria without an expectation that we would be investigating a crime, I was somewhat surprised.

"You thought to bring your glass," I remarked.

"I generally have found it better to be prepared," he replied without looking up at me. "I had no expectation there would be a crime scene to investigate, but it is always prudent to have the tools of my trade with me rather than safely nestled away in their box at Baker Street, wouldn't you agree?"

Without waiting for my reply, he began to crawl about on the rug near the door, grunting from time to time, picking up bits and pieces of the shattered detritus that covered the entry way, and then brushing it all aside to peer at the base of the door itself. He scurried backward slightly and swung the door open again. Loschek, unmoved from his stance aside the door, looked on with astonishment as Holmes slinked about on his hands and knees. After examining an item with his lens, he uttered a soft grunt of satisfaction before dropping the discovery into a small envelope he had removed from his waistcoat.

"If you do not mind my saying so, Herr Holmes, you appear to be focusing on inconsequential wood splinters while ignoring the enormity of the human tragedy that lies not three feet away," protested Philipp.

"In fact, Your Grace, I do not mind your making such a statement in the slightest," replied Holmes. "Indeed, I will even forgive the foolishness of your remark. I am quite aware that the Prince lies dead on the bed" he said, making a vague gesture in the direction of the Prince's body. "But as is self-evident, he is quite dead and therefore not going anywhere. It is far more important that I examine this evidence on the floor before it is swept away by an inadvertent housemaid," he

## Chapter 6: The Locked Room

explained. "I assure you, Your Excellency, I will not overlook the body of the dead Crown Prince."

He gently brushed aside some additional wood shards near the door and uttered a familiar cry that signaled a significant discovery.

"Ah, here is a key!" he cried triumphantly, pointing to a metal key nestled underneath a large pile of chips. He picked it up and displayed it as the men leaned forward to take a closer look at the object.

"Yes, it certainly is the key," said Loschek. "There is no doubt. It must have been dislodged from the lock when I pounded on the door."

"That certainly would seem to explain its presence just inside the entryway, would it not?" said Holmes as he stood up and brushed some bits of wood from his knees. "But let's assume nothing, shall we? There is really no substitute for experimentation."

Opening the door, he pushed the key into the locking mechanism. It fit perfectly and despite the substantial damage to the door, Holmes was able to turn the key to move the bolt back and forth.

"Watson, would you indulge me for a moment? Close the door once I step into the hallway and turn the key to engage the locking mechanism."

Holmes strode into the hallway, pulling the door shut behind him. Following his instructions, I turned the key and heard the bolt fall into place.

Holmes heard it as well and began pounding on the fractured door, giving it perhaps twenty strong bangs as close to the door's hardware as possible.

"Thank you, that will quite do," he said. He reached through the hole in the shattered door and grasped the key, turning it to allow him to re-enter the room.

"Yes, as I had suspected," he commented without explanation. He dropped to the floor and examined the sill and sweep underneath

## Chapter 6: The Locked Room

the door. The Austrians looked quizzingly at me, mystified by Holmes' seemingly inexplicable behavior.

He crawled on hands and knees several yards into the room, peering intently through his lens at the intricate carpeting.

"Look here, Watson," he called. I went over and knelt down next to him.

"Careful, careful!" he warned. He pointed to several spots, barely noticeable on the multi-coloured rug. Taking a white handkerchief from his pocket, he dapped at the tiny stains and showed me the bright red spots on the cloth.

"Fresh blood," I said, "I would imagine."

"Indubitably," he replied. "Were we in London, we could apply the Holmes hemoglobin test to determine that it is human in origin. I regret not bringing it along as well as my lens. However, given the sanguineous scene in this room," he added, looking over his shoulder towards the bed, "it seems reasonable to conclude this is blood. In any event, we can assemble the necessary chemicals to validate the theory."

He stood and carefully folded the cloth before returning it to his pocket. Glancing about the rug and nearby floor, he finally seemed satisfied.

"Who else has a key to this door?" Holmes asked.

"Only the Prince," Loschek volunteered.

"And no one else?" Holmes queried. "Other servants? The military guards? Not even you?"

"*Nein, nein,*" Loschek insisted. "The Prince demanded his privacy! He wanted no one to enter the room without his permission."

"So the key that was inside the room is, to the best of your knowledge, the only one of its kind."

The valet nodded affirmatively.

Hoyos and Philipp continued to watch the scene with wonderment and some impatience.

"Aren't you going to examine the Crown Prince and the young woman?" asked Hoyos impatiently.

## Chapter 6: The Locked Room

"Most assuredly," Holmes explained, offering no additional answer to what seemed to me a most reasonable question. "But why did the Prince lock the door?"

"Why is that important?" Philipp demanded.

"Perhaps he feared someone else might enter the room when they were undertaking their suicides," I postulated.

"But we are told everyone in the house was under the strictest instructions never to enter his room without permission," Holmes responded.

"Well, then, perhaps he wanted to delay anyone from discovering him and the young lady after they had committed these horrific acts?" suggested Hoyos.

"What difference could it possibly make if both of them were already dead?" Holmes closed his eyes in a manner that I knew meant that he was attempting to reconstruct the scene in his own mind. At such times, it was crucial that he not be disturbed.

"Why make it more difficult for someone to enter the room?" he asked. "It is not as though he needed time to escape, after all. What could have been his motivation for locking the door?"

"And yet he most assuredly did!" I reminded him.

"Perhaps," said Holmes, "and perhaps he did not."

# Chapter 7: A Gruesome Examination

Holmes finally turned his attention to the bed on which the two bodies were sprawled. The air in the room had become thick with the tell-tale, iron-tainted scent associated with significant quantities of blood. The smell instantly conjured up terrible memories of the frontline surgical tents in which I had frantically laboured over horribly wounded young men in Afghanistan. I had hoped, even in my surgical practice, to avoid encountering it ever again.

Against the far wall of the room was situated the bed which had an elaborate frame of carved wood. The headboard rose five feet and was topped with four small carved spindled columns and finials that were visible from where we stood across the room. Closer to us was the foot of the bed, a solid block of wood between two shorter but similarly spindled columns running from the floor to the top of the frame, which largely obscured our view of the carnage on the bed. It was not until we stepped closer that the full horror of the scene came into view.

"Good Lord!" I involuntarily cried, both repelled and transfixed by the terrible tableau before us.

On the right side of the bed was the body of a young woman, partially covered by the ample bedclothes that had been pulled back to reveal her head and upper body. She was wearing a flimsy sleeping gown that concealed little and her arms had been folded across her chest. A small bouquet of wilting flowers had been placed in her hands.

Her face was turned towards her right shoulder. Her left eye had been dislodged from its socket and, barely connected to her body by the strands of the optic nerve, lay perched in a macabre fashion on her left cheek. Her left temple was obscured by a mass of thick, clotted blood and hair.

## Chapter 7: A Gruesome Examination

"That is Mary Vetsera," Hoyos declared, transfixed by the sight. "She is the daughter of Baron Vetsera, a diplomat, and his wife, the Baroness Helene." He paused to clear his throat.

"There is no point being coy, Herr Holmes," he continued. "Most of us were aware of the illicit relationship between the Crown Prince and this young lady. Last night at our dinner, although the baroness had remained in this room, I was aware that she would spend the night with Prince Rudolf."

"Did she arrive with him?" Holmes queried.

"No, she did not," said Hoyos. "In fact, the Prince told me that he discovered her presence only when we arrived and that he had not anticipated her being here. She must have wanted to surprise him."

"You never actually saw her or interacted with her?" Holmes asked.

"No," Hoyos acknowledged.

"Nor did I," added Phillip.

Loschek confirmed that as on her other visits to the lodge, the Baroness had discretely remained out of sight.

"Everyone knew what was going on," Hoyos said. "There was no need to flaunt it and feed the insatiable curiosity of the press."

Holmes surveyed the scene and turned back to the trio of men watching his every move.

"So, you are all familiar with their relationship," he said. "Have you reached any preliminary conclusion about what you think happened here?"

"I think it quite likely that out of jealousy or despair, she shot herself," said Philipp. "I would imagine that the Crown Prince placed these flowers in her hands, covered her body with the bedclothes, and then, in a fit of grief, did away with himself. He had, on numerous occasions, discussed suicide with several of his intimate friends. That is certainly what this horrifying scene presents to me. But of course, I defer to your skilled judgment, Herr Holmes."

Holmes sniffed and looked back at the bed.

## Chapter 7: A Gruesome Examination

"I rather doubt that was the course of events," he contradicted the Prince.

"How can you possibly know?" Philipp countered.

Holmes ignored the question and moved closer to Mary's body. Pulling up his sleeves to keep his cuffs from becoming soiled, he began to examine the wound in her temple. "Would you terribly mind bringing me a cloth and a basin of water," he said to no one in particular. The eminent men did not move a muscle in response, but Loschek quickly scurried away to find the requested items.

"Surely a self-inflicted shot, wouldn't you say, Mr Holmes?" Philipp posed, not hovering too close to the hideous wound.

The clotted blood had begun to dry and formed a barrier that almost obstructed a clear view of the wound. Holmes parted the woman's long brown hair to expose her left ear and then gently turned her head slightly from side to side. It was obvious that both temples had been encrusted with gore due to a bullet having passed through the temporal portion of the poor girl's skull.

Loschek had returned with a hand cloth and a silver basin filled with water, which he offered to Holmes. Dipping the cloth into the water and then squeezing it tightly, Holmes gently wiped some of the blood-soaked hair away from the baroness' face and again looked to each side of her head, issuing a brief snort as he did so. He removed the wilted bouquet and moved her hands. He asked me to do the same in order to assess the state of *rigor mortis* in the body, which would help to establish roughly the time of death. As I was doing so, he walked to the window and pushed aside the heavy drapes, presumably to allow more light into the room.

"See here!" he cried, pointing to a pane in the leaded glass on the door leading out to the garden. The men leaned closer to the window, straining to see the object of Holmes's attention.

"Someone has broken the glass!" Hoyos observed.

## Chapter 7: A Gruesome Examination

"Why, it looks like a bullet hole," added Philipp. Excitedly, he added, "Perhaps someone stood *outside* the room and fired in, killing them both."

Holmes looked disbelievingly at the men.

"The most important rule of detection," he explained with some irritation in his voice, "is to discover the facts *first*. Assume nothing, I always say. Then one must allow the facts to guide the thought process, not adapt the facts to fit a pre-conceived and, in this particular case, exceptionally ludicrous theory."

I quickly stole a glance at Hoyos and Philipp, both of whose expressions left little doubt that they were unused to having their opinion dismissed so curtly. Holmes was completely indifferent to the impact of his words on the two aristocrats.

"A shot fired from outside this room would have to have been one of extraordinary precision," he said didactically.

"We have great marksmen in Austria," Philipp insisted,

"I have no doubt, but not likely any who can fire at two figures that were at best obscured and perhaps unseen due to this drapery that largely covers the window. And even your most proficient marksman would have had to have been remarkably skilled to shoot both the Prince and Miss Vetsera in the head, especially since, given the location of this bullet hole in this drape and in one of the lower panes of glass, he would have had to be firing from a prone position. No, I think we can eliminate the theory of the outdoor assassin quite conclusively."

"Now it seems to me that *you* are jumping to conclusions, Herr Holmes," Philipp protested.

"Not all, my dear Prince," Holmes responded. "There is, after all, the matter of broken window glass."

"I see no broken glass on the floor," the Prince responded.

"Yes, that is the point, you see. Had the bullet been fired from outside, it would certainly have left glass fragments here in the room, But there are none. However, I have no doubt that a cursory

## Chapter 7: A Gruesome Examination

examination will reveal that the bullet passed through the drape and thence the window on its way towards the garden."

"But who would have fired a bullet at the window," I asked, "and why?"

Holmes said nothing but looked back at the bed and then again towards the broken pane of glass. He walked to where Rudolf's body was sprawled and reached down to remove a small black pistol that was clutched in his right hand as it rested on his abdomen. He checked the chambers and looked up.

"Two bullets fired," he proclaimed.

"Well, one for the baroness and one for himself," said Hoyos. "That seems obvious." A puzzled look suddenly swept over his face. "But if that is true, then from whence came the bullet that broke the pane of glass?"

Holmes replaced the pistol near the Prince's hand.

"Once again, you are jumping to conclusions," he corrected. "Perhaps there were more bullets fired." He paused, looking down at the bodies. "Perhaps there were more guns."

Philipp expelled a loud breath signaling his frustration.

"And where are they now?" he said with exasperation, looking around the room. "Did they just vanish into thin air? It seems to me you have a simple open and shut case of murder and suicide, or perhaps, a double suicide. In either case, I do not look forward to informing the Emperor that his son took his own life, which is of course a great sin in the eyes of the church, or that he murdered this poor, unfortunate girl, should that be determined."

"I am quite convinced, Prince Philipp, that there is little 'simple' or 'open and shut' about this matter," said Holmes. "Fortunately, I have a little experience in untangling what often begin as 'open and shut' cases but which, by applying the science of deduction, are revealed to be far more diabolical than they appear at a superficial first glance."

## Chapter 7: A Gruesome Examination

Holmes walked back to the bed where Rudolf's body lay diagonally with his legs dangling off the mattress. On the gore-soaked pillow lay what remained of his head, the upper portion of which, just above his eyebrows, had been largely blown away. A ghastly mass of shattered bone shards, blood and brains coated the bedclothes and sprayed upwards onto the bed's wooden frame and the nearby wall. I had seen innumerable gruesome injuries during my war-time service in battlefield hospitals, but the carnage of the scene I now observed was sickening, all the more so because of the realization that this was the body of the young man who, just a few hours earlier, had been the heir apparent to the throne of the Hapsburgs.

Holmes seemed utterly unaffected by the gore. With utter dispassion, he flexed the Prince's arms, testing them for the tell-tale rigidity. He carefully held Rudolf's shattered head in his hands, gently turning it one way and then the other. Using one of the cloths that Loschek had provided, he gently brushed aside some of the matted viscera, trying to avoid contact with the gore. He looked first under the Prince's chin, at his temples and then finally, he then into the top of the open skull. He looked again at the pistol that had been lodged in Rudolf's hand. When he was finished with the examination, Loschek offered him another moistened towel and a clean basin of water to wash his hands.

"Well, Holmes, do you see anything that suggests the sequence in which these deaths occurred?" asked Hoyos.

"I see a great deal, Count," he responded without elaboration. "I suggest that we adjourn to a sitting room to review the facts in hopes that doing so away from this ghastly sight will refresh your memories about the events of last evening."

Loschek, who knew the lodge best, led us down the hallway to a parlor where a fire was already blazing in the large stone hearth. We arranged ourselves in the comfortable upholstered chairs. But for the unimaginable horror we had all just witnessed, we might have been preparing to take afternoon tea.

## Chapter 7: A Gruesome Examination

As Loschek related the events of the prior evening and that morning in greater detail, Holmes sat still with chin perched on the tips of his tented fingers, his eyes closed, almost appearing to have drifted off to sleep. (For the ease of the reader, I will recount the following conversation in English.)

"My room is next to that of the Prince," Loschek began. "As you may know, he complained of feeling ill yesterday. A bad head cold, he said, which is why he decided against returning with Prince Philipp to the Hofburg palace last evening as he had intended,"

"Indeed," Holmes said. "A head cold too debilitating to return to Vienna, but not sufficiently incapacitating to interfere with a dinner with you, Count Hoyos, or a rescheduled hunt in the morning. Might I ask what the menu for the meal was?"

"The kitchen staff had prepared a delicious soup, goose-liver pie, roast beef, venison and pastry," said Hoyos.

"Hardly a meal for someone complaining of feeling poorly," I interjected.

"Certainly not!," Holmes responded. "And what was his mood during this feast, if I may ask?"

Hoyos shrugged. "Oh, he was quite engaged during most of the meal, but as we began the dessert, he grew quite pensive."

"Did he identify any particular subject as the source of his agitation?"

"He expressed considerable concern about the national defence bill that under debate in parliament," Hoyos said. "You may not be aware that it has been stirring up quite a controversy. He had grave qualms about the legislation, and he had learned of criticisms being circulated by Archduke Albrecht, whom he had just replaced as the inspector-general of the army."

"Why had Albrecht been replaced?" asked Holmes.

"He had been *promoted* – after thirty-six years – to the position of Field Marshall," he explained. "The Emperor evidently wanted to

## Chapter 7: A Gruesome Examination

provide Rudolf with additional military experience before serving as Emperor himself someday."

"And what are the major objections in parliament to the defence bill?"

"Many fear it could worsen our relationship with the Hungarians," Philipp interjected. "The alliance has been a strong one since the treaty of 1867 that created the dual kingdoms. But there has been growing unrest in Budapest. Dissidents are insisting upon greater independence. The Emperor's most senior advisors in the government – Albrecht and Minister-President Taaffe in particular – are concerned by the protests and have shared those concerns with the Emperor. My impression was that Rudolf feared these men were conspiring to undermine the father's confidence in his son by linking him to the Hungarian independence campaign."

The Minister President Edward Taaffe (left)
and Field Marshall Archduke Albrecht (right)

"Why would they foment such apprehension?" asked Holmes.

"If one is to believe the rumors circulating through Vienna, they believed that Rudolf was ill-suited to the position of Emperor and

## Chapter 7: A Gruesome Examination

feared Franz Joseph was preparing to confirm his son's status as Crown Prince."

"The possible dissolution of the alliance would presumably represent a serious blow to the Empire," Holmes observed. "Did Rudolf indeed hold sympathies for the Hungarian nationalists?"

No one said anything for a moment, and then Hoyos spoke, choosing his words carefully.

"The Crown Prince is, I am sorry, *was* of a different generation and a more modern time than these venerable leaders. He had strong ideas about initiating reforms in the Empire, including the relationship with the Hungarians. Such views were certainly viewed skeptically by the likes of Albrecht and Taaffe. While he may have expressed such unconventional views to his father, I cannot believe he would have lent open support to the dissidents."

"But you believe him capable of holding such views?" Holmes interrupted.

"Yes, but incapable of taking action in support of such views," Hoyos responded. "Such engagement certainly would have represented a most serious challenge to his father and the nation!"

Holmes turned to Loschek. "You spent a great deal of time privately with the Crown Prince. Did you hear him voice opinions on such matters?"

The valet shook his head from side to side.

"I know nothing about such things," Loschek protested.

Holmes seemed to consider these observations for several moments before returning to the events of the prior evening.

"After the dinner with Count Hoyos, did the Crown Prince retire to his room?"

"*Ja*, Herr Holmes," Loschek said. "I walked him there myself, as I always do."

"And was Baroness Vetsera already awaiting him in his room?" Holmes asked.

## Chapter 7: A Gruesome Examination

The valet looked pleadingly to Count Hoyos and Prince Philipp whose faces disclosed no emotion before turning back to Holmes.

"She had arrived earlier in the day and had gone directly to his room. I had not seen her depart and so, yes, I believe she was in the room when the Crown Prince retired.

"When we arrived at the door, he asked me to wake him at 7:00 in the morning for breakfast so that he might be prepared for the hunt with Count Hoyos and Prince Philipp."

"And then did you go to your own quarters next door and retire immediately?"

"*Nein*, not yet," he replied.

"Why not?" I asked.

"Sometimes the Prince decides that he wants a glass of sherry or port and he will call me," he said. "So, I waited for a short time, but I did not receive any call. Shortly, however, I heard footsteps in the hall outside my room and I opened the door slightly. The fiacre, Bratfisch, was knocking on the Prince's door. I saw the door open and the driver went inside."

I found the account highly dubious and could not restrain myself from asking for clarification.

"That seems rather peculiar," I remarked. "Pray, why would the Crown Prince admit Bratfisch if his mistress was with him in the room?"

Loschek shrugged his shoulder.

"Bratfisch is a very fine whistler," he said. "Also, a singer of Viennese songs. He had performed for the prince in earlier times and I presumed the Prince and baroness wished for some musical entertainment."

Holmes and I looked incredulously at each other.

"Before they killed themselves?" I remarked. "Bratfisch must indeed be a very accomplished whistler!"

*Chapter 7: A Gruesome Examination*

"Oh, he is, *Herr doktor*!" replied Loschek, failing to appreciate my skepticism, although a slight smirk appeared on Holmes's face. "He most certainly is."

"And did you hear his singing and whistling through the walls?"

"*Ja*, it went on for maybe a half hour or so. I could hear it very clearly. Then I heard the Prince's door open and close and I opened my own door slightly to see what was happening."

"And did you see Bratfisch leaving the room?" I asked.

"*Ja*, I saw him walking down the corridor towards the entry way. Naturally, I presumed he was heading back to the cabin where he stayed while at Mayerling, just on the other side of the stables."

"Did you call out to him?"

"*Nein*," Loschek said quickly. "It was no business of mine."

"But you watched as he left the lodge through the front door?"

"No, Herr Holmes, I gave it no thought. I closed my door and I went to sleep. We were expecting an early morning of hunting."

'Now, this is very important, Loschek," said Holmes, leaning in towards the diminutive vale. "Did you hear anything else during the night from the Prince's room?"

The valet's face took on a look of great consternation, and again, he looked pleadingly towards Hoyos and Philipp, seeking their guidance."

"They cannot help you!" Holmes asked sharply. "Did you hear anything, anything at all, during the night?"

The valet swallowed with difficulty and wet his lips with his tongue.

"*Ja*, I could hear them talking."

"The Crown Princed Rudolf and the Baroness Vetsera. Could you discern what they were saying?

He shook his head in the negative.

"I could hear them, but so faintly. Maybe for another hour. But I could not hear the words. Then it became quiet and I must have fallen to sleep."

74

## Chapter 7: A Gruesome Examination

"Are you a very heavy sleeper?" Holmes asked.

"No, no. A valet cannot be a sound sleeper!" he advised. "In case the Prince calls me, I must wake up."

"So, did anything awaken you during the night?"

Loschek's breaths came in a short staccato. He suddenly looked old and very fatigued, and he seemed oblivious to Holmes's question. His eyes closed, seemingly lost in thought, he sat so still that I wondered if perhaps he had drifted off to sleep.

"Did you hear anything else in the night?" Holmes sharply demanded, moving closer to the frightened valet.

Loschek opened his eyes and a look of alarm filled his face.

"*Ja*, a loud noise woke me up. I thought it came from the Crown Prince's room next door. But I could not be sure. Perhaps it was a dream, I thought. I lay very quiet and I could hear nothing for a long time. Then, after a while, there came another loud noise. This one I could hear clearly, since I was awake, and I thought it sounded like a gunshot."

"Surely you could not ignore such a sound coming from your master's room!" I insisted.

"Of course not, doctor! I quickly dressed and walked down the hall to the door of the Crown Prince's chamber. I put my ear to the door and listened, but I could hear only sobbing. I knocked on the door but there was no response, so I turned the handle but the door was locked."

"You are certain of that fact?" Holmes said.

"Yes, yes," Loschek replied. "I knocked again and again and finally I heard a fumbling at the lock and the door opened slightly. It was the Crown Prince, and he looked a fright. His hair was all messed and his eyes were quite red."

"'Why have you disturbed me in the middle of the night, Loschek?' he demanded.

"I attempted to look into the room, but the door was opened just a crack and I could see nothing.

75

## Chapter 7: A Gruesome Examination

"'I heard loud noises,' I said, 'and I feared it might have originated in your room, your Grace.'

"'No, there has been nothing like that from this room,' he said with assurance. 'It might be some poachers shooting in the woods,' he suggested. 'Remind me in the morning to have Herr Zwerger investigate if someone has been stealing the royal game. Now, do not worry yourself; all will be well soon enough.'"

"Herr Zwerger?" I asked, unfamiliar with the name.

"The game warden," Loschek clarified. "He lives in a cottage not far from the stables."

"Please continue," requested Holmes.

"Well, he again reminded me again to call for him at 7:00, told me 'good night' and began to whistle a gay tune while closing his door. I heard the key turn in the lock. I admit I thought this was a most curious conversation, but I had my instructions and I followed them. Returning to my bed, I soon drifted off again and slept soundly, rising at about 6 o'clock as is typical for me.

"But then something most peculiar did occur. I was walking to the lodge's entrance to get some fresh air – I do this every morning before summoning the Crown Prince -- when suddenly the door to the Crown Prince's room opened. To my great surprise, he was standing in the doorway, already fully dressed for the day."

"Was that an unusual event?"

"Most assuredly! The Crown Prince is rarely awake before I summon him, and I have almost never known him to be dressed at such an early hour."

"Did he now seem agitated?" Holmes inquired.

"Most assuredly he did, Herr Homes!" the valet replied. "He once again asked me to return at 7:00. I went off to check on the preparation of his breakfast and returned to his room to waken him, as he had requested, in about one hour. I knocked on the door, expecting that he would again open the door, but now there was no response. I called his name repeatedly and finally he did respond, although in an

## Chapter 7: A Gruesome Examination

unfamiliar tone. But he insisted that all was fine and that I need not remain. He would join me soon."

"You say his voice sounded unfamiliar?" Holmes pressed.

Loschek became pensive and mulled the question for a moment.

"He did not sound like himself, it is true, Herr Holmes," he finally said. "Perhaps it was due to his head cold, I thought. Even so, I was uneasy and I wanted to assure myself he was well.

"'Please, your Grace, open the door,' I asked.

"'Go away!' he commanded.

"His tone seemed unusually unfriendly since I was only doing precisely what he had requested of me. But despite my continued knocking and my cries, I could elicit no further response from within."

"Did you attempt to enter the room?" asked Holmes.

"I was forbidden to do so, Mr Holmes," Loschek reminded him. "But I did try the door anyway but it was locked."

"So, you had reason to become alarmed," I said.

"Yes, I was fearful, especially after the strange events of the preceding night. I knew the Prince was sometimes inclined towards melancholy and I was worried, Mr Holmes, about his state of mind. I went outside to find Herr Zwerger and together we went to Count Hoyos' cottage."

"And you were still at your cottage?" Holmes asked the Count.

"I had just arisen," he replied.

"I told him about my conversations with the Crown Prince," Loschek continued, "and implored him to come with me and Herr Zwerger. He immediately agreed and together we set off for the lodge. On the way, I picked up a heavy hammer as we passed the stable. I suspected I might need it to gain access to the room if the door was locked."

"Did you see anyone else in the vicinity of the lodge? Anything out of the usual?"

Loschek stuck his lower lip out and covered up his upper lip.

## Chapter 7: A Gruesome Examination

"No one," he insisted, "except for the carriage near the stable. I supposed it had been arranged to take the Crown Prince back to Vienna after the hunt. It was not Bratfisch's usual carriage but it certainly was an official-looking one of the sort that the Prince uses frequently."

"It must have been my coach," the Prince responded. "I imagine that I had arrived whilst you were gathering up Hoyos and the gardener. Perhaps the driver was watering the horses before returning to Vienna."

"Philipp was waiting at the front entrance to the lodge as we arrived," Hoyos confirmed.

"I see," Holmes sat thoughtfully. "So now there were the four of you: Loschek, Hoyos, Philipp and Herr Zwerger, is that correct?"

"Yes, and as we hurried down the corridor to the Crown Prince's room, I provided an account of the morning's events."

"'Might he not be sleeping soundly?' Prince Philipp had asked."

"Yes, that was my thought," interjected Count Hoyos. "We had consumed a rather filling dinner last night, and a good bit of wine. He was probably again sleeping very soundly, I conjectured."

"But I reminded these gentlemen that I had already seen the Crown Prince, awake and fully dressed, only an hour earlier," Loschek declared. "Moreover, I had spoken with him through the door just before going off to find the others. It seemed very unlikely that he had returned to bed and fallen asleep in the intervening time."

"How long would you say you were absent from the lodge when you went to find Zwerger and Hoyos?" Holmes asked.

"Perhaps ten minutes, that is all," he reported. "Their lodgings are not far from the main building. Once we arrived at the Crown Prince's door, I again called out his name, but received no response."

"I also called for Rudolf," interjected Hoyos, "and we banged sharply on the door, but there was no sound whatsoever from inside the room. Finally, we all agreed there was no alternative but to force open the door using the hammer Loschek had brought with him."

The others all voiced their agreement that this account accurately described the scene outside the Prince's room.

## Chapter 7: A Gruesome Examination

"I raised the hammer and began banging through the door," the valet said. "As you could see, the door is a heavy one, made of thick planks, and it took several minutes, but I finally was able to reach in to locate the locking mechanism."

"And the door had been locked?" Holmes pressed.

"Yes, although the key was not in the lock, but I was able to manipulate the locking mechanism from inside the door and then we all pushed together and forced the door open and rushed in. *Mein Gott im Himmel*! May I never see such a sight again!" he shrieked.

"From the doorway, we could see clearly Rudolf lying on the bed," said Hoyos. "His head was terribly disfigured and there was a great amount of blood splattered on the bedposts and wall above where he lay."

"I looked around the room and was relieved not to see the Baroness Mary anywhere," Loschek offered. "Perhaps, I thought, she had returned to Vienna already and had been spared this horror!

"But then, I noticed the blankets next to the Prince's body were piled up in an unnatural way and seemed to be covering something on the bed. I walked to the bed and pulled the covers back. May God save me! It was the Baroness who lay as you saw her, with those terrible injuries.

"'It is Mary Vetsera!' I declared. 'She has been shot as well!'"

"'Is she dead?' Prince Philipp had demanded.

"'Most certainly,' I had replied.

Recounting the experience had utterly depleted the valet and he buried his head in his hands and wept uncontrollably. The other men sat stoically looking at Holmes, their royal breeding precluding any outward display of grief before a stranger.

"Which of you entered the room?" Holmes demanded, looking to the two royal gentlemen.

"Just Loschek," declared Count Hoyos.

"Weren't you curious as to what had happened, or whether perhaps the Prince might still be alive?" Holmes asked.

## Chapter 7: A Gruesome Examination

"You have seen the injury to his head, Mr Holmes," said Hoyos. "I know something of battlefield injuries. There was no question in my mind the Prince was quite dead. Frankly, my first thought was not to tramp about and interfere with the evidence. I am," he acknowledged to me, "a reader of Dr Watson's stories and understand your disdain for the clumsiness of Scotland Yard's inspectors."

"Since I had met you at the Hofburg dinner last evening," Philipp said, "we agreed to take advantage of your presence and summon you to examine this terrible scene before anything is moved. We sent the wire to your hotel. I hope we have done the right thing."

"Very much so," Holmes said, "although I fear the Emperor will understandably be extremely displeased that I was unable to prevent this tragedy."

Hoyos shook his head in agreement. "Yes, Holmes, it seems you have arrived too late."

Holmes looked curiously at the group of men.

"Yes," Holmes said, "But perhaps I can unravel what happened here last night, which might be of some comfort to his parents." He paused momentarily. "By the way, have the Crown Prince's parents been informed of the tragedy?"

"I will leave momentarily to convey the sad news to the Emperor and Empress," Hoyos declared. "This will be a devasting blow. The Empress, in particular, will be inconsolable. To take his own life! As a Catholic, he will not even be eligible for burial in the royal vaults! The Emperor has lost his only son and heir! The very fate of the nation has been altered. And poor Princess Stephanie! A widow at just 24 years old! I am not sure how I can explain the circumstances to them."

"True," Holmes agreed, "and there is the inconvenient presence of the Baroness Vetsera. I do not wish to minimize the grief of the family or the nation from the loss of the Crown Prince, but there is a certain awkwardness about this situation. Let us remember that she,

## Chapter 7: A Gruesome Examination

too, is a victim. The circumstances surrounding her death will have to be fully explained as well, and doing so may well prove to be embarrassing to Rudolf's family."

"I presume you will need some time, Mr Holmes, to further examine the room for details. I have wired Dr von Widerhofer, the Prince's longstanding physician, and asked that he come to Mayerling with his preservative fluids, although I did not mention whom he would be embalming," said Hoyos, looking at his pocket watch. "He should be arriving within the hour."

"And Miss Vetsera?" Holmes asked. "Is she to receive the same attention as the Prince? Her death is no less consequential in a purely legal sense, at least not under British law."

"We must await instructions from the palace," Philipp said authoritatively. "Until we do, there can be no mention whatsoever of the Baroness' death. On this point there can be no disagreement. We cannot risk the scandal or the political intrigue that might well follow any disclosure that she had died alongside the Crown Prince."

"I appreciate your giving me time to conduct my investigation," Holmes replied, "but it is not clear how long it will take to establish what precisely occurred here, Your Excellency."

Prince Philipp assumed a dismissive tone.

"Surely the chain of events is clear," he brusquely told Holmes. "Either Baroness Mary Vetsera killed herself or, God forbid it, she killed Rudolf and then took her own life! In the case of the former, it seems obvious that a distraught Rudolf took his own life."

"Could it be the Prince, angered by her unexpected presence, might have killed her -- by accident or intentionally -- before turning the gun on himself?" Holmes speculated.

"Or perhaps each committed suicide," I proposed. "We shall never know, since only the two of them were in the room, the door was locked, and they are now both well beyond being able to explain how this horror came to be."

## Chapter 7: A Gruesome Examination

"However, we cannot allow such revelations to become the subject of the Viennese gossip circles," Philipp declared. "We will have to fashion an explanation for this terrible mess."

"Any of the scenarios you have mentioned surely could become the topic of irresponsible speculation," Holmes agreed. "However, I must caution you that none is the correct explanation since they all are unquestionably at variance with the facts."

Every head in the room turned to him.

"You question whether the facts are as we have stated them?" demanded a clearly perturbed Philipp.

"The facts are almost assuredly *not* as you have stated them," Holmes declared. As Philipp noticeably started, Holmes added, "I am not accusing you of misrepresenting on purpose, Your Excellency. But even the rudimentary observation I have made demonstrates unequivocally that the true account of what occurred here last night remains yet to be discovered."

A look of shock had registered on the faces of the three men.

"You can, for instance, quite dismiss any notion that the Baroness bore any responsibility for the death of the Crown Prince," Holmes pressed forward.

"How can you be certain of that assertion?" asked Hoyos.

"Because, my dear Count," Holmes declared, "she was already quite dead long before the Crown Prince expired," Holmes continued. "As to his death, there is no chance whatsoever that he took his own life, as the presence of the gun in his hand was intended to have us believe."

"But what other explanation is there?" asked Hoyos. "They are dead, the door is locked from the inside. There is no other way into or out of the room without being detected."

"All true, all true," said Holmes. "And yet I am quite certain that neither Crown Prince Rudolf nor Baroness Mary Vetsera committed suicide!"

# Chapter 8: Seeds of Doubt

Our companions greeted Holmes's declaration with a silent amazement that was broken only by a sharp knock on the door, which then creaked open. A distinguished looking middle- aged man with a receding hairline of dark curls and a mustache and goatee of pure white walked into the room. He quickly surveyed the occupants of the room, several of whom appeared to be known to him.

"What is going on here?" he demanded of the two aristocrats, and then pointing towards my friend and me. "Who are these people?"

"My name is Sherlock Holmes, and I am here on behalf of Emperor Franz Joseph," my friend said with a forced friendliness. "This is my colleague, Dr John Watson. But now you have the better of me, sir."

Hoyos and Philipp confirmed we were as Holmes had declared, explaining that we were investigating the recent events at Mayerling lodge.

"I am Dr Hermann Freiherrn von Widerhofer," the new arrival declared. "I have the honour to serve as the personal physician to the Crown Prince."

"And have you come to examine your patient?" Holmes asked.

"I was prohibited from entering the room," the doctor said, adding in a frustrated tone, "on the orders of an *English* policeman!"

"I am a *private* detective, Dr von Widerhofer, not a policeman," Holmes said, "and I have no interest whatsoever in keeping you from examining the Prince and his companion."

"His companion?" von Widerhofer exclaimed, looking around to the other men. "What is the meaning of this?"

"Come along," said Holmes, moving towards the doorway. "I am most curious to hear your opinion of the injuries."

*Chapter 8: Seeds of Doubt*

We followed the detective and doctor back down the hallway, past a guard at the door and into the chamber where the two bodies remained sprawled in a macabre fashion on the bed. Upon viewing the Prince's body, von Widerhofer convulsed in shock and uttered a vile profanity that did not require translation.

"What has happened to this man?" he cried, stepping toward the bed. "And Mary Vetsera! My God, what has happened here?"

Holmes restrained him by the arm.

"If you do not mind, let me guide you to the beside so possible evidence is not damaged by your footsteps."

Together, the two men walked to the bedside where Rudolf's corpse was sprawled. Von Widerhofer leaned over to peer closely at the damage to the Prince's head and then turned away in revulsion.

"You mentioned that you were the Prince's personal physician," Holmes said. "May I ask the last time the Price consulted you, *Herr Doktor*?"

The physician looked back to the young man he had treated since childhood.

"It was several months, I should say, but I found nothing amiss."

"So this sore on his nose is a recent problem?"

The physician looked perplexed.

"I know of no such injury."

"It may not be an injury," Holmes suggested. "Perhaps it was not evident when you last saw him but I could not help noticing it when I examined him."

The doctor became exasperated and threw up his hands in frustration.

"Herr Holmes, my Crown Prince is lying in bed with his brains blown out and you are worried about a bruise on his nose? Really, sir, which are we to be more worried about?"

## Chapter 8: Seeds of Doubt

"I worry about everything that may pertain to the solution of the case, Herr Doktor, even something as innocuous as an unexplained canker on the Prince's nose."

"Whether the problem is a canker or a bullet," Philipp said, assuming an authoritative tone, "the explanation of the Prince's death must remain confidential, at least until we have discussed the tragedy with the Emperor and determined how the news is to be disseminated. We cannot have the nation know that the Prince of Austria and his paramour have killed themselves in some sort of suicide pact!"

"But as I have advised, we do not know any such thing," Holmes interrupted. "Nevertheless, I understand the need to break the news most compassionately to the Prince's parents."

"Until Dr von Widerhofer had completed his post-mortem examination," suggested Philipp, "I propose that we ascribe the Prince's death to a sudden and unexpected heart failure. Count Hoyos will return to Vienna to convey that version of the terrible news to the Emperor and Empress." He looked to Hoyos, adding, "I do not think it is important to bring the death of Mary Vetsera into the account you give to their royal highnesses."

I would gladly have joined Hoyos in leaving the curséd house but Holmes insisted on our remaining at Mayerling to interview additional members of the lodge's staff concerning anything they might have heard or observed during the night and early morning. We would return to Vienna later that afternoon when the Prince's body was transported back to the palace.

Several soldiers were enlisted to remove the Prince's corpse to a room where von Widerhofer could conduct his post-mortem examination and initiate the embalming process. As we prepared to follow them, Philipp raised a concern .

"Despite Mr Holmes' wild conspiracy theories, it is obvious that he died by his own hand," he protested to von Widerhofer. "Is it really necessary that you desecrate his body further, which can only be additionally distressing to the Emperor and Empress."

## Chapter 8: Seeds of Doubt

Holmes looked disdainfully at the Prince.

"Your Grace, I have come over a thousand miles to consult with the Emperor about the stability of his kingdom. It was he who instructed me to conduct an interview with his son, the Crown Prince. Even before I had an opportunity to meet the young man, let alone to assess any risks to the Empire, the Crown Prince has been struck down in a very violent act."

"By his own hand," Philipp interjected yet again.

Holmes cast him a cold eye. "As you know, I do not subscribe to that conclusion, however anxiously some may wish me to do."

"Your suspicions appear to me without a basis in fact, Herr Holmes," Philipp brusquely declared. "This seems to have been a double suicide and nothing more."

"That may be the version of events with which you are comfortable, but I have no doubt that the facts fail to support such a conclusion," said Holmes. "Unless you have evidence to offer to warrant your conclusion …"

Prince Philipp had dug into his pocket and withdrawn an envelope and piece of white paper.

"These may help to remove any remaining doubts," Philipp said. He opened the envelope and withdrew several pages of paper which he unfolded, holding them up for us to observe.

"*Zu meiner Mutter*," was scrawled across the face of the envelope. "To my mother."

"These are notes from the Crown Prince and baroness declaring their intention to take their own lives," said Philipp. "These were obviously written in their own hands and left on the writing table." He pointed to a small table not ten feet from where the bodies lay. "What could be clearer?" A look of supreme satisfaction spread across his face. "This may be one situation where your famed deductive skills are not required, Mr Holmes."

My friend took the papers from Philipp's outstretched hand. Reading them over, his face grew increasingly grave.

## Chapter 8: Seeds of Doubt

"Do you mind?" he asked Philipp as he handed the notes to me. The Count nodded his assent and I took the papers from Holmes.

The letter in the envelope had apparently been written by Mary Vetsera on *Schloss Mayerling* stationery embossed with the royal crest of the House of Hapsburg. I had earlier noticed blank sheets of the same stationery on the writing desk.

> *Dear Mother* [I translated for Holmes],
> *Please forgive me for what I've done. I could not resist love. In accordance with Him, I want to be buried next to Him in the Cemetery of Alland. I am happier in death than life. Please forgive me for what I've done, I could not resist love. Mary*

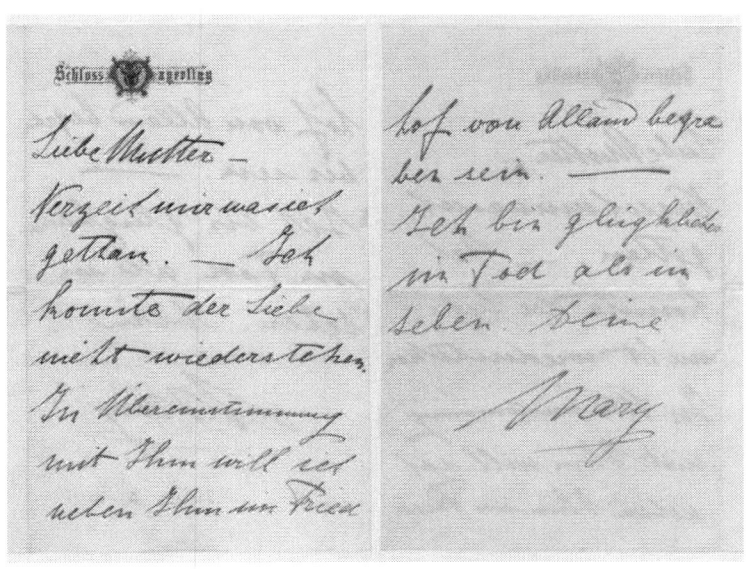

Baroness Mary Vetsera's suicide note to her mother, written on stationery from the Mayerling lodge

The second note was addressed to the Crown Prince's wife and was written in a man's scrawl on a piece of cheap white paper.

*Dear Stephanie,*

## Chapter 8: Seeds of Doubt

*You are now rid of my presence and annoyance; be happy in your own way. Take care of the poor wee one, she is all that remains of me. To all acquaintances,* [here he listed a number of names with whom I was unfamiliar] *say my last greetings. I go quietly to my death, which alone can save my good name. I embrace you affectionately. Your loving Rudolf.*

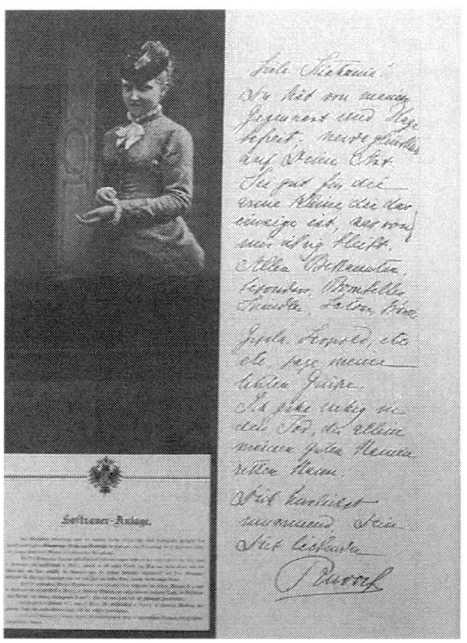

The suicide note from Rudolf to his wife, Crown Princess Stephanie

"Where did you find those?" Holmes asked sharply.

"I took the liberty of removing them earlier from the Prince's bed chamber," Philipp replied. "To safeguard them."

"I thought you said you had not ventured into the bedroom before my arrival," Holmes said.

"And I did not. There were found by Loschek."

## Chapter 8: Seeds of Doubt

"Were they?" Holmes responded, turning to the valet. "How very interesting that he had failed to mention them to me during our earlier interview."

"I decided not to leave them lying about where they might fall into the wrong hands," the valet explained.

"Wise thinking," said Holmes unconvincingly. "Do you mind if I retain them for the time being?"

Philipp strode to where I stood holding the letters.

"I think not, Mr Holmes," he responded, taking the notes from my hand and placing them back in his jacket pocket. "I am certain you can appreciate the very delicate nature of this situation. I recognize that you are completely trustworthy, but it is best if this material remains in the custody of the royal family. If you require these notes during the course of whatever investigation you may undertake, I assure you they will be made available to you."

Holmes looked chagrined but nodded to the Prince.

"As you wish, of course," he said. "However, I entreat you to handle those notes with the greatest of care. Given the uncertainties as to precisely what transpired in this room, they may well prove to contain crucial information."

"You seem intent upon making this terrible situation into something far more complex than it evidently is, Mr Holmes," protested Philipp, his frustration with Holmes evidently growing. "We have these notes, incontrovertibly written by the baroness and Crown Prince. We found the revolver in the Prince's hand with two bullets fired, corresponding to the fatal wounds of the baroness and Rudolf. They were found inside a room sealed by a locked door with the only known key on the inside. It would appear there is no reasonable doubt about what transpired. Perhaps you are seeking to create one of your little mysteries where none exists?"

"I do not seek to create mysteries, Your Grace, great or small. And when there are two dead people, both members of the Austrian aristocracy, the case can hardly be termed 'little.' Those letters, the revolver, the locked door; it is true, they constitute *some* notable features of the case, although their significance remains to be proven. My career has been based upon the application of scrupulous standards to every aspect of a case combined with the discipline to avoid drawing premature conclusions.

"It might seem evident that, on first observation, the circumstances of the tragedy are as self-evident as you describe them. The Crown Prince slips away from his wife and family in the Hofburg palace for a relaxing hunting trip at Mayerling with Hoyos and yourself. He promises to return for the important dinner the following evening, as requested by his father.

"Plans for the hunt are upended when Rudolf complains of a sore throat and head cold. He not only declines to participate in the hunt but announces he will not return to the Hofburg palace for the aforementioned dinner. Surely he knows that his absence means he will miss his opportunity to speak with his father before the Emperor's departure for Hungary the very next day, even though matters concerning the Empire's relationship to Hungary have caused considerable tensions between the two men. He requested that you, Prince Philipp, return to the palace in order to explain his absence to the Emperor.

"The Baroness Mary Vetsera has unexpectedly arrived at Mayerling and has been ensconced in the Prince's bedchamber, as he discovers at some point before his dinner with you, Count Hoyos, at which you have said he displayed no evidence of illness."

"That statement of the facts is all quite true, Mr Holmes," Hoyos confirmed. "At about 21:00 hours, he professed fatigue and announced he would retire to care for his cold. He wished me a good evening and expressed enthusiasm about partaking in the rescheduled hunt after Philipp's return from the palace."

"Just before retiring, he instructed Loschek to prepare his breakfast for the next morning," Holmes continued, surveying the room to see if anyone cared to challenge any of the account. Seeing no

## Chapter 8: Seeds of Doubt

opposition, he concluded, "I think we can all agree that those are the essential known facts prior to the shootings."

"I begin to appreciate your point, Holmes," Philipp mused.

"It does not seem to me that the Prince was exhibiting the kind of melancholy one might of expect of one preparing to take his own life," Holmes said. "Eating a heavy meal, drinking liberally, talking of a hunt the next day, planning a breakfast. And then, of course, there was a very attractive and, apparently, very willing young woman waiting for him in his bed."

"Mr Holmes!" Loschek interrupted. "You are speaking of the Crown Prince!"

"I have no patience for discretion and niceties!" Holmes interrupted sharply. "There are questions that I will not be intimidated from asking, even if the answers may not place the Crown Prince in the best light. I assure you I will do my best to ensure the reputation of these two young people is not besmirched for the benefit of the tongue-waggers and sensationalists. But facts are facts. They are dead and many individuals may have potential motives for wishing them so. The circumstances remain murky, the timeline is uncertain and the whereabouts of various individuals in question – including all of you – await further investigation."

I carefully watched the faces of those in the room: Count Hoyos, Prince Philipp, the driver Bratfisch, Dr von Widerhofer, the valet Loschek. None betrayed anything by their response but each watched Holmes intensely.

After several uncomfortable moments, Hoyos broke the silence.

"Of course, we defer to your well-deserved reputation, Mr Holmes," he said. "You are, of course, the detective, not us." He swept his arm around the room to indicate his compatriots. "I am sure I speak for all of us when I say you will have our complete cooperation. At the moment, however, I must depart for the palace for the unpleasant task of conveying this news to the Emperor and his wife. Our conversation, I have no doubt, will continue in Vienna."

## Chapter 8: Seeds of Doubt

"I reiterate Prince Philipp's wise admonition against discussing the exact circumstances of the Prince's death other than to his parents," Holmes said. "The less said about suicide or shootings, let alone Miss Vetsera, the better for the moment. The less scandalous explanation of the Prince's death -- a heart attack or stroke – might serve for the next day or two to keep the gossip under control until the facts become clearer."

The meeting broke up with Hoyos boarding his coach for the return trip to Vienna and his interview with the Empress and Emperor. Philipp retired to his room, explaining he needed to lie down to calm his nerves.

Holmes remained momentarily in the hallway and naturally, I waited with him.

"That was quite a statement you just made," I remarked. "Do you genuinely believe there is more to this tragedy than meets the eye?"

"Almost without question," he responded.

"But I see no obvious clues," I said.

"That is because there are none that are readily apparent," Holmes replied. "Murderers, at least those with a semblance of intelligence and cunning, do not strew clues about willy-nilly for detectives to discover! But even my cursory examination of the bodies and the bedchamber convinced me there was far more devilry afoot here than many would like for us to believe."

"With all due respect, Holmes, I looked at the same injuries. You obviously have discovered evidence that I missed entirely, which is hardly the first time that has been the case!"

"But there are clues, Watson, even if they are not so obvious. The key on the floor, for example. The notes on the writing table. And the spots of blood on the carpet. All offer conclusive proof. But for the moment, let us hurry to von Widerhofer's examination, which I have little doubt will reveal additional fascinating evidence."

*Chapter 8: Seeds of Doubt*

Utterly confused, I followed Holmes into the makeshift mortuary where the Crown Prince's physician was to prepare the Crown Prince's body for transport back to Vienna.

# Chapter 9: A Curious Angle

We found the Prince's physician in a small, windowless room on the ground floor that served as the lodge's medical clinic. Although not equipped for a comprehensive post-mortem dissection, von Widerhofer had modified the table to facilitate an examination. Von Widerhofer was already dressed in a white surgical gown and had donned rubber gloves that reached almost to his elbows. On the examination table, the Crown Prince lay on its back, his eyes closed, his body unclothed except for a towel modestly draped across his loins. A pillow covered in towels lay under his head, soaked with blood. Despite the evidence of the brutal injury that had taken his life, he appeared at rest. Indeed, his large mustache remained carefully combed into a thick handlebar.

"A terrible injury," the doctor observed as Holmes and I entered the room.

"Be careful, Holmes!" he warned as my friend advanced towards the table. "I would strongly advise you not to touch the Prince's body unless you are wearing protective gloves!"

After we had both donned the gloves proffered by the physician, Holmes invited me to join in a quick perusal of the Prince's body. He looked over the front of the corpse and gently rolled the body to the side to gain a view of the Prince's back. Finally, he reached for the towel that covered the midsection, but the doctor grabbed his hand.

"Please, Mr Holmes, let us be discrete! This is the Crown Prince, after all."

Holmes nodded in agreement and turned his attention to Rudolf's shattered head.

## Chapter 9: A Curious Angle

"Fortunately, the bullet miraculously did not damage his face," von Widerhofer said with a sigh. "With a head bandage, he will appear almost lifelike. That will be a great comfort to the Empress."

"I am less concerned with his appearance than with determining the cause of his death," Holmes responded curtly.

"'The *cause of death?*'" von Widerhofer echoed in a disbelieving tone. "Can you look at what remains of this poor boy's head and doubt 'the cause of death'?"

I could not argue with the doctor's conclusion that the gunshot wound appeared to be the undeniable explanation for the Prince's demise.

"This wound to the Prince's head would have killed any man," Holmes agreed, "and I do not see evidence of other injuries. But that fact does not answer several other pertinent questions."

Von Widerhofer seemed exasperated by Holmes's statement.

"Such as?"

"I will certainly want to see the results of the chemical analysis of the Prince's blood."

Von Widerhofer remained quizzical.

"His blood?" the doctor asked, seemingly dumbfounded.

"In the event he was poisoned or drugged before the fatal shot was fired."

"Poisoned or drugged?" the doctor repeated incredulously. "Why on earth would the Prince do such a thing before committing suicide?"

"Perhaps to calm his nerves or to give him courage. Of course, you are making the assumption that Rudolf himself fired the shot that blew off half of his head."

"That still seems a plausible conclusion, wouldn't you say?" I interjected. "The young woman was incapable of performing such an act. She was already dead hours before Rudolf died, as we know from the state of rigor mortis."

## Chapter 9: A Curious Angle

"Which leaves us with suicide, however unpalatable that may be," said von Widerhofer. "The door was locked from the inside, I am told, as were the doors out to the garden. No one else could have been in the room and left, locking the door behind them."

"That seems true enough," I advised Holmes. "And the only key to the room was the one you found inside the locked room."

"All perfectly reasonable opinions, doctors. But as Watson knows, I believe it is far easier to see than to observe, and there are most certainly several observations in this case that require a good deal of explanation."

The physician looked nervously towards his two assistants who were closely listening to the conversation. He ordered them out of the room with a strong admonition against discussing anything about what they had seen or heard. Then he turned back to my friend with a combination of wonder and concern.

"Alright, Herr Holmes, what have I missed?"

Holmes smiled thinly and placed his hand on the old physician's shoulder.

"The autopsy of a Crown Prince is not the typical responsibility of a pediatrician, is it?" he said. "I expect you have undertaken this unsavory assignment because of your loyalty to the Crown Prince and the royal family, not because of your skills as a coroner."

"Count Hoyos and Prince Philipp have directed me to examine the Prince's remains," he affirmed.

"Yes, well, I can see there is no intention to conduct a proper autopsy," said Holmes.

The doctor's face revealed displeasure with Holmes's cold evaluation.

"There would be little point in further violation of the Prince's body," he insisted. "We know what caused his death."

"However I need more information than you have offered thus far about Rudolf's medical condition *before* his death," the detective

## Chapter 9: A Curious Angle

pressed. "The infection on his nose was something new, you insist. What else can you tell me about his overall health?"

The doctor shook his head. "Nothing of great consequence. A touch of rheumatism. An inflamed bladder that has been treated for several years by Dr Auchenthaler."

"Do you maintain a complete list of the medicines used to treat his illnesses?" I asked. "Medicines that would be detectable in laboratory tests of the Prince's blood, for example?"

Dr von Widerhofer looked at me cautiously.

"A variety of treatments," he responded. "Perhaps not one that are employed in London hospitals: zinc sulfate, oil of Copaiba balsam, all quite effective."

"Mercury chloride?" Holmes suggested.

Von Widerhofer's eyes narrowed. "I was not aware you had completed medical training, Herr Holmes," he commented, warily watching as Holmes moved toward the end of the examining table where the Prince's head lay. "Again, I advise you to be exceedingly careful about handling any of his bodily fluids. You must be careful about exposing yourself to dangerous bacteria, even from a corpse, you are doubtless aware."

Holmes and I exchanged glances at this pointed admonition.

"We you able to retrieve much of the brain?" Holmes asked, peering into the largely vacant cranium..

The doctor shook his head. "Not much," he said. "However, from the small amount of the cerebellum I have retrieved, I can see there has been some subsidence of the brain passages," he ventured. "Perhaps enough to explain his increasingly erratic behaviour and his decision to take his own life."

"A finding of such illness would help persuade the Church to overlook the act of suicide and allow his burial in the royal crypt," I noted. A similar situation had presented itself in my practice in London several years earlier in the case of Mad Mary O'Shaughnessy who dove into the Thames from the top of the Tower Bridge with her infant

97

## Chapter 9: A Curious Angle

daughter in her arms. Based on my testimony to the local prelate, the church had waived its proscription against permitting the burial of a suicide victim in its cemetery.

"I would not be terribly surprised if that diagnosis had been suggested to you, doctor," Holmes added. Another scowl was directed towards him by the Prince's doctor but Holmes missed the glance, having turned back to examine the wound in Rudolf's head.

The Prince's shattered skull certainly was an horrific sight. The assistants had cleaned away much of the gore and the enormity of the damage to the top of his skull was striking. Holmes focused his attention, however, at the base of the skull. Gently, he used his gloved hands to lift the Prince's head up from the blood-soaked towels on which it rested. With his face just inches from the dreadful injury, he turned the Prince's head to one side and then the other, examining it closely.

"Look here, doctor," he said, "have you noticed this singular piece of evidence?" He had turned Rudolf's head far to the right and pushed up the hair behind his left ear. As von Widerhofer ventured closer, Holmes pointed to a perfectly round hole that had been drilled into the Prince's mastoid bone. "Unquestionably, this must be the entry wound for the shot that tore through his head, would you not agree?" he asked.

Von Widerhofer leaned forward to examine the wound and shook his head in agreement.

"I have found no evidence of any other entry wound," he said, "and so I concur this is where the fatal shot must have entered the skull."

"It is beyond doubt!" Holmes declared. "See here – the unmistakable powder burns caused by a pistol fired close to the skin. A gun was held not an inch or two away and fired!"

I could see the tell-tale blackened markings on the scalp just behind the left ear.

## Chapter 9: A Curious Angle

"Hand me that probe, if you will, Watson," Holmes requested, pointing to the instruments von Widerhofer had laid out on a small table.

I gave Holmes the metal shaft that was about 8 inches in length, which he proceeded to carefully insert into the bullet hole, precisely following the path drilled by the projectile through the bone.

"You can see the bullet's trajectory was nearly straight upward towards the vertex of the Prince's head," said Holmes, pushing the probe deep into the skull until the metal tip emerged from the bloody morass remaining inside the skull.

"Is that important?" asked von Widerhofer.

"I should say so," responded Holmes. "The shot was indisputably fired from the lower left side of the head, behind the left ear. As the probe demonstrates, it traveled upwards so as to pass through the head, shattering the skull and brain. Death was violent and instantaneous, wouldn't you agree, von Widerhofer?"

"It appears inarguable," the physician replied.

"Well, there you are, then," said Holmes, a self-satisfied tone affecting his voice as he triumphantly withdrew the probe and pulled off the rubber gloves, signaling his analytic work was complete.

"I do not understand," the confused von Widerhofer declared. "Have you been able to determine something definitive?"

"Most certainly," Holmes replied. "It was clear to me the moment I stepped into the bedroom, even before I examined the body. It is the key to the entire matter!"

Von Widerhofer and I stared at Holmes in utter confusion.

"Then whom do you suspect, Herr Holmes?" asked the doctor.

"Given the intrigue, jealousy and secrecy that surrounds this royal family and its associates," said Holmes, "I suspect everyone."

The doctor started at these words.

"Everyone?" he repeated.

"Yes, doctor, everyone," Holmes affirmed. "This examination certainly confirms my earlier statement. Prince Rudolf neither committed suicide nor was he shot by his lover, Mary Vetsera. And unless I am very much mistaken, the did not commit suicide either. They were both murdered. Most assuredly."

# Chapter 10: The Second Bullet

While Dr von Widerhofer initiated his embalming work in preparation for transporting the Prince's remains back to Vienna, Holmes and I ventured back to the room where the bodies had been discovered. To our surprise, the remains of the young girl had been removed from the bed in contravention of his explicit instructions. Moreover, the soiled bedclothes already had been replaced by crisp, white sheets and the headboard and wall behind scrubbed clean of blood and other viscera.

Holmes was understandably alarmed since the cleansing had certainly removed many important clues.

"What has become of the Baroness Vetsera's body?" he sharply asked of the guard stationed by the shattered door. I quickly translated into German, and the guard stiffly pointed down the corridor towards the front door of the lodge.

Outdoors, we encountered several soldiers milling who were doubtless discussing the terrible events of the morning. Holmes asked them if they knew where the young girl's remains had been taken. Most stared blankly at the ground, doubtless following instructions to say nothing. One gazed involuntarily to a small out-building about thirty yards from the main house. I followed Holmes as he strode over and pushed open the door.

Inside the building, one of von Widerhofer's young assistants was bent over, examining Mary Vetsera's remains, which had been placed unceremoniously on a plank of wood balanced between two large barrels. The assistant, startled by Holmes's unannounced entry, straightened up and put down the instrument he had been using to examine the corpse.

"What is going on here?" Holmes demanded.

"A preliminary post-mortem while awaiting Dr von Widerhofer," the young man reported.

## Chapter 10: The Second Bullet

The young woman was covered up to her neck by a rough blanket that Holmes removed, revealing her naked body. The light in the small room was dim but that did not stop Holmes from minutely inspecting her body. He examined her from head to foot and then turned her over briefly before repositioning the blanket for the sake of modesty.

"What is the plan for returning the Baroness' body to her family? Holmes pressed, covering her remains with the blanket.

"I do not know," the physician replied. "I believe the gentlemen at the lodge have assumed that responsibility."

Holmes looked uncertainly at him and back at the body on the wooden plank.

"It is important that I make a closer examination of the injury caused by the bullet," he insisted. The doctor nodded in approval and Holmes began a close examination of the ugly wound in Mary's right temple.

"Yes, you can certainly see that the gun undoubtedly was held very close to her head," he said, pointing to a small hole just in front of the tragus, where powder burns were evident. Holmes took the probe from the young doctor's hands and inserted into the bullet hole in the right temple. As he pushed the rod, it exited not out the other side of her head but just above her left eye socket.

"As I suspected!" Holmes cried. He grabbed a cloth and wiped away the large clot that had formed, concealing the point where the probe exited.

"Yes, there never was any doubt in my mind. This shot was almost certainly self-inflicted by the Baroness," he said, "and it was poorly aimed. You can see from the probe that the bullet failed to traverse her head but exited here, near her left eye. I think we will find that it was this bullet that, upon exiting, shattered the window in the bedchamber."

"But wasn't that injury sufficient to have killed her?" asked the physician.

## Chapter 10: The Second Bullet

Holmes look to me for advice.

"It could well have missed the brain entirely," I said. "Indeed, from the angle shown by the probe, I would say it passed through the sinus cavity and out the eye socket. It would have caused a great deal of bleeding and certainly terrible pain, but had it been treated promptly and professionally, it is possible that she might have survived."

"But if this bullet exited from her eye socket," the doctor insisted, "how can you explain the damage to the left side of her face that we presume to have been the exit wound?"

Holmes withdrew the probe and turned Mary's head so that her chin was nearly resting on her right shoulder, as it had when we had first seen in on the bed. Taking a wet cloth, he carefully wiped away the blood that had caked in her hair around her left ear.

"There is your answer!" he triumphantly cried, pointing to a small hole in the skull just in front of and above her left ear. "The entry point of a *second* bullet!"

"How did you know to look for this entry wound?" the doctor wondered.

"I knew it must be there because of the way Mary's head rested on her pillow," Holmes explained. "When we found her, her head was turned to the right. Since Mary was right handed, it is all but certain that she would have held the gun in her right hand and fired into her right temple."

"That surely seems reasonable," I agreed, "although you cannot be sure she was right-handed."

"Unquestionably she was," Holmes answered. He removed her right hand from under the blanket to reveal a spot of ink on one of her fingers. "She spilled this ink on her finger when she wrote the suicide note.

"Why, then, was her head turned to the right, the opposite direction one would have expected? I hypothesised that a second shot had been fired from the other side of the bed. That is precisely what

## Chapter 10: The Second Bullet

occurred," he said triumphantly, pointing to the newly discovered wound in the left temple. "*This* is the shot that killed the poor girl!"

"But she certainly could not have fired the gun that caused this wound!" I said. "However poorly the first shot was aimed, there is no question it would have left her utterly incapacitated and in an advanced state of shock. She could not have pulled the trigger again."

"No, of course, the second shot was fired by someone standing on her left as she lay, gravely wounded, on the bed. Remember that the valet Loschek reported hearing *two* shots before he left his bedroom to check on the Prince? It seemed puzzling to him since the Prince answered the door and clearly had not been injured. Why were two shots fired? And who fired the second shot, if not the Baroness?"

I admit I was puzzled. "Why, the only other person in the room, we have been led to believe, was the Prince himself!" I said. "Loschek has said Bratfisch had departed already, and he was in his own room when he clearly heard the retort."

"Do you mean that the Prince murdered his young mistress?" I cried incredulously.

My head was spinning when suddenly, the door to the little building flew open and the lodge's military commander, Captain Brüder, barged into the darkened room accompanied by several junior officers.

"Who are you?" he demanded of Holmes, who stood his ground, glaring at the military official.

"I am Sherlock Holmes, and I am here by command of the Emperor," he announced.

"If you do not mind, I am going to continue my examination of this unfortunate girl's body."

"That will be unnecessary," Brüder insisted curtly. "We have assumed responsibility for these remains."

"Nevertheless, a complete examination of Miss Vetsera's wounds is crucial to understanding what transpired in the lodge last

## Chapter 10: The Second Bullet

evening," Holmes said sharply. "I must insist that I be present for the post-mortem examination."

"Dr von Widerhofer is perfectly competent to conduct such an examination, should it be required," Brüder declared.

"Yes, I am," insisted von Widerhofer, who had suddenly materialized behind the captain. "Your participation is unnecessary, sir," he said sharply. "I have known Mary Vetsera since she was a little girl." He became emotionally undone and took several moments to recompose himself.

"This girl was a 'pure angel,'" he declared. "That is what Rudolf called her, and I loved her very much as well. I served as her doctor throughout her life and I shall see her through this final tragedy as well."

He turned to Holmes and me and his face assumed a determined look.

"May I suggest you concern yourself with the circumstances involving the death of Crown Prince Rudolf and not trouble yourself over an insignificant figure like Mary Vetsera?" he insisted. "Her death, while lamentable to me personally, is unlikely to affect the future course of this Empire and is therefore no concern of yours."

"I have the authority under these circumstances, Herr Sherlock Holmes, and I must agree wholeheartedly with the doctor," Brüder insisted. "I must ask you to return to the lodge at once and prepare for your departure! Please do not bother yourself further with the death of the Baroness Vetsera. This situation is well in hand, I can personally assure you."

I did not feel assured in the slightest, but as frustrating as it was, the presence of a battery of armed guards persuaded us that there was little point in challenging the captain's explicit order.

"Very well," Holmes said in a resigned tone. He nodded to me to follow him out and, as we reached the door, he stopped and looked back at the doctor. "But I think we both know, von Wiederhorn, that the death of Mary Vetsera is very much at the center of the Mayerling

## Chapter 10: The Second Bullet

mystery, however concerted may be the efforts to remove her name from the story."

Feeling quite maligned, we returned to the lodge to gather our possessions for the return trip to Vienna. We would not, it appeared, have the opportunity to interview other staff at the lodge. Shortly before we departed, the shrouded and newly embalmed body of the Crown Price, surrounded by a solemn phalanx of uniformed soldiers, was placed in a casket and taken from Mayerling lodge for the last time to begin its solemn journey back to the Hofburg palace. We watched as the parade of soldiers wound its way down the drive to where a train was waiting, enormous clouds of steam rising from its engine into the chill.

We clambered aboard and were racing back to the capital. Along the way, Holmes composed a list of people we would have to interview immediately, before the efforts to fabricate a false account of the Mayerling tragedy had time to congeal into a twisted and tortured official narrative. There could be little question that even as we sped back to Vienna, a whitewashed version of what had transpired was being fabricated -- one that undoubtedly bore little resemblance to the truth.

# Chapter 11: A Visit to Mizzi Kaspar

Arriving at the Hofburg palace in the late afternoon, we were welcomed by a somber Count Hoyos who had performed the unenviable duty of informing the royal couple of the death of Crown Prince Rudolf. Despite years of training as an ambassador and government official, the veteran diplomat appeared to have been deeply shaken by his experience.

"I have never faced a more challenging assignment," Hoyos explained. "Upon returning from Mayerling this morning, I summoned the Emperor's adjutant general, *Graff* Paar and *Freiherr* Nopcsa, the controller of the Empress' household, to explain I must speak immediately to His Highness. I had no choice but to disclose the reason for my urgent request, and both men were deeply distraught when I explained what had transpired. They insisted that I must first inform the Empress, for only she could possibly announce the dreadful news to the Emperor.

"The Empress was engaged in her Greek lesson when I arrived at her rooms and I was informed that she could not be interrupted before completing the day's study. Of course, the guard had no idea of the magnitude of the message I was conveying. After a half hour, however, I insisted my news could not wait any longer and forced my way into the chamber. The Empress was startled by my intrusion but seeing the serious look upon my face, she waved off the guards who had rushed in to seize me.

"'What can possibly warrant your intrusion into my private quarters against my explicit instructions, Hoyos?' she demanded.

"I begged her forgiveness for my intrusion and guided her to a chair, requesting that she be seated as I had the most painful disclosure to make to her. Warily, she sat and then looked to me with great fear in her eyes.

## Chapter 11: A Visit to Mizzi Kaspar

"I informed her that the Crown Prince had died suddenly at Mayerling. As we had agreed, I reported that the cause of his death appeared to have been a rupture of an aneurism in his heart."

"And her reaction?" asked Holmes.

"Why, what would you imagine her response to the death of her child might be?" he responded impatiently. "No sooner were the words out of my mouth than she turned a deathly white. She was incredulous, defiant! She insisted it could not be true. I begged her forgiveness for having conveyed such grim news, but I assured her that I spoke the unfortunate truth. As the reality of the tragedy began to take hold, she became distraught. Her shrieks brought the Emperor rushing in from the adjacent room, demanding to know what had occasioned such an outburst. As he comforted her, he stared coldly at me, realizing I must have been the source of her frenzied behavior. Her cries became less feverish and after several moments, she had regained her composure and shared the news with him."

"And his response after she delivered the terrible news?"

"Stoic. Disbelieving, of course, but without emotion, as one might expect of an emperor."

"And their understanding continues to be that he succumbed to heart failure?" Holmes asked.

"Yes, but it will not be for long," Hoyos said. "The Emperor will surely insist upon viewing the body, and it is only a matter of time before the press will pry the truth from someone at Mayerling. In a day or two, I predict, the truth will be known in all its shocking details. Of course, they will bear their grief expressed strictly in private. Their duty is to accept all news – good or bad – with equanimity."

"How did they respond to news of Baroness Vetsera's suicide?" I inquired.

Hoyos' face grew grim.

"I could not tell them. The Crown Prince's death was devastating enough," he said. "To learn that he had died alongside his

## Chapter 11: A Visit to Mizzi Kaspar

mistress – well, they simply could not have accepted such a revelation. There will be time for that part of the story to emerge, but not today."

"But when they learn of that piece of the story soon enough," I commented, "will not your credibility will be in tatters!"

"I did not deny Miss Vetsera was there," Hoyos said. "I have no doubt the Empress, at least, suspects that was the case. In the days ahead, we will construct the complete account that will provide the Empress and Emperor some measure of comfort."

"What do you propose?" Holmes asked.

"Perhaps we might suggest that Mary poisoned the Prince after learning that he was breaking off their liaison and returning to the Crown Princess Stephanie. That version would provide his mother some contentment since such a reconciliation was a great wish of hers."

"But that would be a preposterous misrepresentation!" Holmes reprimanded. "The physical evidence will incontrovertibly contradict such a ludicrous account!"

Hoyos' startled reaction signaled that he was unused to being publicly upbraided.

"You are right, Mr Holmes," he acknowledged. "The official record will be corrected in a few days, after the initial shock of the Prince's death wears off. For now, it is important to downplay any version of the story that mentions the issue of suicide or refers to the Baroness' presence.

"The relations between father and son were strained and might even have become worse if Rudolf did not accept his father's entreaties to abandon his advocacy of reforms the Emperor found objectionable. But for all his faults, the Empress remained quite close to her son. She had great hopes that he would abandon his frivolous ways and comport himself as a Prince. She certainly believed him to be capable of responsible and intelligent behavior and even shared his sympathy for the Hungarian reformers. Of course, that was a sentiment quite at odds with men like Taaffe and Albrecht, her husband's closest advisors," the count recalled, "or the Emperor himself."

## Chapter 11: A Visit to Mizzi Kaspar

"So there is no question that the Prince and his father did not get along?" Holmes inquired.

"There were differences of opinion," the Count acknowledged. "On several occasions of late, I was aware that tensions had flared between them."

"What 'occasions,' if I may ask?" pressed Holmes.

Hoyos had ushered us into a room in the palace where we could speak privately and we drew our chairs even closer together so that we could speak in hushed tones.

"Let me speak plainly," Hoyos said, a strained look on his face. "Rudolf was an intelligent young man, an avid reader and an impassioned reformer, which raised concerns within the royal family and among some of the political leadership of the country. Suspicions about his flirtation with the Hungarian revolutionaries inflamed these concerns significantly.

"But he was also personally reckless. He had confided to me his frustrations with a marriage into which he was coerced with a very plain 17-year old girl. He had grown bored with his wife and impatient with the lack of any substantive role for him to play while his father sat on the throne, a situation that he knew could extend for years or even decades into the future.

"The Emperor had come to appreciate that impatience and was prepared to concede some more responsibility to him."

"That is why he recently appointed him to replace Archduke Albrecht as the inspector general of the army," Holmes noted.

"Yes, very much to the consternation of Albrecht and Taaffe. But despite his father's initiatives and concessions, Rudolph showed little inclination to end his undignified conduct. The misbehavior that had marked his youth, before his marriage to Princess Stephanie, continued into years when he should have been paying attention to mastering statecraft."

"Women?" I ventured.

Hoyos took a deep breath.

## Chapter 11: A Visit to Mizzi Kaspar

"More than you could count, of every station: royalty and actresses, sophisticated and nearly illiterate. Whoever could satisfy his momentary desires and then," he clapped his hands for emphasis, "he would cast them off as though they were yesterday's newspaper."

"A dangerous game when one's name includes a title," Holmes noted. "Such indiscretion carries with it an ever-present vulnerability to blackmail."

I knew he was recalling his recent case in Bohemia but, of course, I remained silent.

"And how did Princess Stephanie react to such abysmal behavior on the part of her husband?" he asked.

Hoyos became noticeably uncomfortable.

"The Crown Prince and the Princess were," he hesitated, choosing his words cautiously, "not close. Not for some time. On more than one occasion, the Prince has admitted to me that whatever love there had ever been had long since gone out of the relationship. Over the past several years, they had little to do with each other but for official palace events and their daughter. But he did not simply ignore her; he also could be unspeakably cruel over the most petty of matters."

"In public settings?" Holmes interrupted.

"Why, just the other night at a reception at the German Embassy, he behaved in a most abysmal manner. As they were preparing to leave, Stephanie asked him to fetch her ermine cloak. It was a perfectly reasonable request and a courtesy he had doubtless performed for her on dozens of occasions. This time, however, his response was very ungentlemanly. In fact, he became almost uncontrollably irate!

"'Go to blazes with your silly cloak!' he yelled loudly enough for many of the guests to overhear, to her understandable mortification." Hoyos grew reflective and solemn. "Indeed, those may well have been the last words he ever spoke to her."

"She must have been terribly jealous of her rivals for the Prince's affections," I mused.

## Chapter 11: A Visit to Mizzi Kaspar

Hoyos laughed harshly. "She did not consider them 'rivals.' They were the Prince's dalliances."

"Even the Baroness Mary?" I asked.

"She ridiculed Mary's efforts to attract the attention of the Crown Prince," he recalled. "She found it almost comical how aggressively she pursued him, not that capturing the Prince's eye was an exhausting challenge for any attractive young woman."

"How did the Prince meet the Baroness Vetsera?" Holmes asked.

"Ah, that is a contentious matter. It seems the Prince had noticed her at the Opera one evening when she was exerting every effort to assure he did just that. He insisted that his cousin, the Countess Marie Larisch, introduce him to the attractive young lady, unaware that Mary had been secretly maneuvering to meet him for several months. It was an awkward situation since the Countess has long been an exceptionally close confidante of her aunt, the Empress, and expressed great discomfort with arranging a liaison between the Prince and this young girl."

"Was the Countess Marie Larisch yet another of the many women with whom the Prince was intimate?" asked Holmes.

"Not in the way you infer," Hoyos corrected Holmes, "although Rudolf was exceedingly fond of her. He believed there was a kinship between them since she was also trapped in a loveless marriage arranged by his own mother. They had known each other as childhood playmates, and as they grew into adulthood, she became something of a confidante. He did her many favours, including paying many of her bills."

"Did her husband fail to honour his wife's obligations?" Holmes asked. "I understand he is a gentleman of some considerable affluence."

"As I have said, her marriage to Count Georg Larisch is apparently ... unsatisfying," Hoyos continued. "There have been four

## Chapter 11: A Visit to Mizzi Kaspar

children thus far, but it is a well-known fact that only the first two are the offspring of her husband."

I was astonished that such a humiliating fact was apparently common knowledge, but I bit my tongue and remained silent.

"And the others?" Holmes inquired.

"The presumed father is Heinrich Baltazzi, himself an uncle to none other than the late Baroness Mary Vetsera!" Hoyos exclaimed.

"I shall require a chart to keep track of all the names and liaisons," I involuntarily exclaimed, taking out my notebook and pencil. "How do you keep the scandals straight?"

"Our police chief, Baron Krauss, does a very good job of keeping track of who is spending time in the company of whom."

"Does *no one* in the royal family possess any ethical scruples or personal morality?" asked Holmes with a decided air of incredulity.

"There are many more such intrigues in Vienna, Mr Holmes," Hoyos assured with a sigh. "Many more."

"Then Watson, you shall indeed have to fabricate a chart! Every liaison is a piece of the puzzle that may explain these tragic events."

Hoyos appeared confused following Holmes's statement.

"Are you suggesting that Marie Larisch, Count Georg or Baltazzi might somehow be implicated in the events at Mayerling?" he demanded incredulously. "Why not accuse me as well?"

A slight tilt of his head, which perhaps only I recognized, told me that Holmes would most certainly not rule out the possible involvement of the former ambassador, but outwardly, he adopted a conciliatory tone.

"I should not have made much of a career for myself if I were in the habit of excluding potential suspects simply because they have a title in front of their name!" he explained with a smile. "I am suggesting, my good Count, that one cannot discard any piece of evidence until being certain it fits nowhere in the puzzle. It seems half of Vienna is connected by blood, friendship, intimacy or politics to

## Chapter 11: A Visit to Mizzi Kaspar

Rudolf, the Baroness Mary Vetsera, or both. Such linkages invariably present the possibility of a motive."

Hoyos seemed calmed by Holmes's explanation and readily agreed to secure us appointments with others who might possess valuable information to aid our inquiry. Holmes stressed the need to complete our interviews as quickly as possible; the funeral for the Crown Prince would take place in just three days, at which time all of the principal family members, friends of the Crown Prince and political players would assemble. Such a gathering would provide an excellent opportunity for all of those attending to agree to a single narrative of the life of the late Crown Prince and his death that might well make it impossible for Holmes to distill the facts from the fiction concocted to protect the Prince's reputation.

At the top of our list to interview was Mizzi Kaspar, an actress of middling achievement whose penchant for entertaining prominent men – most notably the Crown Prince – was evidently not limited to the stage. No one in Vienna seemed particularly concerned about her longstanding liaison with Rudolf, which neither did very much to conceal. Indeed, he had apparently spent his last evening before departing for Mayerling with her rather than with his wife or mistress, Mary Vetsera. Perhaps annoyance over his preference for Miss Kaspar helped explain the Baroness' uninvited arrival at Mayerling the next afternoon.

Loschek confessed that he frequently had facilitated the Prince's many liaisons with Miss Kaspar and provided us with the location of her home, which was situated not far from the city center.

"Miss Kaspar has quite an ingratiating manner," Loschek frankly noted, "but she is more complicated than your typical courtesan."

"Perhaps you would care to shed additional light on that statement," Holmes urged.

"She is known to have extensive associations amongst the official Vienna, including Krauss, the police chief," he said. "Krauss is

## Chapter 11: A Visit to Mizzi Kaspar

not a man to be trifled with. She provides him with information she has gleaned from, well, let us say, her less public performances with prominent men in return for a considerable financial reward and protection from prosecution."

"She is a police informant?" I exclaimed bluntly.

"A distasteful appellation that nevertheless may strike close to accuracy," he admitted. "Certainly, you can understand why we would not want to formally acknowledge the Prince's relationship with a woman of that class!"

"I can assure you that any discission between us will remain very discrete," Holmes assured.

Without waiting to make an appointment, we set off immediately for the ornate building where Miss Kaspar resided. A ring of the bell brought no response, but Holmes was insistent and after several vigorous knocks with the head of his walking stick, the door finally cracked opened slightly.

A young woman, barely visible behind the door, asked tentatively, "Who is there?"

"We wish to speak with Miss Kaspar," I responded in German.

"Oh no, that is not possible," the voice said. "She cannot see anyone today. You must go away!"

She tried to push the door closed but Holmes had placed his foot in the narrow opening and pushed back against her efforts without much difficulty.

"I am afraid I must insist," he said brusquely as the door opened. The flustered young woman fell back, unsure how to respond to this unwelcome intrusion. As we strode past the servant and into the vestibule of the townhouse, a voice rang out from the corridor.

"What is it that you want?" the voice demanded. As it came closer, we could see the plain and yet attractive face of a woman in her mid-twenties. Her dark hair was somewhat disheveled and piled high on her head. She had a weak chin and prominent nose, and in her hands, she clutched a large, light blue handkerchief with which she dabbed at

## Chapter 11: A Visit to Mizzi Kaspar

her reddened and puffy eyes. It was evident that the woman had been distraught for some time.

"*Fräulein Kaspar?*" Holmes inquired.

She looked steadily at him, gauging how to respond to his greeting.

"*Ja, Ich bin Mizzi Kaspar*," she replied. "I can understand some English with you."

Holmes offered a wan smile at the woman's fractured diction.

"*Danke*," he said. "I have no doubt your English is quite superior to my German. If we find ourselves in need of translation, my friend will do his best to assist us." He looked into the parlor. "May we sit down?" he asked.

Mizzi Kaspar, actress, courtesan.and police informant

The young woman dismissed her housemaid and motioned us into the well-furnished room. She chose a stuffed chair covered in a floral design and sat down, motioning for us to do the same on a comfortable settee.

"My name is Sherlock Holmes," he repeated. "Does that mean anything to you?"

*Chapter 11: A Visit to Mizzi Kaspar*

The young woman looked blankly at him and shook her head in the negative.

"And this is Dr Watson, my associate. We come from England, where I am a detective."

She instantaneously grew alarmed; the word clearly required no translation.

"*Detektiv!*" she cried, rising from her chair. "*Ich habe nichts falsch gemacht!*"

"I have done nothing wrong," I translated, leaning over to explain the statement to Holmes.

He held up his palms to her and smiled.

"Then there is no trouble, I assure you. I am a *private* detective. I only wish to speak with you."

"About what?" she asked, reclaiming her chair, her eyes narrowing although her voice quivered with fear.

"You are, I understand, a friend to Crown Prince Rudolf," Holmes said.

A sharp, little cry escaped from her lips and a look of panic returned to the young woman's eyes.

"I have heard!" she cried out. "I know!" An outpouring of tears rushed from her eyes and she buried her face in the handkerchief. It had not taken long for the grim news to spread throughout Vienna.

"Fräulein Kaspar, we need information to help us understand what led to the Prince's death," Holmes said. "No one is accusing you of anything ... inappropriate, I assure you. Do you understand?"

She blew her nose gently into the handkerchief and looked up at us with her large dark eyes that were rimmed in scarlet.

"I was not there," she said defiantly in English. "I was not at Mayerling, where I hear he is dead." Her face became quizzical. "I hear he had a heart illness." She looked pensively at me. "Strange for young man, *Doktor*? Heart illness?"

"Very strange," I repeated. "Did you know if the Prince had any serious medical problems?"

## Chapter 11: A Visit to Mizzi Kaspar

The woman looked uncertainly at me.

*"War der Prinz gesund?"* I translated.

Fräulein Kaspar did not respond immediately. She clasped her hands in her lap and looked blankly back and forth from Holmes to me.

"You tell what I say?" she asked cautiously.

"No, no," Holmes assured. "The Prince's family has asked me to help them in this difficult time. Privately. I assure you that I need not share what you tell me with the Crown Prince's family, the police, or with anyone, if that is your preference."

She ruminated about his words for a moment.

"Rudolf such a nice boy, but very sad, many troubles," she finally said. "His father so stern. His mother, his wife!" Her face grew dark. "He is very unhappy with his wife. And he don't like to be Prince." She began to cry again.

"I am sorry," Holmes said softly. "I know this is a most difficult situation for you." But I knew he had grown excited by the prospect that this young woman might be able to shed light on Rudolf's state of mind. "I understand, Fräulein Kaspar, that you saw him the night before he went to Mayerling."

She nodded affirmatively in agreement., *"Ja,"* she said. "He stayed with me like always."

"Was he ill that evening?" I asked.

She shook her head from side to side but hesitated before responding.

"*Nein*, he was not sick. But he was so sad, so very tired. His eyes so red, maybe from no sleep, maybe from crying, I don't know. He wanted to go away, go to Mayerling with his friends, get away from the Hofburg, his family. Only his daughter he loved. Only little Elisabeth. So sad." Her voice drifted off.

Holmes looked at me deliberately and I caught his meaning immediately.

"Fräulein Kaspar, this is very important, *sehr wichtig, verstehst du,* do you understand?" I asked.

## Chapter 11: A Visit to Mizzi Kaspar

She nodded her head slowly.

"Was he despondent?" I insisted.

She looked uncomprehendingly at me.

"Do you think he was so sad that he might have considered committing suicide? Do you understand? Doing away with himself?"

She seemed confused, and I tried to find the German words to describe what I needed to know. *"War er verärgert? War er verzweifelt? Hat er geklungen, als ob er sich verletzen könnte?"* ["Was he upset? Was he desperate? Did he sound as though he might hurt himself?"]

Her head nodded almost imperceptivity.

*"Oh, ja,"* she repeated. "He told me, 'Mizzie,' he said, 'I am so tired of life.'"

Holmes abruptly sat up straight in his chair.

"What is that you say?" he asked.

"He talk about that, about hurting himself, even killing himself! Once, he even wrote a note to show me he was serious. Maybe a month ago."

"Do you have that note?" Holmes eagerly pressed her.

She shook her head.

*"Nein,* I gave it to Baron Krauss, the police chief." She looked guiltily at us. "I thought they need to see that note," she said. Realizing the admission revealed her relationship to the police, she added, "to protect Rudolf." She allowed herself a voluminous, and perhaps theatrical, wail. *"Ach,* my poor boy!"

"So, you have no doubt that Rudolf was thinking about committing suicide, is that the case, Miss Kaspar?"

She nodded he head sadly in response.

*"Ja, zusammen,"* she paused, straining to find the proper words in English. "Rudolf, he ask for me to do it with him."

"What is that?" Holmes asked excitedly.

Sadness filled her face.

*Chapter 11: A Visit to Mizzi Kaspar*

"He said, 'Perhaps we both die *zusammen*,' Mizzi Kaspar recalled. 'We die together.'"

# Chapter 12: The Go-Between

"So, Rudolf may well have committed suicide alongside Baroness Mary Vetsera after all," I said to Holmes as we walked to our hotel through the brisk Viennese evening. "According to Miss Kaspar, Rudolf had raised the subject of a joint suicide with her some weeks ago."

"Remarkably, not only had he proposed it earlier, but with a different one of his paramours," Holmes responded. "Unquestionably, a highly peculiar and unappealing offer to be peddling to young women with whom one is romantically entangled. But another factor must now be considered."

"What is that?" I responded.

"It is evident that the Prince's desperation with his life was more commonly known than we might have presumed. Miss Kaspar was aware of his depressed state of mind, but so was police chief Krauss thanks to that note she had given to him. Krauss sounds like a man who might know what to do with such information. Which means …"

"That someone may have known of the Prince's twisted thinking and capitalized on it," I completed the thought.

"Capital!" Holmes cried. "I believe you are on your way to developing outstanding deductive skills, Watson!"

I was gratified by this expression of confidence in me by Holmes, who rarely missed an opportunity to express disdain for my propensity for overlooking or misinterpreting a clue.

"So, you think Miss Kaspar might have been involved?" I questioned.

"It surely cannot be ruled out," Holmes replied. "The Crown Prince undoubtedly disappointed her by ruling out any permanent relationship with a common actress. He might as well consider a

## Chapter 12: The Go-Between

teacher at one of their kindergartens! You can be certain no heir to the British throne would consider such folly! She might well have resented his taking up with the Baroness Vetsera whose title, however diluted, made for a more acceptable liaison should he determine to throw off his wife.

"It is certainly instructive that she admitted giving the Prince's note to Baron Krauss. I would imagine a suicide letter signed by the Crown Prince would be a most valuable piece of information for any police chief to possess! Its travel from Miss Kaspar to Krauss to the writing table at Mayerling lodge was indubitably an fascinating journey."

"So, Krauss, also, must be added to the list of potential suspects?" I ventured.

"Most certainly," Holmes replied. "At the very least, he will have to explain how a note written by Rudolf that had been given to him for safekeeping was later found with the dead Prince and his mistress at the Mayerling lodge."

Holmes certainly had identified a most curious and as yet unanswered question regarding Rudolf's suicide note, although I was left no closer to an understanding of what had transpired at the lodge or why.

"Who is next on our list of interviews?" I asked.

"I should be most interested in a conversation with Countess Marie Larisch," Holmes ventured.

"Do you suspect she was yet *another* doxy of Rudolf?" I exclaimed.

Holmes shook his head. "No, Hoyos was quite insistent she was not, although amongst these royal family members, shared blood lines hardly discourage intimate relationships. I am also intrigued by the relationship between the Countess Larisch and the Empress."

"They were quite close, I believe," I recalled.

"So close the Empress sometimes refers to her as a 'daughter' rather than as a 'cousin.' Indeed, you may remember that it was the

## Chapter 12: The Go-Between

Empress who bears the responsibility for having introduced Countess Larisch to her rather disappointing husband. It was with some irony that the countess subsequently became something of a matchmaker of her own when she acquiesced in introducing Baroness Vetsera to the Crown Prince."

The Countess Marie Larisch was willing to speak with Holmes, we were informed, but declined to conduct an interview at the palace. Instead, we awaited her in a private area of our hotel's lobby. Promptly at 3 o'clock, the young woman appeared in the doorway with an attendant. As she strode confidently towards us, Holmes and I rose to greet her. After introductions were completed, Holmes ordered tea and some light refreshments.

Marie Larisch was an attractive woman of perhaps 30 years old, possessing all of the aristocratic bearing expected from one with her title. In fact, her provenance was somewhat more convoluted. As we had awaited her arrival, Holmes had informed me that she had been born out of wedlock to an actress, Henriette Mendel, and the Bavarian Duke Ludwig Wilhelm, the older brother of Empress Elisabeth. That relationship helped explain the unusual closeness between the Empress and the young woman notwithstanding Marie's besmirched legitimacy. A similar closeness had developed with the Crown Prince, and for years, she had been granted unrestricted access to the Hofburg palace.

## Chapter 12: The Go-Between

Countess Marie Larisch (R) with Baroness Mary Vetsera

The Countess was dressed entirely in mourning black. Her mood was somber but her emotions, befitting a member of the aristocratic caste, were admirably under control.

"I am sorry to have to request this interview so soon after the tragic loss of the Crown Prince," Holmes explained, "but I am certain you understand the necessity of my gathering facts whilst recollections are fresh and more likely to be accurate."

She held a handkerchief to her lips and nodded several times affirmatively as Holmes spoke.

"I am not certain what information I may possess that would be of value in this matter," she responded, "but I certainly want to discover what lies behind this great tragedy."

Holmes murmured appreciatively. "And I must apologize in advance if any of my questions appear impertinent or cause you embarrassment," Holmes said. "I assure you, I ask them only to serve our mutual interest in uncovering the truth behind the tragic events at Mayerling lodge."

Again, the countess nodded and then looked expectantly at Holmes.

## Chapter 12: The Go-Between

"I understand the Baroness Mary Vetsera is not unknown to you," he said.

"Of course, I know her -- all of us in this extended family know each other," Miss Larisch responded. "We have all grown up together and as young ladies of the court, we have naturally participated in many events and parties together. But Mary was," she hesitated for a moment, "she is, of course, much younger than I. Seventeen, think, nearly eighteen perhaps. Little more than a child, which is how she often behaves."

Holmes looked at her intently.

"You corrected yourself at a most suggestive moment, Countess," Holmes said. "I think you have a more complete account of events at Mayerling lodge than has been officially reported."

I could see an involuntary tightening of the young woman's jaws. She removed the afternoon newspaper from the bag she was carrying and laid it on the table before Holmes and me.

"His Royal and Imperial Highness, Crown Prince Archduke Rudolf, died yesterday at his hunting lodge of Mayerling, near <u>Baden</u>, from the rupture of an aneurism of the heart," declared the story that covered the front page, which also included a portrait of the late Crown Prince surrounded by a thick black banner.

"The Crown Prince," she said measuredly, looking directly into Holmes' eyes. "He is dead."

Holmes's steely gaze fixed on her.

"Come now, Countess," he said firmly. "Let us not play games at so calamitous a moment. I know not how you came by the information that was to remain private, but surely you must realize I am aware that you have heard far more details than are revealed in this newspaper account."

She dropped her gaze and stared at the floor.

"*Ja, Ich bin mir bewusst,*" she said quietly, and then translated her own remark. "I am aware." She heaved a deep sigh and looked up at Holmes and me, tears welling up in her dark eyes forcing her to raise

## Chapter 12: The Go-Between

her handkerchief to catch them before they cascaded down her powdered cheeks.

"Mary, dear, such a silly little girl, but so provocative. Not a great beauty, but pretty enough with that long hair, those beautiful eyes, and a cute little nose." She smiled thinking of her friend's face. "Her smile. Little 'mouse teeth,' I would call them.

"She was a coquette by instinct. She would walk with a sway, so seductively; she knew that made all the men looked at her. She fell in love effortlessly, like a little schoolgirl, and she had quite modern views about romance! I think it must have been because of the books her governess gave her." She lowered her voice even further. "Naughty books. *French* books -- with drawings! You know?"

A rush of color came to her cheeks that burned through even the generous amount of powder that had been layered on. She shifted self-consciously on the chair, paused for a moment and then looked imploringly at Holmes.

"I warned her, you know."

"Warned her? About what?" asked Holmes.

"Why, about Rudolf, of course! 'He is a rather heartless and fast man,' I told her. 'Wolves like Rudolf only eat up little lambs like you.'"

"Why would you warn her about the Crown Prince?" asked Holmes. "I thought he was a great friend of yours."

"Of course, he was. But that does not change the fact that he could be a perfect cad in his dealings with women," she insisted, adding "especially young women. Loyalty meant nothing to him. Even after he began to see Mary regularly, he also continued to see his actress."

"You mean Mizzi Kaspar, I presume. Or was there another?"

She laughed caustically. "There were *many* others, Mr Holmes, all of whom must have gone home from their royal liaisons dreaming of replacing Elisabeth on the throne one day. But Rudolf had no such plans. He used women like hand towels. He would wipe his dirt on them for as long as he wished and then declare he had to go on maneuvers or offer some other excuse to push them away."

## Chapter 12: The Go-Between

"But he remained involved with Mizzi Kaspar, it is my understanding," I said.

"Yes, because it was never a serious affair. She surely must have had no expectations that their relationship was anything but what it appeared to be. She is," her voice dropped barely above a whisper, "a woman of rather low morals. You understand?"

We indicated that we understood exactly what she was alleging.

"When did Rudolph and Miss Vetsera begin their ... friendship?" Holmes asked somewhat awkwardly.

"She was quite enthralled with him long before he gave her a second glance. I have no doubt that Rudolph knew that a 17-year old girl pushed the bounds of propriety even for him, a Prince. His mother was even younger when she met Franz Joseph, but he was, of course, not already married. But Rudolf did not care about anyone's disapproval; he was Crown Prince and for him, it was a frivolity. It was perfectly absurd, of course, and childish."

A wistful smile crossed her face.

"She was what you would call in English 'a flirt.' 'A passion was born in me' for the Crown Prince,' she revealed to me. "Isn't it preposterous – they had not even met!" She laughed softly and in a derisive manner before gathering her emotions into a more serious mien.

"But for Mary, it did not matter. She resolved to do anything she could to attract his attention. There was no barrier for her: his marriage, his parents, his position. All she wanted was him. In that irreverent way, they were quite suited for each other.

"She rejected my entreaties to find someone her own age, someone unburdened by marriage, but she dismissed my pleas. Late last year, when I was in Bohemia with my husband -- he prefers to live there although I do not – she wrote me of her plans to ensnare Rudolf. I dismissed her scheming as the immature dreams of an impassioned girl, somewhat like an immature daughter. I implored her to drop the flirtation but she would heed no admonitions, no criticisms. Each time

## Chapter 12: The Go-Between

I returned to Vienna, Mary's infatuation had grown even stronger. It was increasingly clear that my pleas were falling on deaf ears."

"And this bizarre behavior went on for months?" I inquired with disbelief.

"On yes," she replied. "She remained resolute about meeting him. As weeks passed, she conceived quite a fantastical romance in her own mind and sent him note after note pleading for an assignation."

"And how their first meeting occur?" asked Holmes.

"I am afraid I must admit to playing a role in arranging their *rendez-vous*. Rudolf had grown quite curious about the author of these impassioned notes. Who could blame him? When they were both at the Opera last fall, she finally had her opportunity. She made quite an effort to attract his attention, preening, smiling and waving to him as he sat in the royal box. For days afterwards, he asked his friends, myself included, who she was. He spoke admiringly about her clothes, her smile, her figure! Finally, he asked me to arrange a meeting."

"Why would he agree to meet her?" asked Holmes.

The baroness looked somewhat mystified by his question and looked at me for assistance. She hesitated before speaking.

"Perhaps I have not been sufficiently clear," she said. "Rudolf was indiscrete. He was, like many in his family, easily influenced by a pretty smile or an exposed calf. Why should he not be captivated by this fawning -- and very willing -- young woman? He made it clear to me that he desired to meet her without delay."

"How would he accomplish that goal without drawing unwanted attention?" Holmes interrupted again. It was becoming painfully clear that the great detective had little practical knowledge of courting.

"Rudolph sent a carriage driven by his loyal fiacre, Nockerl, to await Mary in the *Salesianergasse* park every night until she was able to sneak out and meet him."

"Nockerl?" repeated Holmes, obviously searching his brain for the name. "I thought the Prince's driver was named Bratfisch."

## Chapter 12: The Go-Between

"Ah, yes, that is his true name," Marie said. "But Rudolf always called him Nockerl. Mary's mother, the Baroness Helene, shared my distress over her daughter's obsession, and she watched Mary with great vigilance, adamant that such a meeting should not take place," the Countess continued. "She was well aware of his reputation and forbade Mary from meeting with the Prince. But about two months ago, one evening after her mother had retired early, Mary escaped to the carriage that Rudolf had sent. As arranged, Nockerl drove her to the Prater, the large park not far from the palace. No sooner had they arrived than from out of the shadows emerged my cousin Rudolf! And that was the beginning of the affair."

"Did anyone else know of your role in arranging this meeting?" asked Holmes.

She shook her head. "No, I dared not tell anyone! Rudolf quickly was smitten with her, of course. Soon, he was begging for me to bring her to the palace as often as possible, and I could not refuse his entreaties.

"You must think me quite horrible, Mr Holmes, but I did insist on serving as a chaperone during their early meetings in the Imperial palace. As relations between them progressed, they insisted that I leave them alone in his private apartments. Of course, it was impossible to keep the liaison secret, especially since Mary boasted rather openly about Rudolf's affection for her."

"And how did the Crown Prince's wife respond as the affair became more public?" I asked. "Surely she felt humiliated and angered by her husband's deceit."

"There was a terrible confrontation between Mary and the Crown Princess at the German Embassy ball," Marie Larisch recalled.

"I had heard of a particularly unpleasant exchange between the Prince and his wife at that party," Holmes interrupted.

"Yes, undoubtedly provoked by the argument between Mary and the Princess earlier in the evening. She outrageously proclaimed to Princess Stephanie that she considered herself a rival for her husband's

## Chapter 12: The Go-Between

affections. Such effrontery was scandalous, to say the least; to make such an assertion to the Crown Princess of Austria! Of course, such a confession raised many eyebrows, including those of the Empress.

"But Mary was undeterred. Despite many warnings to control her behavior, she continued to flaunt her relationship with the Prince."

"Did not the Crown Princess intervene more decisively?" asked Holmes. "After all, her reputation and perhaps even her marriage were at stake and with it, her future as Empress."

"She seemed reconciled to Mary's substituting for her in Rudolf's affections. When he was thrown by his horse some months ago, it was she, not his wife, who nursed him through his recovery!"

"Infatuated, like a schoolgirl," Holmes said, repeating the Countess' description.

"Exactly," she sighed wearily, "a schoolgirl. But Rudolf was culpable as well. He was besotted – that is the termed, yes? Besotted? He cared not a whit what others thought. He wished only to spend time with her! He even missed the opening of the new opera season to spend the night with her! The entire royal family attended, but Rudolf," she shook her head disapprovingly, "Rudolf was in the arms of his 'little devil.' That is what he called her, and I have no doubt it was a well-chosen term of endearment."

"Do you think he was truly in love with Miss Vetsera?" Holmes asked.

"I do not know whether Rudolf loved her or anyone, for that matter," the Countess said thoughtfully. "But their involvement certainly became more serious earlier this month."

"How do you know that to be the case?" Holmes pressed.

"This embarrasses me to tell you, Mr Holmes, but Mary confessed to me that something very special had occurred between the Prince and her on 13 January. 'We both lost our heads,' she said, 'and I became a woman! Now we belong to each other in body and soul.' That is what she said. 'We belong to each other.' I supposed I knew what *that* meant."

## Chapter 12: The Go-Between

"How can you be so certain of the date?" he asked.

"Mary bought a silver cigarette case a few days later and had it engraved with that date," Marie said, her face growing increasingly grim. "The frivolity had gone too far. I warned her she must break it off, that no good could come of the flirtation, but she laughed at me."

"Did she not have any other suitors, perhaps closer to her own age and perhaps more available for matrimony than the Crown Prince?" Holmes asked. I imagined he was considering the possibility that a rejected rival might have had a motive contributing to the dual murders.

"You mean someone who might resent the Crown Prince's treatment of her?" She thought for a moment before answering. "There is Miguel, I suppose. He does love her and I think he even had hopes of marrying her."

"Miguel?"

"Ah, yes, of course, you would not know. He is the Duke of Braganza, a member of the royal house of Portugal."

"Do you know if he was in Vienna recently?" Holmes pressed.

"Perhaps," the countess responded. "He came often to see Mary. But she paid him little attention."

"When did you last see the Crown Prince?" I inquired.

"On 28 January," she noted, "just before he left for his last hunting trip at Mayerling. I brought Mary Vetsera to the Hofburg. It was stupid and dangerous for her to be in the palace with so many people there who might identify her.

"Before I left, I became determined to confront Rudolf, especially since I now was aware how intimate their relations had become. Given my closeness to Her Majesty and the trust she placed in me, I did not feel I could continue with the deception any longer. While Mary waited in another room, Rudolf and I had the most terrible row. I told him he was behaving in a most dishonourable and disreputable manner. I insisted that he break it off with Mary and return to his wife and child. If he refused, I warned him I would tell all of the details to the Empress."

"How did he respond to that threat?" Holmes asked.

"He became very agitated," Marie said. "He grabbed me hard by my wrists," she explained, holding up her hands, "and he threatened to kill me unless I remained silent."

Her eyes grew wide in alarm remembering the scene.

"To *kill* you" I asked. "Do you think he was serious?"

"Most certainly, but I refused to retract my statement! I told him he was ruining his life -- and her reputation. I pleaded for him to consider his responsibilities if he cared for her at all but my appeal was futile. He dropped my hands roughly and went to his writing table. From the drawer, he withdrew a small black revolver."

"Perhaps the one used at Mayerling!" I suggested quietly in an aside to Holmes.

"'Do you want me to shoot you?' he threatened. Then he grabbed me by the throat and pressed the weapon against my forehead. His eyes blazed in anger, almost fanatical and rimmed in bright red!

"I had never seen him behave in such a manner. I could not believe this was my cousin, my friend for our entire lives. I did not even know he had such a violent side to his personality, which had always seemed so carefree and gay. In that moment, I despaired for our future – as friends, as cousins -- even perhaps as a nation, if this was the man who would one day lead us.

"'Yes, shoot me,' I answered miserably. 'It would be a kind thing to do for I have betrayed Princess Stéphanie and the Empress – and so have you!'

"He was enraged by my blunt talk, but the fury quickly dissipated from his face and he let go of my neck. He found a chair and lowered himself into it. He begged my forgiveness for his atrocious behavior. Placing the revolver on the table, he buried his face in his hands.

## Chapter 12: The Go-Between

"'The fact is, cousin, I'm in a devil of a mess,' he admitted, 'in more ways than one. Mary has lost her head. I have gotten myself in too deeply with this girl, I admit, and I must find a way of breaking it off. Of course, she will not hear of it. I fear she is intent of causing a regular scandal unless you are able to steady her.'

"I thought to suggest that he find her a more appropriate suitor.

"The Duke of Braganza makes a fool of himself for her," I noted, but Rudolf hung his head forlornly.

"'She won't be shaken off by him. Goodness knows I have tried my utmost to persuade her,' he insisted. 'I have tried time and time again, but now, it is likely too late.'"

"Too late?" Holmes repeated. "Too late for what?'"

"I think I probably know, Holmes," I interjected, looking to the countess for confirmation. "You suspect she might have been with child?"

Silently, she nodded her head in agreement.

"Yes, which of course means she either had lied to me about the date of their first intimacy or that 13 January was the day she realized her condition, or perhaps even the day she told Rudolf."

"I would imagine this was not the first time this situation presented itself given the Prince's history of indiscrete behaviour," I mentioned. "Surely there are ways in Vienna, as there are in London, to address such a condition."

"Yes, I think Rudolf might even have approached Dr von Widerhofer, who coincidentally had served as pediatrician for both of them. He flatly turned her down. But even if he had agreed, Mary would never consent to such a procedure, not even with a highly skilled physician. Never! She knew that having his child gave her leverage."

"Leverage? What sort of leverage?" I asked.

"I presume she might have thought such a development might help persuade Rudolf to leave Stephanie and marry her instead so that she would become Empress."

## Chapter 12: The Go-Between

"That is somewhat preposterous," I insisted. "How could she possibly believe his mistress would be accepted as Empress? Indeed, how could she even believe he would divorce the Crown Princess? How could a child conceived out of wedlock be regarded as a legitimate heir to the Hapsburg throne?"

"You are being far too logical, Dr Watson," the Countess explained. "She was a child, with a child's lack of sophistication! But I fear Rudolf had encouraged such frivolous thinking by telling her, before his passions had recently cooled, that he was seeking an annulment of his marriage. He told her he had even broached the subject with his father, suggesting an appeal to the Pope himself."

"What an extraordinary proposition!" I interjected. "A royal annulment!"

"Of course, the Emperor considered the request preposterous and turned him down with his typical abruptness.

"'You must be insane to propose such a course,' he told Rudolf, making no effort to conceal his contempt for his son's chronic womanizing. 'You should be attempting to produce an heir to the throne with your wife, not gallivanting about with whores and schoolgirls.' It was a humiliating reminder of Rudolf's failure to produce a male heir with the Crown Princess.

"After that terrible argument, they did not talk for several days. So, I was not surprised to hear that Rudolf had ignored his father's request to return from Mayerling to attend the dinner on the night he died."

Here, she choked back tears and we waited in silence until she regained her composure.

"I thought no one knew of my role in having arranged the meetings between Mary and Rudolf, but I was naïve. There are no secrets in Vienna! Someone had revealed my role in the affair to the Empress, whom I have long considered my closest friend as well as my aunt. She castigated me in the most reproachful of terms, accusing me

## Chapter 12: The Go-Between

of undermining the Prince's marriage and abusing her friendship and trust."

She paused and motioned around our settings.

"Imagine my despair when I was told that I would no longer be welcome at the palace! That is why we are meeting here in this café, Mr Holmes." She looked around our austere surroundings. "She is so angry with me that I fear she will now blame me for the Prince's death, which is something I would never have wished for or expected!" She again dabbed her eyes with her handkerchief.

"You can hardly expect her to be grateful!" I said reproachfully, but Holmes threw me a disapproving glance and I immediately regretted the remark. He shifted the conversation back to the Crown Prince.

"What became of the engraved cigarette case?" Holmes asked, focusing in on a piece of evidence that could certainly prove embarrassing were it made public. "I did not see it among Miss Vetsera's belongings or those of the Prince, to whom I suppose she had given it."

"Oh, no, she gave it to her sister, who presumably still has it in her possession." She paused for a moment, and then continued. "But she kept a gift he had given to her, one that she doubtless considered far more valuable."

Holmes raised his head like a dog responding to a whistle undetectable by human ears.

"And what pray was that gift?"

"Nothing of real value," Miss Larisch said. "Just an iron ring."

"That does not sound like the kind of a gift a Prince would bestow," I observed.

"That is true. It was not a ring encrusted with rare jewels as one might expect from a Crown Prince. It was a very common type of ring – the kind lower class women receive from their men and wear about the neck. But it was precious to her, especially since he wore one just like it when they were together."

## Chapter 12: The Go-Between

She suddenly started as if she had thought of something.

"Oh, my, Mr Holmes. I just remembered that Rudolf had both rings engraved."

"Do you recall the engraving?" Holmes asked.

"Oh, yes, I remember it exactly," the Countess Larisch insisted. "The engraving consisted of just seven letters -- 'I.L.v.b.i.d.T.' Many people engrave items with that message. It stands for '*In Liebe vereint bis in den Tod.*'"

I sat up abruptly in my chair as I translated the words in my own mind.

"In love united," I translated aloud, "until death!"

# Chapter 13: The Hungarian Question

"She certainly provided us with quite a bit of useful information," I remarked to Holmes after the Countess had departed, "and perhaps some evidence the Prince's death was truly a suicide."

"She withheld quite a bit as well, I suspect," he replied. "But I have no doubt that the Countess knows a great deal more than she has revealed. I was especially intrigued by her mention of the Duke of Braganza."

"The Duke of Braganza!" I exclaimed. "The Countess of this; the Baroness of that! Dukes and Archdukes. The cast of characters is beginning to resemble one of those silly operettas by Gilbert and Sullivan!" I admitted to becoming confused with the sheer number of characters in the evolving story not to mention the intricacy of their familial relations.

"Might she have been trying to throw suspicion on him? He certainly has reason to be very displeased by Rudolf canoodling with the woman he hoped to marry. Perhaps he became aware of the child."

"If there *was* a child," Holmes interjected.

"Perhaps he became enraged at both Rudolf and Mary Vetsera for ruining his prospects for marriage to the Baroness?" I speculated. "Perhaps he had learned of the Prince's hunting trip to Mayerling lodge and went to the remote location to confront him. When he found Mary in his company, he killed them both and made it appear to have been suicide."

I felt some satisfaction with the hypothesis I had concocted. Admittedly, there were several loose ends, but the narrative had the makings of a dramatic plot that appealed to my literary side. My friend was unimpressed with my speculation.

## Chapter 13: The Hungarian Question

"A dubious hypothesis," Holmes said dismissively. "You are forgetting the suicide notes. And the locked door. Still, greater obstacles to covering up traces of a crime have been overcome, as we know! For the moment, the Duke of Braganza will join our burgeoning list of suspects."

"Who else has been awarded membership on that list?" I asked.

"Well, we have already identified Mizzi Kaspar who might have a reason to feel jilted by the Prince had she learned of Mary's possible pregnancy."

"And she does have connections to the secret police through Krauss," I noted. "Might she have entreated a disreputable member of the force to punish the two lovers?"

"Perhaps," he responded without much conviction. "And let us not forget the Crown Princess, Stephanie."

"The Crown Princess?" I gasped. "Can you possibly think she would become engaged in the murder of her own husband, the father of her child?"

"She certainly has a motive. Had she learned that the Crown Prince was contemplating a divorce or annulment, she would doubtless have realized how close she might be to losing her chance of becoming Empress of Austria."

"But she does not appear to have known that her husband was at Mayerling until just before he died, and she was nowhere near Mayerling when the murders actually occurred," I countered. "I am no detective, but that certainly seems to me a credible alibi."

"True enough," said Holmes. "But most assuredly she possesses the resources to engage agents who would carry out her instructions, even if they were given on short notice."

"That makes no sense," I protested. "After all, as with an annulment or divorce, Rudolf's death would also preclude her becoming Empress someday," I reminded him.

"Yes, but if one is to live the rest of one's life without a husband, is it not far preferable to be the grieving widow of the Crown

## Chapter 13: The Hungarian Question

Prince, permanently ensconced within the royal family, than to become the object of humiliation and exclusion if an annulment were granted? Given the intrigue coursing through the royal family, I suppose it conceivable that were the extent of Rudolf's follies became widely known, there might have been formidable pressure for him to abandon his claim to the throne or abdicate, which also would have cost Stephanie her role as Empress."

"And the other suspects?" I asked.

"Well, I could not rule out the involvement of our most recent interview, the Countess Marie. She presents herself as a loyal friend of both Mary and Rudolf, not to mention the Empress Elisabeth, but might she not have also been an avenging angel, exacting punishment on one or both for their sins?"

"Perhaps we are approaching the problem the wrong way altogether," I proposed. "Suppose Rudolf was never the intended victim. Suppose one of these paramours of the Crown Prince arranged for Mary Vetsera to be killed at Mayerling. Perhaps, having witnessed or discovered that tragedy, the Prince killed himself in despair!"

"A most intriguing idea, Watson, given Rudolf's propensity for angering his female companions. However, your scenario overlooks the suicide notes and the timing of Mary's death. If she were shot by a third party around midnight, when Loschek heard the two gunshots, would a despairing Prince have waited for six hours to shoot himself or would he have called for assistance?"

"Perhaps whoever killed Mary Vetsera was discovered by Rudolf and killed him, too."

"The how would you account for the lengthy time period between the two deaths, as established by the very different state of rigor mortis in the two bodies," Holmes said, closing his eyes and thinking deeply. "Remember as well that Loschek claims to have spoken with the Prince several hours after Mary was already dead.

"Even so, it would be a capital mistake to remove any of these people from suspicion simply because of their relationship to the royal

## Chapter 13: The Hungarian Question

family. In fact, the more I learn about the dynamics of Hapsburgs, the more I marvel there are not bloodstains on the hands of the lot of them."

With additional interviews arranged for the following day, we devoted the evening to supper at the Cafe Sprel, one of Vienna's finest restaurants, courtesy of the royal household. Although Holmes ate sparingly and seemed enmeshed in thought for much of the meal, as was common during complex cases, I enjoyed hearty portions of schnitzel and roasted vegetables as well as a memorable cream-filled Viennese confection for my desert. Afterwards, we attended a performance of an outstanding string quartet. The mellifluous melodies and virtuoso performances provided a welcome diversion following the tiring days of travel, the horrific scenes at the lodge and the terse interviews since our return to Vienna. Holmes, sitting erect in his chair with his eyes closed, unconsciously traced the violinists' finger movements on an invisible instrument.

The next morning, I arose later than I had expected, undoubtedly due to the prior evening's heavy Austrian fare and soothing performance. Since Holmes had already gone out, I waited in the hotel's lobby for his return, writing a quick note to my dear Mary to assure her all was proceeding satisfactorily and attempting to improve my German by reading several newspaper stories about events at Mayerling. The lurid accounts continued to attribute his death to "heart failure" but remained completely silent on the presence of Baroness Maria Vetsera. It took some effort on my part not to laugh out loud at the preposterous distortion in some of the stories given the overall somber air of the lobby, where black crepe and portraits were being hung in honour of the late Crown Prince.

Holmes arrived back at the hotel just before lunch and we found a charming café – of which there appeared to be no shortage in Vienna – not far from the Parliament building. After perusing the inviting menu and ordering a light meal, I eagerly asked Holmes about the morning's sleuthing.

## Chapter 13: The Hungarian Question

"Well, Watson, the Duke Miguel may have had aspirations for Baroness Mary but he seems to have little prospect of ever claiming the throne of Portugal," he reported. "Neither the government nor the citizenry of that nation has any interest whatsoever in restoration of the monarchy. Wisely, the Duke has chosen to insinuate himself into Austrian high society by way of his marriage to the niece of Empress Elisabeth, the Princess Elisabeth of Thurn and Taxis."

"Thurn and Taxis!" I exclaimed. "You had a remarkable case involving their new ruler, Albert, just a few years ago, as I recall.[4] I must congratulate you, Holmes; you are developing quite an impressive inventory of clients of Germanic royalty!"

"Yes, and a strange and demanding clientele it is!" Holmes admitted with a chuckle.

"So he was pursuing Mary Vetsera at the same time he is married to this Princess?" I wondered disapprovingly. "Is *everyone* in Austria possessed of habitual indiscretion and faint morality? Has no one given a thought to honouring their matrimonial vows?"

Holmes smiled wryly.

"It is ironic that you should raise such a question," Holmes responded. "In fact, a young physician named Freud in this very city is undertaking studies of the brain to determine the origins of such libidinous behavior."

"A rich practice amongst the royal family awaits him," I observed, "although I rather doubt he will amount to very much through such a theoretical approach to medicine."

Holmes held up his hand. "In this rare case, however, your approbation is misplaced, Watson. The Duke, alas, is a widower and quite free to pursue a new wife. Still, I look forward to interviewing him as to his whereabouts on the night of the double deaths. There is no question that he is very familiar with the intrigues of the Hofburg

---

[4] John Lawrence, "The Case of the Duplicitous Suitor," *The Undiscovered Archives of Sherlock Holmes* (London, MX Publishing, 2022).

## Chapter 13: The Hungarian Question

palace and is quite disapproving of his rival for the affections of Mary Vetsera."

As it turned out, the Duke was in Vienna that very day and a meeting was quickly arranged at the Hofburg palace. He was a formal man in his mid-thirties, hardly a suitable age for marriage to a 17-year old like the Baroness Vetsera. He was of average height and generally undistinguished in appearance -- with heavy-lidded eyes set above a handlebar-style mustache of impressive size and waxing. He was accompanied by an aide who explained that, as the Duke lacked proficiency in English, he would serve as his translator during our conversation.

"As you wish," Holmes responded breezily.

The Duke, we were informed, had been briefed on Holmes's assignment and through his interpreter assured us of his full cooperation. Unfortunately, he professed, he could offer no insights into the events at Mayerling lodge resulting in Rudolf's demise. He betrayed no awareness of the fate that had befallen Mary Vetsera.

"Your Grace, it is my understanding that you serve as a military aide to the Emperor despite being a pretender to the throne of Portugal?" Holmes began.

"That is correct, sir," the translator explained after the Duke had finished speaking. "It was my honour to serve in the campaign against the rebels in Bosnia and Herzegovina in defense of the Emperor. Afterwards, I returned to Vienna where service to Austria and Karl Joseph has been my only duty these past eight years."

"Other than your responsibilities to your children," Holmes added.

The Duke's eyes narrowed as he realised Holmes had been looking into his background. He settled into his chair more comfortably and removed a silver case from his jacket. I looked to Holmes, certain that he had observed that such a case might well have been a present from Mary Vetsera, who we knew had purchased and engraved one to commemorate some milestone of her relationship with Rudolf. After

## Chapter 13: The Hungarian Question

offering both of us a cigarette, he placed one in his lips, struck a match and lit it. He took in a deep breath and closed his eyes before expelling a significant quantity of blue smoke into the room. Finally, he opened his eyes and smiled in our direction.

"Come, Mr Holmes," he said in flawless English, which revealed that his fluency in our native tongue was far from as elementary as he had originally insisted. "What is it you *really* wish to know?"

"I am pleased to have our conversation elevated to a higher level of forthrightness," Holmes said. "My research into your background had, of course, revealed your attendance at British university, which undoubtedly required a thorough proficiency in the English language." He cast a dubious glance at the Duke's translator. "I wondered how long it might take for you to abandon the pretense of requiring the services of whoever this gentleman might be."

The Duke bowed slightly in Holmes's direction.

"I have learned in diplomacy that it is often helpful to employ such a third party so that any disagreeable 'misunderstanding' may be attributed to a faulty translation."

Holmes noted his appreciation for the deception, and the Duke spoke a few words quickly in Portuguese to the translator, who hurriedly rushed from the room, closing the heavy carved wooden door before him. The Duke's eyes followed his path before returning his gaze to Holmes and myself. We settled back into heavy wooden chairs.

"As I said, Mr Holmes," he repeated, "what is it that you really wish to know?"

"I have a familiarity with your family," Holmes said. "I was of some assistance to the family of your late wife."

"I am aware of your assistance, for which her father remains deeply grateful."

"I do not wish to be indiscreet, your Grace, but my immediate concern involves your relationship with the Baroness Mary Vetsera."

The Duke's face rapidly transformed into a mask of annoyance.

## Chapter 13: The Hungarian Question

"I fail to see how that is any business of yours, Mr Holmes," he said disapprovingly, standing up abruptly to signal his displeasure. "My private affairs are my own business, and hardly relevant to the sudden death of the Crown Prince, which, I understand to be the objective of your presence here in Vienna."

"Your Grace, the Baroness is very much my business," Holmes declared brusquely. "I am afraid I must inform you that Mary Vetsera is dead." He cautiously scrutinized the Duke's response to the revelation.

Miguel appeared as if struck by a club and his mouth fell agape. The gilt-edged cigarette dropped from his hand to the carpeted floor. I quickly retrieved it, tossing it, still smoldering, into the fireplace. He stood and swayed slightly before sitting back down in his chair and grabbing the arm rests tightly.

"What!" he cried in a loud voice. His face had twisted swiftly into a mask of utter grief. "Mary dead? No, it is not true! It cannot be true!"

"I am afraid there is no doubt, your Grace," I advised, standing in preparation for offering any medical assistance that might be required. "We saw her remains with our own eyes just yesterday."

"She is but a child! How can she be dead?" Involuntarily, he again stood and began to pace around the room.

"I advise you to be seated," I said. "This will not be easy for you to hear."

He returned to his chair and slowly lowered himself to the seat, burying his face in his hands as Holmes began to explain.

"There has been no public disclosure of this tragedy as yet," I said, "but she died at the royal hunting lodge at Mayerling, alongside the Crown Prince." The Duke looked up at me and then stared blankly at Holmes.

"But how?" he asked with exasperation.

"She was shot."

"Shot!" he echoed in disbelief. "In a hunting accident?"

## Chapter 13: The Hungarian Question

"There is no question of that," Holmes assured. "She was deliberately shot in the head."

"I am confused! She is but a young girl. She has no influence, no power. Why would anyone kill her?"

"Perhaps no one did," said Holmes. "The injury may have been caused by her own hand."

"So, I have Rudolf to thank for this!" he seethed. "You think she may have become distraught following the Prince's heart attack."

Holmes carefully studied the shaken man.

"The Crown Prince did not suffer a heart attack," he disclosed. "It will be become public knowledge soon enough and so I will not deceive you. He was also shot in the head. He may well have taken his own life. It is plausible that he did so as part of a pact with Mary Vetsera, although other explanations must be considered as well."

"Such as?" inquired Miguel.

"It is possible," Holmes said, "that someone else killed one or both of them and attempted to make it appear to have been a mutual suicide."

"But who would do such a thing?"

"I was hoping that you might offer some thoughts on that subject. I know you were disappointed that Mary Vetsera's affections for you diminished once she became infatuated with the Crown Prince. Would you say that is an accurate account?"

The Prince struggled to control his emotions.

"She declared I was no longer going to be in the picture," he said, his voice choking. "Oh, she was very apologetic but she professed her heart had been stolen by Rudolf. It seemed a quick, childish romance, even preposterous to me. I am not even sure she had met him more than a few times. I must say I found her decision inexplicable.

"The Crown Prince was a charming man, to be sure. But as I presume you have learned, he possessed the most disreputable morals and questionable loyalties, and I do not only refer to his wife. But I accepted her decision. Even though the Prince was married, I knew

## Chapter 13: The Hungarian Question

Mary would never voluntarily disavow him, and I had resolved to look elsewhere for companionship."

A look of concern had appeared on Holmes's face. He stood, hand on his long chin, and paced about the room thoughtfully before turning back to the Duke.

"You just intimated your suspicions that questions about the loyalty of the Crown Prince extended beyond his obvious infidelity with Princess Stephanie." He stared hard into the Duke's face. "What did you mean by that?"

The Portuguese pretender wrestled with Holmes's question for several moments before offering a qualified response.

"I am a guest in this house, Mr Holmes, and it is not my place to impugn the Crown Prince who lays dead in his coffin. I am loyal to the Emperor; that is all that matters now."

"What matters, Your Grace, is determining accurately what transpired at Mayerling lodge," Holmes challenged him. "I do not doubt your loyalty to the Emperor, but it is on his behalf that I have been retained to determine what befell his son and heir, no matter how distasteful a man you or anyone else believes him to have been. Questions about his 'loyalty' are doubtless very pertinent to that investigation. You have my word that anything you tell me will be kept in the strictest of confidences, if at all possible. But I must insist that you withhold nothing from me at this time."

Once again, I saw a look of displeasure that crosses royal faces when Holmes employs a brusque manner that conveys insufficient deference to rank. But the force of his statement, reinforced by the commission from the Emperor, had the desired impact. After a long pause, the Duke shifted in his chair.

"I have gone to war to defend this country and crown from those who have sought to tear this Empire apart: Croats, Bosnians and many others," he began. "A decade ago, during the battle for Sarajevo during the Ottoman war, I came close to losing my life. Today, Mr Holmes, there again are those who once seek to violate treaties to divide our

## Chapter 13: The Hungarian Question

Empire. There are threats everywhere: Prussia, Hungary, Serbia, Russia. Even England, if you do not mind my mentioning your own country. The influence of your Queen is heavily felt in the royal houses on the continent, to which she is intimately linked."

"I really do not concern myself with matters of political intrigue, to the extent that I can avoid them," Holmes said.

"Then you will be quite handicapped in assessing the treachery that festers throughout the Hapsburg Empire, I assure you," the Duke responded. "There is little *but* intrigue, and few inside the walls of this palace are innocent of involvement. Perhaps you have heard of the recent parliamentary machinations over the defence bill."

"Hoyos mentioned there are issues of concern," replied Holmes breezily. "However, I rarely devote a substantial portion of my day to the deliberations of the Austrian parliament."

The Duke ignored his flippant tone.

"There has been little else of such consequence considered during the past several weeks," he explained. "The controversy surrounds provisions responding to Hungarian insistence on greater autonomy than provided under the joint monarchy arrangement. Supporters of Hungary have been scheming to defeat this important bill."

"So Hoyos mentioned to me," Holmes responded indifferently.

"And you believe Rudolf might have supported these dissidents?" I asked. "Was he foolish enough to embrace those who voiced opposition to his own father, not to mention to the Empire he was destined to inherit?"

"Frankly, doctor, I cannot answer your question authoritatively. But some of the Emperor's closest advisors – including Archduke Albrecht and the Minister-President Taaffe – believe that Rudolf's position on the defence bill, and perhaps the Hungarian question, constitute something less than the unequivocal support the Emperor has every right to expect from a member of the royal household, let alone his heir. Several articles have appeared in the newspaper of late – the

## Chapter 13: The Hungarian Question

identity of the author concealed by the use of a pseudonym – that evoked reformist views that Rudolf was known to share. It was a poorly kept secret. Around the palace, many say 'Oh, Rudolph is chatting again' whenever these diatribes appear."

"Would it be fair to say that the question of Rudolf's loyalties had become an acrimonious issue within the royal family?" asked Holmes.

The Duke thought for a moment before beginning his reply.

"There is no question the Prince's views were creating grave tensions," he agreed. "I have been told – I am afraid I cannot share the source with you – that the Crown Princess has described her husband's dalliance with the Hungarians as 'wholly repugnant.' On the other hand, the Empress may have shared some measure of sympathy with the Hungarians, although I could not swear that to be the case."

"Rhetorical sympathies for the Hungarians and nothing more?" Holmes asked.

"To be accurate, Mr Holmes, there have been rumors of a clandestine visit by Rudolf to meet with the reformers in Budapest. Some even speculated that he might aspire to be crowned King of the Hungarians!"

"The Emperor must have been alerted," Holmes said.

"Most assuredly he was," the Duke agreed. "I think there was a fear, when Rudolf failed to appear at dinner the other evening that he might be preparing to depart for Hungary so that by the time Franz Joseph arrived in Budapest, his son's assumption of the Hungarian crown would be a *fait accompli.*" His voice trailed off as he contemplated the enormity of the treason he was describing.

The weight of the Duke's words fell heavily in the room. His grave allegation impugned the loyalty of the Crown Prince who was no longer able to defend himself from such accusations.

"Now, if you do not mind, your news about Baroness Vetsera has deeply affected me," he insisted, "and I have responsibilities to attend to before the funeral." He stood and with a formal bow, the Duke bade us adieu and took his leave.

Holmes stood up and lit the pipe he had been carrying in his hand. For a few moments, he thoughtfully sucked at the mouthpiece of the old briar as the orange flame rose and fell. Removing the pipe from his mouth, he blew a stream of blue smoke to extinguish the match and a lazy curl of dark smoke rose into the room from the pipe's bowl, along with the odour of burnt wood.

"Rudolf plotting to become King of the Hungarians against his father!" I repeated. "Now, that is a most disturbing bit of gossip." I waited to see what Holmes might think.

"It is not simply 'gossip,' my dear Watson," Holmes said, taking another deep mouthful of smoke and expelling it. "It provides a most potent motive – for murder!"

# Chapter 14: A Terse Interview with Hoyos

The Portuguese Duke had no sooner departed than a knock on the door was followed by the entrance of Count Hoyos who, we had come to believe, was one of the few reliable individuals in Vienna interested in cooperating with our inquiry.

"If you do not mind, Herr Holmes, I thought, on behalf of the Emperor, that I should receive an update on your investigation," he explained. "Even though this was not the original reason for requesting your presence, he is deeply grateful that you have agreed to stay on in Vienna to inquire into the circumstances surrounding the death of the Crown Prince. Have you reached any conclusions about what actually transpired in that locked room?"

"I just completed a most instructive discussion with Duke Miguel," Holmes responded. "Your arrival is most timely as I have some additional questions for you. I believe that your answers might shed additional light on the matter."

Hoyos looked cautiously about the room to ensure we were alone and then walked over to where Holmes and I were standing. "Yes, of course," he responded.

"At your dinner with the Crown Prince on the night of the tragedy," he began. "I am wondering if he discussed his relationship with Mary Vetsera."

The Count's lower lip jutted out to cover his top lip and his head cocked slightly to the side.

"Not that I recall," he said indifferently, shrugging his shoulders. "The subject may have come up. He sometimes spoke to me of her professions of love for him."

"Did those declarations make the Prince uneasy?"

## Chapter 14: A Terse Interview with Hoyos

"I would say yes, increasingly so," Hoyos responded thoughtfully. "I think he was worried that her affections were becoming too intense, her expectations unrealistic."

"At the time of your dinner, were you aware that the Baroness Vetsera had already arrived at Mayerling lodge?" Holmes pressed.

"I was not told that she was present or that she was not, and I hardly thought it my place to ask. But I certainly would not have been surprised to have learned that an attractive woman was waiting to spend the evening with the Prince after our dinner."

"And why would you suspect that?"

"Because, Mr Holmes, one almost always was! I am sure you have discovered by this time that the Prince was a man whose taste for women was matched by his disdain for solitude."

"Which helps to explain his relationship with the actress Mizzi Kaspar."

Hoyos burst into a sharp laugh at the mention of the name.

"'Actress!' Hah! How droll, Herr Holmes!" He quickly collected himself and resumed a more serious demeanor. "Yes, this 'actress' was frequently in the Prince's company."

"But evidently not because of her prowess as a performer?"

"Not on the stage, no. She was, as I am sure you have already determined, a woman of rather low morals. According to our police, with whom she collaborates, she may even be a German spy. The intrigue runs deeply in this country. You can understand the reasons for our concern about her prying secret information from the Prince when," he hesitated and searched for the right words, "his guard was down."

"Had you not alerted him that she might be an espionage agent?" I asked.

Hoyos shrugged his shoulders. "It would have done little good," he explained. "Rudolf trusted and confided in her. He would not have tolerated any question about her loyalty, which is questionable, any more than about her virtue, of which there is painfully little."

## Chapter 14: A Terse Interview with Hoyos

"Might she, like Mary Vetsera, have harboured illusions of becoming the Prince's wife," Holmes declared.

"Hs wife? Why, you know, of course, that the Prince is already married to Princess Stephanie!"

"But I understand the Prince was very unhappy in his marriage," Holmes pressed. "Is it not true that he had envisaged a divorce or an annulment of his marriage to the Princess Stephanie, and perhaps had even raised the topic with his father?"

"I would not know about such intimate matters," Hoyos quickly insisted. "But I will tell you this; that is a preposterous scenario. The Emperor would never sanction divorce or annulment of the Prince's marriage – most assuredly not with a child already born of the union and hopefully more – including a male heir – to come."

"If the Emperor proved unmovable on the subject, might not the Prince have considered making his own appeal to the Pope, perhaps citing as a basis that Stephanie had failed to produce an heir to the throne," I inquired. "That would hardly be the first time a king or Prince had sought to end a marriage on such a basis." The multiple marriages of our own King Henry VIII provided more than a sufficient precedent for such schemes.

Hoyos shook his head sharply.

"No, I think such action would be very unlikely. The Emperor would certainly prohibit Rudolf from succeeding him if he pursued such a course on his own. I do not exaggerate the Emperor's dedication to fidelity in marriage. Indeed, he has indulged in indiscretions of his own but his marriage to the Empress has never been in doubt. A divorce by Rudolf would mean scandal, and Franz Joseph is far too much of a traditionalist to have such scandal besmirch his house. He would rather have allowed the crown to fall to his brother, Karl Joseph or even his nephew, Franz Ferdinand, of whom he has a rather low opinion."

"So either of those men might have a motive for seeing Rudolf removed from the line of succession," I reflected "since they stood to benefit."

## Chapter 14: A Terse Interview with Hoyos

Holmes and Hoyos both looked at me but said nothing in response to my observation.

"And what of Princess Stephanie?" asked Holmes. "How much of all this did she know?"

Hoyos shrugged his shoulders again.

"She knows about the Prince's dalliances, of course. And to be frank, she is not without some peccadillos of her own. Few begrudge her these dalliances given the Prince's obvious disinterest in their marriage. But divorce; no, I do not think she would countenance ending her marriage and facing disgrace for herself and her daughter.

"It is true they had grown apart, but it was not beyond the realm of possibility that they might still have had a son who would someday succeed Rudolf. That was surely the most important consideration. In any event, even if he were to have freed himself of Stephanie, I refuse to believe he would have sought the hand of Baroness Vetsera. She was too young, too frivolous. She was a plaything for him, nothing more."

"I need to raise a rather delicate matter," Holmes said, watching Hoyos intently. "What is the exact nature of your knowledge of the Crown Prince's collaboration with the Hungarian independence movement?"

A bombshell exploding next to the startled Count could hardly have had a greater effect. He stood quickly and a deep red flushed onto his face.

"You are very significantly out of your depths, Mr Holmes!" he said tersely. "That comment is a gross insult to the memory of the Crown Prince and an unpardonable slander upon his honour and legacy. This interview is at an end!"

He turned and walked to the door, looking back at Holmes as he placed his hand on the doorknob.

"In the strongest possible terms, Herr Holmes, I direct you to abandon this line of inquiry. No good can come of it, but a great deal of evil may result should such perfidy circulate. Now, please excuse me. I must make further preparations for the Prince's funeral."

*Chapter 14: A Terse Interview with Hoyos*

With that, he grabbed his hat and quickly exited the room leaving Holmes smiling grimly and myself staring in disbelief.

# Chapter 15: Disposing of Mary Vetsera

By the late afternoon, any hope of containing the true account of what had transpired at Mayerling had evaporated into the chilly Vienna air. Rumors were rampant throughout the city as dozens of reporters from Austria and other countries swarmed over the lodge, interviewing anyone they could find in a frantic effort to glean details of the tragedy. Unsurprisingly, facts we had hoped might remain unspoken had begun to slip out of the mouths of indiscreet servants and into the press.

"The truth is," the French journal *Le Figaro* definitively proclaimed, "no one knows anything." But some clearly knew more than others.

The family of Mary Vetsera, however, remained distraught at her unexplained absence. Her mother, Baroness Helene Vetsera, had become convinced that the young woman's disappearance was somehow connected to her illicit and poorly-concealed affair with the dead Crown Prince, whom the palace had acknowledged to have died by a self-inflicted gunshot wound. Her anxiety only increased as further details concerning Rudolf's death flooded the capital while her daughter's disappearance remained unexplained.

Two days after the Prince's death was disclosed, the Baroness appeared at the palace, half-crazed with anguish and raving to anyone she encountered that someone must have absconded with her daughter. Understanding a mother's anxiety over her child, the Empress agreed to set aside her anger over Mary Vetsera's scandalous behavior and grant her one-time intimate friend an audience. Here I relate that encounter, the details of which were confidentially shared with me by one of the Empress' trusted attendants.

"My unhappy child, what has she done?" Madame Vetsera pleaded to Elisabeth upon being admitted to the Empress' waiting room. "What has become of her?"

## Chapter 15: Disposing of Mary Vetsera

The Empress stared stonily at the panic-stricken Baroness, who fell to her knees, her hands outstretched, begging for information.

"Mary -- my daughter," she wailed in despair.

The Empress remained cold and drew away from the distraught woman.

'Helene, it is too late," she said brusquely and without emotion. "They are both dead – and by their own hands!"

A look of horror and disbelief immediately swiftly overcame the kneeling Baroness, who pitched over onto the floor in a dead faint. Impassively, the Empress simply walked into another room and shut the door, asking her attendant to revive the unconscious woman and escort her from the palace. Palace aides helped to revive the distraught Baroness and to accompany her to the ground floor and the exit from the palace where she encountered the Minister-President Taaffe, a longtime acquaintance who had been lurking about, waiting for her to appear.

"Is it true, Eduard?" the baroness cried. "Is it true Mary is dead?"

He gathered her in his arms to calm her and spoke soothingly.

"Helene, I promise you that Mary will have a most respectful burial," he tried to reassure her, "but we cannot allow the press to create a great scandal over her misbehavior. That would embarrass the Emperor and could have even more serious political ramifications than you can imagine. I know you do not want her name associated with such scandal. I ask that you trust me to treat her, and you, with the greatest of respect but also the greatest of discretion."

The elderly Baroness was utterly confused by this unexpected turn of events.

"What shall I do?" she pleaded.

"Send George Count Stockau and Alexander Baltazzi to Mayerling at once to collect her," he requested, referring to the dead girl's uncles. "I will find her a decent grave without arousing public

## Chapter 15: Disposing of Mary Vetsera

scrutiny. And I make a personal promise to you that it shall be in consecrated ground."

The distraught Baroness nodded her head in silent agreement.

"But can I see my girl?" she pleaded.

Taaffe shook his head negatively.

"She suffered a most terrible injury, Baroness," he said. "You must believe me when I advise you in the strongest terms against viewing her remains. In fact, we ask that you not even visit her grave until the insatiable curiosity of the press calms down. Perhaps you would consider traveling abroad for a time to put all this behind you, perhaps to London. I am certain the Queen would welcome such a visit. The palace will make all the arrangements for you."

The Minister-President was certainly correct that the press was turning Mayerling into something of a macabre circus. Reporters seeking additional information about the Prince's death were still unaware of Mary Vetsera's presence, creating a challenge in removing the young girl's body without being detected. Once her uncles Stockau and Baltazzi arrived, they were taken to the unheated outbuilding and shown a large laundry basket covered by a sheet. Around it, ostrich feathers were strewn on the floor together with articles of woman's clothing.

Throwing off the sheet, they peered into the basket and were horrified to discover Mary's body, still naked and with no sign that any effort had been made to cleanse the gore or prevent the onset of decomposition, which had been delayed by the cold weather alone. The outraged uncles demanded that her clothing be brought to them immediately and that attendants clean and dress her corpse and fix her hair to make her appear to be alive.

The guards informed them that arrangements had been made for the Baroness to be interred in a nearby churchyard. But first, they needed to concoct a charade that would enable them to depart Mayerling without alerting the press. A broomstick was lashed to the back of the fully dressed corpse so that the gruesome cadaver would appear seated upright, as if out for an evening drive. Before the reporters could follow, the remains of Mary Vetsera were hurriedly placed into a cab and the uncles clambered in next to her. Pretending to be engaged in merry conversation with their dead niece, they drove out from the lodge and sped along the roadway, far from the indifferent eyes of the reporters.

When the carriage arrived at the nearby monastery in *Heiligenkreu*, however, the planning appeared to go awry. The local abbot insisted upon viewing Mary's body before sanctioning the burial and he recoiled at the sight of wounds he suspected had been inflicted by her own hand. Burial of a suicide in the churchyard was impossible, he insisted. The distraught girl, the uncles implored the cleric, had lost her senses when she fired the fatal shot and could not be held accountable for her act.

After much persuasion by a military aide accompanying the carriage and the likely exchange of a considerable amount of money, the abbot relented. Mary's act of self-destruction was attributable to her mental instability, an exception to church dogma that allowed burial in the consecrated church yard, as Taaffe had promised. With no religious ceremony and few mourners, the body of Baroness Mary Vetsera was consigned to an unmarked grave while the attention of the press remained focused on the late Crown Prince.[5]

---

[5] Editor's footnote: At her mother's request, Mary's coffin was relocated to a new grave within the *Heiligenkreuz* cemetery shortly thereafter. In 1955, it was revealed that Soviet occupying troops had desecrated Mary's tomb after World War II, perhaps searching for jewelry. The bones were examined by Dr Gerd Holler four years later and then reinterred. In 1991, a Linz furniture dealer obsessed with the Mayerling case again removed the bones from the grave. Forensic tests confirmed these were Mary's remains. The young baroness' bones were reburied a final time in October 1993.

# Chapter 16: The Crown Princess' Account

"Well! What do you make of that?" I asked after Count Hoyos had rushed from the room following Holmes' mention of Rudolf's association with the Hungarian independence movement.

"We seem to have struck a decidedly raw nerve, Watson!" he said with a grim look. "Now, I fear, time is most certainly conspiring against us. We must accelerate the pace of our interviews. The mere hint of an entanglement with Hungary provoked grave concern from a seasoned diplomat like Hoyos whose loyalty to Rudolf seems above reproach. I can understand why the palace wishes to avoid any public speculation about of a connection between this movement and the Crown Prince's death."

"How shall we proceed?" I inquired.

"By seeking interviews with several elusive figures who have not yet deigned to share their knowledge about the events leading up to the tragedy," he explained. "And perhaps also with some we have already spoken with since, I have little doubt, they have been somewhat less than fully candid in their recollections. It is essential that we complete our interviews before the funeral takes place. Once the service is over and the Crown Prince is sealed in the family crypt, our opportunity for prying loose information with become decidedly more difficult, if not impossible."

"Who must we interview first?" I asked.

"Let us seek out the bereaved widow, Crown Princess Stephanie," he declared. "Then, it will be critical to secure an audience with Archduke Albrecht and Minister-President Taaffe!"

I wondered aloud if he thought it likely we would be granted access to the highest officers of the Austrian government at a time of national distress.

## Chapter 16: The Crown Princess' Account

"It is essential that we question them!" he demanded. "They would almost certainly be aware of any attempt by the secret police to monitor the Prince's comings and goings and thereby know with whom he was engaged."

"Spying on the Crown Prince, Holmes?" I asked incredulously.

"Have you really any doubt such espionage was being conducted?" he answered. "In this part of the world, Watson, the most serious challenges to power often arise from within one's own family. Indeed, it is difficult to name a situation where the most malevolent of adversaries is *not* a cousin or uncle. No one can be excluded as a potential assassin or terrorist unless one is fully prepared to live with the catastrophic consequences that might follow such a sentimental decision.

"Only after we have completed these background meetings will we have the information we need to bring our findings to the Emperor and Empress, however distressing those conclusions may be for them to learn."

Arranging to see the newly widowed Stephanie proved vexing. She was, as any number of reports had predicted, a challenging person – hot-headed and stubborn – doubtless born of having been involuntarily locked into an unhappy and loveless marriage when little more than a child. With little formal education and the chronic disposition of a gawky schoolgirl, the young Princess had been publicly dismissed as "a burden" by the worldly Rudolf. She preoccupied herself with their daughter Elisabeth and, as we had been informed, a succession of suitors nearly as inappropriate to her rank as the women who entertained her husband.

We were immediately struck by her peculiar calm given that she had just lost both her husband and her opportunity to reign as Empress, presumably her singular ambition since her wedding eight years before. We were, however, quickly disabused of such a presupposition.

## Chapter 16: The Crown Princess' Account

"I do not care a fig about being Empress," she insisted to Holmes after we had tendered our condolences. "As to my husband, of course, I am sorry for the nation and his parents and for our daughter. But it has been some time since he has been a real husband to me. I tell you this to be truthful, Mr Holmes."

"Can you enlighten us about your husband's state of mind or his plans prior to departing for Mayerling?" he asked.

She gave a harsh laugh in response.

"My husband was not in the habit of sharing his thoughts or his schedule with me. Our last conversation took place at the German Embassy the night before he left. He was beastly rude, as anyone in our immediate vicinity would confirm."

"Yes, I have heard of his behaviour, which I confess to find loutish," Holmes agreed. "I wonder, may I trouble you with the subject of that conversation, beyond your request that he fetch your coat?"

"I entreated him to attend the Emperor's upcoming dinner. I thought it would be best for them to clear the air between them before the Emperor departed for Budapest."

"And what was his response?"

"He reproached me, insisting the matter was none of my business and that I should not advise him on matters of state or his relations with his father. He communicated this message in the most extremely rude manner. Even so, he did indicate his intention to return from Mayerling as he had promised our daughter. She was so looking forward to seeing him. After that most unsatisfactory conversation, I did not see him again."

She hesitated before she continued.

"I am told," she said distastefully, "that he spent the night in the arms of one of his paramours: that preposterous 'actress,' Mizzi Caspar." She spat out these words with a strong disdain. "Perhaps you should direct such questions to her," she said, waving her hand in a sign of disgust. "They're all strumpets as far as I am concerned."

## Chapter 16: The Crown Princess' Account

"And you heard no more from him before learning of his death?"

She had a look of extreme boredom on her face when she turned to face the detective.

"Not a word, until Prince Philipp showed me the note."

"You refer to the note the Crown Prince had written to you before supposedly taking his life?" Holmes responded.

"Yes, Philipp presented it when he informed me what had transpired. I will never forget his insipid and insincere words." She uttered a cackle that positively made the hairs on my neck stand straight up.

"'*I go calmly to my death, which alone can save my good name,*' she recited. "Well, that may be true enough with all the scandal he was inviting our political enemies to exploit. Not to mention the reporters! That note was little more than a contrivance to convince our countrymen that he was a man of honor. In fact, he has been a dastardly cur!

"'*I embrace you warmly,*' she quoted. "How absurd! How preposterous!"

"Surely he must have once expressed true affection for you," I observed.

The Princess' face conveyed utter boredom with the notion.

"It would be the first embrace in a very long time from my husband, I assure you. And as for 'warmly,' his only warmth came from the maladies his whores infected him with!"

I admit to being shocked to have such sentiments expressed in my presence from a woman we did not even know, let alone the Crown Princess of Austria-Hungary. Such was the Princess Stephanie's contempt for a man she felt had so grievously betrayed her.

"Princess," Holmes began gently. "Have you been told the actual circumstances of his death?"

"You mean the speculation that he and that ridiculous, love-addled little girl shot themselves?" she said disdainfully. "Yes, I heard

## Chapter 16: The Crown Princess' Account

the report. I certainly did not believe the initial report that he had suffered a heart attack! Frankly, I am skeptical of such a chronology. I suppose Mary Vetsera might have had great pluck, but it is difficult for me to believe that Rudolf had the courage to pull the trigger. And you just stated your opinion that he 'supposedly' took his own life, didn't you Mr Holmes?" She offered the thinnest of smiles. "You see, I was paying attention!"

She softened for a moment, and I presumed some ancient memory of a tender time must have come into her memory, but I was mistaken.

"I suppose I must not be so cold towards Baroness Vetsera," she surprisingly said. "After all, she was little more than a child who had become infatuated with a grown man she barely knew. And I am certain that she was easily manipulated by Rudolf's practised insincerities. I doubt she realized how little he really cared about her."

"So, you dismiss the rumor that he was contemplating a request to the Pope to have your marriage annulled so he might marry Mary Vetsera?" Holmes asked.

The Princess looked incredulously at Holmes and then burst into a shriek of disbelief.

"Annul our marriage?" she cried in astonishment. "Preposterous, as I am certain the Archbishop and his father would have informed him. The Emperor and Empress are not fond of me, I admit; but there was no possibility they would sanction an end to our marriage let alone accept a silly child like Baroness Vetsera."

Her tone softened a bit.

"In truth, I do not bear true animosity towards Mary Vetsera. Perhaps she bears some culpability for what occurred, but she is hardly the only person in Vienna who might have wished my husband disposed of, one way or the other."

I looked at Holmes, whose right eyebrow had raised by this last remark.

## Chapter 16: The Crown Princess' Account

"I beg your pardon," said Holmes, "but are you suggesting that you are aware of others who might have plotted against your husband?"

Stephanie caught herself and suddenly assumed a coy demeanor.

"I am sure I do not know," she ambiguously said. "There are always rumors, of course." She stopped speaking and stared straight at Holmes and me saying nothing, waiting to see if we knew enough to move the conversation forward. I admit I had no idea what question to ask, but Holmes sensed where she was leading.

"You are speaking, of course, of his dalliance with the Hungarian rebels," Holmes said forthrightly.

Had he been mistaken, the breach of propriety in hinting at disloyalty to a member of the royal family would have been grievous, to say the least. But the Crown Princess' gaze remained firmly on Holmes as she measured how to reply to his comment. After several moments of study, she responded with the most miniscule of smiles.

"Well, Mr Holmes, you are as perceptive as the reports profess," she said.

He bowed slightly in her direction but said nothing.

"Yes," she added tentatively, "the Hungary question. Rather a delicate subject around the palace, as you might imagine."

"I presume his parents would understandably view any hint of disloyalty on his part with the gravest of consternation," I suggested.

"The Emperor, of course," she replied. "The 1867 Compact is celebrated as one of his finest achievements. But it is known to some family members and close associates of the Emperor that my mother-in-law has dabbled in the subject of Hungarian autonomy." She looked slyly at us. "Perhaps mother and son were conspiring together to tear the Austria-Hungary partnership apart!"

She stood and pulled a wrap tightly around her shoulder as she strode across the carpet to the large window looking out on the parade grounds in front of the palace.

## Chapter 16: The Crown Princess' Account

"Yes, I heard rumors that Rudolf was involved with the rebels and I let him know I found the entire idea preposterous as well as dangerous."

"And the Empress."

"Oh, I am certain she will find a reason to blame me for his death just as she blames me for failing to produce an heir. His morphine habit, his whores, the conspiracies: they are all my doing, to hear her tell it. She neither knows nor cares about the misery Rudolf spreads to me and probably to Miss Vetsera as well. If she wishes to know why there will be no male heir, she should look no further than that contemptible behavior on the part of her son."

She stopped for a moment and seemed deep in thought. Then she dramatically turned towards Holmes.

"If you are curious about Rudolf's political activities, I would suggest you schedule a meeting with Count Taaffe and the Archduke Albrecht," she advised. "If anything, they are relieved the Emperor has been spared further diplomatic and military embarrassment from the antics of the Crown Prince."

"Are you suggesting those gentlemen might know something about the death of the Crown Prince," I asked.

"I am only suggesting that they likely feel little sadness from his death. Little happens in Vienna of which they are unaware or, in many cases, in which they have not been engaged.

"I have read some of your stories about Mr Holmes," she said to me. "'When you have eliminated the impossible, whatever remains.' Isn't that how your little observation goes, Mr Holmes? I have no reason to believe they were involved, but I do know they are shedding no tears over his removal from the picture, by whatever good fortune it occurred."

"Well, *that* certainly was a remarkable conversation!" I exclaimed as we left Princess Stephanie's sitting room and walked towards the exit to the palace garden.

## Chapter 16: The Crown Princess' Account

"Yes," mused Holmes, as we found ourselves outdoors, "perhaps *too* remarkable. We learned that some within the highest ranks of the government believed that Rudolf was engaged in seditious activities. And we heard a degree of indifference towards his death that must raise suspicions about any spouse who holds such an opinion, especially if she has the influence and resources of a Crown Princess! With every conversation, I marvel at the number of people with a variety of motives for wishing the Prince disposed of. I am beginning to lose count of potential suspects!"

"And which of them is next on your list?" I asked.

"I would like to see the Minister-President Taaffe," Holmes said, "and then to check in with Archduke Albrecht."

We had not gone twenty paces, however, when a young man in uniform called out from the same palace door from which we had just exited.

"Herr Holmes, Herr Holmes!" he cried as he trotted up to us, holding a small envelope in his hand. "This was left for you."

Holmes thanked the young man and took the envelope. Waiting until the messenger had retreated towards the palace, he tore open the envelope and held up the paper so we could read it simultaneously.

*"I must see you again, Herr Holmes,"* the brief message read. *"I did not tell you everything but now, I must."*

An address not far from our hotel was given as a site for the rendezvous.

It was signed, "Countess Marie Larisch."

# Chapter 17: The Sealed Box

The countess had chosen an obscure pastry café for our second conversation, which provided another opportunity to sample Vienna's sumptuous treats as we awaited her arrival. The stress of the past several days seemed to me to justify some strudel or perhaps a nice lemon tart to accompany my tea.

"I wouldn't over-indulge in these sweets!" Holmes advised, warily eyeing my waistline. "I suspect the future Mrs Watson will be displeased with me for snatching you off to Vienna in reasonably sound physical condition and returning to her a flabby glutton!"

I was displeased by his gross mischaracterization of my eating habits. I had enjoyed but a single Viennese delicacy since our arrival days earlier -- a delectable *kardinalschnitte* -- but I did have to admit that my trousers already felt slightly tighter. My intention to rebuke Holmes was curtailed, however, by the arrival of Countess Marie Larisch in a hansom pulled by a single magnificent grey mare. She descended from the cab and walked rapidly to the table that Holmes had selected in the rear of the café to assure her maximum privacy.

"Thank you for agreeing to meet with me again," she began, her eyes sweeping the room, doubtless to ensure that no prying ears were close enough to overhear what she was about to disclose. "I am embarrassed not to have been completely honest with you during our last conversation. I was not certain I could trust you to be fair with me, to be perfectly truthful. Now, so much has happened, and I am so confused! I know now that I must make a clean breast of what I know. But can I ask if you might keep this information confidential or must it be shared with others?"

"Such as whom?" Holmes asked.

## Chapter 17: The Sealed Box

"The Empress," she answered, sadness filling her eyes. "Oh, she is already so angry with me." She looked pleadingly at my friend and put her hand on his arm. "I have no one to tell but you, Mr Holmes."

"Do not worry about the Empress," Holmes said. "There may well be opportunities for you to repair the damage to your personal relations with her in the future. The immediate need is for you to tell me whatever you have withheld; hurry, time is short!"

She took a deep breath of air and steadied herself before continuing.

"I told you I did not see Rudolf just before he departed for Mayerling, but in fact, I did," she began. "Indeed, quite early that very day, he appeared unannounced at my room at the Grand Hotel carrying a large leather satchel. I sometimes stay there when my husband is in Vienna.

"Of course, I protested that it was highly inappropriate for him to enter my room when we were alone but he cared little for such formalities. Before he pushed open the door, he looked carefully behind him – down the corridor, this way and that. He was in a very excited state, almost frantic and terribly concerned that he was being followed.

"'You cannot possibly realize the trouble into which I am plunged,' he cried. I could not imagine what 'trouble' he was referring to, but I could see the terror in his eyes. I held his hand and begged him to confide in me.

"'Does the trouble concern Princess Stéphanie?' I asked. "He laughed dismissively.

"'Stéphanie!' he exclaimed. 'Oh, dear me, no; she's merely a domestic complication. The danger which menaces me is far more grave!'

"Then he turned to the satchel he had carried into the room and placed on the bed. He unlatched the top. From it, he withdrew a small metal box and placed it on the table.

"'Listen, Marie,' he said to me, 'you must take this box and hide it away in a safe place.'

## Chapter 17: The Sealed Box

"He must have seen my hesitation and he held up his hand to stop me from speaking.

"'No, do not ask! It is better that you do not know what the box contains. I implore you not to open it, or allow anyone else to do so. For God's sake, tell no one that I have entrusted it to you. Do you understand: *no one*! My life – and perhaps other lives as well – may well depend on your trustworthiness!'

"I was so frightened by his warning!

"'Why can *you* not keep it?' I asked, hoping for an explanation.

"'It is imperative that it not be found in my possession,' he explained. 'At any moment, the Emperor or Krauss may order my personal belongings seized. If the material this box contains were to be found with me, the effect could be most severe.'

"'Why should they confiscate your belongings?' I asked with alarm. 'Whatever this box contains, aren't you better to go to the Emperor and lay your case before him rather than allow your accusers to paint you unfairly?'

"'You fool!' he hissed at me.

"We had been friends since childhood but I have never heard him so agitated! Even so, he should not have spoken to me so, and I am sure he saw the hurt in my eyes.

"'I don't mean that, Marie,' he apologized. 'But if I were to confide in the Emperor, I should sign my own death warrant.'

"Of course, I was taken aback by such language. Imagine suggesting your own father could threaten your life! The conversation was making me ever more anxious about having the box in my possession.

"I asked how long I was to retain the dreadful thing. To be truthful, I was concerned the secret police night have followed him to my home and would find it in my possession as soon as he departed.

"'Until I retrieve it from you,' he explained. His face grew grave. 'But I must be truthful with you, my dear friend. Marie, it is possible I shall never be in a position to retrieve it! Now, pay close

## Chapter 17: The Sealed Box

attention to what I am about to tell you. If I am not fated to see you again, you will be contacted by someone who alone has the right to the sealed box and can be trusted with its contents.'

"'But why would you be unable to come to me for the box yourself?' I pleaded.

"'If this unnamed person approaches you for the box, dear cousin, it is because I have fled Austria, because I have been absconded with, or,' he swallowed with difficulty, 'because I am already dead!'

"I was horrified by his statement and found it nearly impossible to catch my breath.

"'Who will this mysterious person be?' I inquired. "Do I know him – or her? You are placing me in jeopardy, Rudolf! Surely, I have a right to insist upon answers to these questions.'

"'Do not attempt to determine that person's identity, for he will appear to you *incognito*,' he warned. 'He will advise you where and when to meet, and when you do, he will provide you with the password, which you must remember. It is *RIUO*. He alone will know that password, and you must give the box only to him.'

"With that, he gave me a tight hug, placed the box back in the leather satchel and handed it to me. Then, he vanished from my life -- forever."

"What about these initials – RIUO? Have you any idea what they mean?" I asked.

"That is not a mystery," she responded, fear slipping into her eyes. "RIUO are the German initials for *Rudolf Imperator Ungarn Österreich*."

"Rudolf King of Hungary Austria," I translated.

"Precisely! Of course, I understood the implication that that message. I hurriedly took the satchel to my home and hid it in a dark and inaccessible section of the basement, behind some old crates, so it would be undetected should Krauss and the secret police search my house," she recalled.

"And have the police conducted such a search?" Holmes asked.

## Chapter 17: The Sealed Box

She shook her head.

"No, they have not. But two days ago, after Rudolf's death had been announced, I found a note that had been slipped under the front door of my room at the hotel."

"Weren't you frightened?" I asked. "You must have realised you were caught up in some very serious business."

"Oh, yes, I was terrified. It seemed certain that the Crown Prince had become involved in some kind of political intrigue. He could be so trusting and naïve sometimes! Perhaps his mind had been poisoned by traitors for their own nefarious ends."

"Hopefully you have not destroyed the note," Holmes said. "May I see it?"

She dug into her bag and removed an envelope, which she handed to Holmes, who unfolded the paper and handed it to me to translate.

> *If you are fearless and still faithful to your word given to the dead, bring what you know of this evening at half-past ten to the public promenade between the Schwarzenberg and the Heugasse. Be silent for the sake of his memory.*
> *R.I.U.O.!*

Just hearing the message read aloud caused the young woman to tremble, but she quickly gathered her wits and continued with her account.

"I could not refuse Rudolf's request, particularly now that he was dead. Surely you understand my loyalty to him, even though complying with his instruction caused me intolerable dread. I was certain I had been drawn into some nefarious plot that would see me cast into prison or worse.

"Nevertheless, I had given my word and that evening, as I had been instructed, I took the box from the hiding place and took my carriage close to the edge of the Prater. I did not want even my driver to know my precise destination. Although it was quite heavy, I carried

## Chapter 17: The Sealed Box

the box with me for a quarter mile before reaching the precise point where the rendezvous was to take place.

It was not long before the ghostly figure of a man appeared from out of the shadows and approached me with nearly silent footsteps. He was bundled in thick clothes against the cold and his head and shoulders were wrapped in a cloak that almost completely shielded his face from my view.

"'Countess Larisch?' he asked urgently. The voice was not totally unfamiliar, but I could not be certain about his identity. 'You have received my letter?'

"Naturally I was terrified. I did not know if this was the man I was supposed to meet. For a moment, a nonsensical thought entered my mind: it was Rudolf, who was not really dead! Then I worried the man was an imposter, not truly a friend but a member of the secret police who had intercepted our communication and would arrest me if he found me with the box' contents. Still, I felt bound by my pledge.

"'What do you want?' I stammered uncommittedly, moving slightly away from the mysterious figure.

"He softly hissed a single word. '*Rudolf.*'

"I hesitated to acknowledge my identity or reveal why I was alone in the Prater so late in the evening. Perhaps the stranger was unaware of the password.

"'That name means nothing to me!' I declared.

"'Ah,' he said, realizing he had failed to follow the proper protocol. 'I understand. You require the password. Well, here it is: R.I.U.O.'"

I must admit that I found myself utterly captivated by her account. The entire story – the cast of characters, the clandestine meetings, the twists and turns of the narrative – all seemed more suited to a West End playhouse than the corridors of power in the Austrian capital.

"What did you do?" I asked breathlessly.

## Chapter 17: The Sealed Box

"Why, since he knew the code word, I did as Rudolf had instructed and showed him the satchel containing the sealed box. He hesitated before taking possession of it. Perhaps he was fearful that I was a member of the police."

"'Did he tell you what this mystery was about?' he asked me.

"'No!' I replied truthfully. 'I am in complete ignorance. I am here only because of my promise to my friend.'

"'Well, well, it is better that such is the case,' he replied. 'Otherwise, your life might be forfeited.'

"My heart raced at this statement.

"'Please,' I entreated, 'take the box. I want nothing further to do with it!'

"Two hands emerged from under his cloak and I noticed that on one of his little fingers, a most attractive diamond ring glittered in the moonlight.

"He saw me glancing at the ring.

"'I suppose you have no idea who I am, Countess?' he asked as he lifted the satchel.

"'None,' I replied. Nor did I have any desire to know given the obvious peril of being associated in any way with the sealed box. 'I wish only to be done with this business. I have honoured his memory by following his instructions."

"He looked about to convince himself we not being observed, and then he removed the cloak so that I could clearly see his face.

"'Imperial Highness!' I cried. The stranger was none other than Archduke John Salvator of Tuscany, another of the Crown Prince's cousins. Suddenly, I realised the extreme danger into which I had been placed. Salvator was well-known to be a collaborator in the Hungarian independence movement. Involvement with him could easily subject me to accusations of sedition or worse! I immediately realized the implication of his comradeship with Rudolf.

"'You have honoured his cause through your bravery, Marie,' he said, attempting to calm me. 'Had the contents of this box fallen into

## Chapter 17: The Sealed Box

the wrong hands, the Emperor would have had little alternative but to have his own son and heir shot.'

"I gasped at the very thought of such intrigue, and immediately worried again that I had seriously compromised myself.

"'Rudolf remained at Mayerling because he had learned that his plan for an uprising in Budapest were collapsing. Yes, Marie: an uprising!'

"He must have seen the shock his revelation gave me."

"'Yes, an insurrection that would have made him King of Hungary!' the Archduke explained. 'Six days ago, just days before the revolt was to commence, it was uncovered by the secret police and its leaders in Hungary arrested, a fact so far kept from the newspapers. But it was only a matter of time before, under the most excruciating duress, one of the patriots would have implicated our friend in the plot, with the most calamitous of consequences.

"'I saw him immediately after learning of the collapse of the plan, and he was in quite dreadful condition. As a result of the brandy and drugs he was ingesting, his nerves were utterly ruined. He believed he was about to be exposed and denounced. He had fallen apart and behaved like a contemptible coward, seeking comfort in the arms of that mere child, Mary Vetsera.'

"I was offended by his calling Rudolf a coward and chastised him for such a cruel remark, particularly since the Crown Prince had been driven to suicide by his despair.

"'Suicide?' he sneered. 'You think Rudolf maneuvered to escape his father's wrath in order to kill himself at Mayerling? Preposterous! I cannot believe he would have the nerve!'

"Then how?' I asked. 'Who?'

"'There are powerful men who would kill to secure what is in this box,' Salvator declared. 'By exposing this material, they could earn the eternal gratitude of Franz Joseph, who is easily impressed with such acts of loyalty.'

## Chapter 17: The Sealed Box

"I realized the danger the Archduke was facing, which explained his heavy concealment and his determination to ensure the material entrusted to him did not fall into the wrong hands.

"'What is to become of the contents of this box?' I asked.

"'It is better that you should not know,' he replied. 'With luck, these papers will never be revealed and history will never have a definitive answer as to Rudolf's involvement in the plot. As for me, it would be foolhardy to remain within the Emperor's grasp. It pains me to contemplate leaving Austria without achieving the goals of reform I shared with Rudolf. But the despotic forces are too formidable. I have no doubt there is a long list of officials who would relish marching me in front of a firing squad!'

"He replaced his hat and again his eyes again surveyed the park for agents of the Emperor's dreaded secret police.

"'I will not give them that pleasure! I am going to die without dying, Marie' he said mysteriously. 'Within weeks – perhaps just days -- the Archduke Johann Salvator will cease to exist.' With that cryptic statement, he disappeared into the night clutching the bag that contained the metal box."

Miss Larisch's tale thrilled both Holmes and myself.

"Might Salvator also be contemplating suicide?" I asked worriedly.

"It is possible, I suppose," said Holmes, "but it sounds to me as though he is more inclined to escape from the intrigue and danger of the palace: perhaps a new name and identity. I presume he was accurately representing the dangers he faced in Vienna?"

"Oh, yes, Albrecht, that old bureaucrat, hated Salvator as much as he disliked the Crown Prince," Marie said in an outburst. "He believed both of them favored dismantling the Empire, which made Rudolf unfit to rule."

Holmes lapsed into silence for several moments before addressing a question to Countess Larisch.

## Chapter 17: The Sealed Box

"Are there others whom you are confident harbor similarly hostile feelings towards Rudolf – men loyal to the Emperor and disdainful of the man he favoured inheriting his crown?"

She pressed her lips together unconsciously, as if attempting to will herself to remain quiet, but to little avail.

"The President Taaffe was cheered by Rudolf's death, I have no doubt, although he would surely deny it," she professed. "He shares Albrecht's disdain for reforms that he believes would weaken the Emperor.

"Make no mistake, Mr Holmes," she said, her voice rising with urgency. "These are powerful men! They can arrange to cover up any unpleasantness and they are deeply involved in the events of the past several days. It was Taaffe who arranged for Mary's body to be secretly buried without a proper medical examination or even a priest to consecrate her grave. Imagine, the President of the nation involving himself in such pettiness! One can only imagine the depths of the conspiracy they believe they have exposed."

"And yet the Emperor retains confidence in the judgment and loyalty of these men, I would imagine," I said.

"The Emperor has deep affection for Taaffe and trusts him implicitly. I understand that he has given all of Rudolf's papers to the Minister-President for safe-keeping because he feared their contents might incriminate the Crown Prince. Taaffe will surely squirrel the papers away for future political advantage or burn them if they contain embarrassing information about his own conduct."

"Yes, and I expect that there are more papers that contain information of the most incendiary nature," Holmes speculated, "and those papers are in the sealed box now in the possession of Count Salvator. Without question, those are the documents Taaffe covets most."

"Surely those papers cannot fall into the hands of the enemies of Prince Rudolf," I observed.

## Chapter 17: The Sealed Box

"The papers of the Crown Prince belong in the state archives, not in the files of the state President," Holmes said disapprovingly. "Nor," he said, reproachfully looking at Miss Larisch, "do they belong in a sealed metal box secretly squirreled away by the Crown Prince's co-conspirator!"

Miss Larisch looked down at the ground in embarrassment and then met Holmes's glare.

"Now you must tell me, Countess, where may I find Salvator?" he demanded.

"I have not heard from him since our meeting in the Prater," she replied. "But there is no doubt in my mind that he intends to flee as soon as practicable. He knows that Krauss will order his arrest, if he has not done so already. He will do anything to avoid the release of letters that could compromise his friend's legacy or implicate himself in a conspiracy."

I could see Holmes's mind spinning at a furious rate as he calculated the intricate maneuvers at play amongst these conniving aristocrats. If he was grateful to Miss Larisch for finally coming forward, he did not indicate it.

"Your withholding of this information has undoubtedly given Salvator the time he needs to slip out of Vienna," he reprimanded, "or alternatively, to fall into the clutches of those who wish him ill. I cannot do my job if information is withheld! Is there anything else that you desire to share with me," he asked, "perhaps an additional cache of writings that you have hidden away?"

The Countess looked appropriately chagrined.

"I have now told you all I know, Mr Holmes," she insisted. "I realize I have nothing to gain from withholding information. I suggest you interview Albrecht and Taaffe, neither of whom can truthfully make the same profession to you. As to Salvator, he was a true friend to Rudolf, and I cannot help but wish him well!"

"If he is captured with those papers," Holmes replied tersely, "he will need far more than your good wishes."

## Chapter 18: The Case Thus Far

"We must not delay in locating Johann Salvator and the mystery box," I advised Holmes. "Whatever revelations it contains may well be the clue to this entire mystery, if there is a mystery."

Holmes uttered one of those ambiguous grunts that typically connoted dissatisfaction with my observation.

"No, Watson, I think the Countess Larisch is quite accurate," he remonstrated. "Salvator knows he is not safe within the reach of the constabulatory of Vienna, which extends considerably further than the city limits. Efforts to chase him down would, I fear, consume valuable time that we must devote to interviewing those with substantial interest in the Prince's dual flirtations with Hungarian independence and Mary Vetsera."

As we awaited responses to Holmes's requests for meetings with Albrecht and Taaffe we retired to my sitting room in our hotel. The bustle of the prior days was flooding us with information and draining my energies, although Holmes showed no signs of fatigue. We both lit cigars and settled back in comfortable armchairs.

"Let us take stock of what we know thus far," Holmes suggested, a proposal I welcomed since the rapid unfolding of facts and bewildering number of personalities and motives had frankly left me somewhat befuddled.

"I was initially summoned confidentially by Emperor Franz Joseph to assist in evaluating threats to the Hapsburg Empire that he feared jeopardized his own rule and destabilize all of Europe. You will recall I agreed to play such a role only because of the intervention of our Prime Minister through Mycroft. Our schedule for undertaking that inquiry changed dramatically within a day of our arrival due to the absence of our primary subject, Rudolf, from the dinner at which we were to be introduced.

## Chapter 18: The Case Thus Far

"Recall, Watson, that prior to the dinner, our presence in Vienna was unknown to virtually everyone but the Emperor and Empress and some palace attendants like Bratfisch. That is a crucial fact! Any plot hatched against the Prince during these past few days would have been undertaken without knowledge of my presence or any expectation that I might become involved in the investigation.

"Perhaps I flatter myself, but I venture that the execution of any scheme would have been far more meticulously planned had the schemers known that Sherlock Holmes, and not simply the local gendarmes, would be conducting the inquiry."

"Unquestionably that is true," I responded. "The expectation undoubtedly was that the entire matter, whatever the facts could be hushed up to spare the royal family embarrassment. Minimizing the public discussion of the circumstances surrounding the Prince's death would also reduce the risk of its triggering political unrest, especially in Hungary amongst the Prince's extensive network."

Holmes nodded in appreciation of my observations.

"Now, the immediate question facing us is the death of the Crown Prince Rudolf and his lover, the 17-year old Baroness Mary Vetsera, one of numerous women with whom he was engaged in an illicit affair."

"Not an unknown circumstance among men of his station," I added disapprovingly.

"Or any station, you may be quite certain," Holmes knowingly responded. "Those peccadillos amongst royalty can prove highly embarrassing, particularly if they lead to competing claims to the throne in the years to come."

"But surely, an illegitimate child would have no entitlement to such a claim!" I challenged.

"Perhaps not legally," Holmes agreed, "but as any student of history would know, those seeking to challenge established political power will grasp at any available ambiguity, regardless of its legality or even accuracy, to challenge a succession or the outcome of an election. A child with royal blood, even if the bloodline is irregular, often can serve as a most convenient instrument for inflaming such instability."

"Undoubtedly true," I agreed, recalling England's long history of violent claims and counter-claims for the throne. "A most harrowing set of problems!"

"Unquestionably, and a good reason for any plotter to assume the Emperor would seek to have the matter resolved quickly and with little publicity or scrutiny."

"No wonder, then, that your presence may have upended the original plan," I added. "So, you think this entire mystery may be linked to the succession to the crown of Austria."

"The Crown Prince's indiscretions – due to what this Dr Freud calls his 'libido' – was likely not the only concern driving a plot against him," Holmes continued. "Through the influence of his hot-blooded cousin, the Archduke Johann Salvator, he became involved with Hungarian nationalists seeking an end to the 1867 alliance that had created the dual monarchy. His involvement in such a plot, should it come to the attention of the Emperor, would most certainly have demanded a most serious response, since no indiscretion is more unforgivable than treason."

"Well, I can't say your recitation of the facts is making it much easier to untangle the case," I complained. "But you have surely identified any number of Rudolf's associates who have reason to wish him ill: Mizzi Kaspar, Princess Stephanie, Prince Miguel Braganza, not to mention Albrecht and Taaffe, and there may well be others with a strong motive for tarnishing Rudolf in the eyes of his father. And much of what we are being told may be utter rubbish designed to conceal who knows what impropriety? Perhaps Salvator invented the entire story about the box to ensure that his own involvement in the Hungarian plot remains concealed."

"Quite so," Holmes replied. "Each had a distinct motive for removing Rudolf and perhaps Mary Vetsera from the picture. I think it

## Chapter 18: The Case Thus Far

would be fair to say that the Crown Prince felt the walls closing in on him.

"Unbeknownst to us, the pace of events was speeding up even as we were on our way to Austria," he continued. "The Emperor, concerned by the growing unrest, had decided to make a state visit to Hungary there to solidify the alliance. At the same time, he planned a formal dinner at which he would proclaim Rudolf his unquestioned successor, doubtless with the hope such a designation would quash the Prince's involvement in any Hungarian plot."

"But Rudolf may not have known of his father's intentions," I noted. "Perhaps he feared his involvement in the failed plot would be exposed at the dinner, which would mean disgrace and likely imprisonment, if not worse!"

"Capital reasoning!" Holmes declared. "And so, he invents an illness to sequester himself at Mayerling, far from the palace dinner and the political intrigue. Perhaps he planned to abscond to Budapest and take up his role as leader of another Hungarian uprising. But then his plans were upended when he arrived at Mayerling.

"To his astonishment, his love-struck mistress, Baroness Vetsera has unexpectedly appeared in his room at the lodge. They are both despondent although for very different reasons: she may be pregnant and convinced he will never abandon the Princess Stephanie, while he fears exposure as a traitor linked to the aborted uprising in Hungary."

"So while the Prince dines with Hoyos, she composes a suicide note," I commented. "Perhaps she had become aware of his discussion of the subject with Miss Kaspar and anticipates he will join her in perpetuity. That is what they might have been discussing when Loschek heard a conversation taking place in the Prince's bedroom. But there are many other pieces of this puzzle that cry out against such a simple explanation! Perhaps the truth of what happened at Mayerling – and why – will simply remain unknown," I summarized.

## Chapter 18: The Case Thus Far

"Yes, many motives, many suspects! " Holmes said. "Perhaps *too* many! Whoever is behind these dastardly events now must realize the danger of my presence and doubtless regrets the evidence that was thoughtlessly left strewn about. With the application of appropriate pressure, I have no doubt the local constabulatory would have neither the competence nor motivation to recognize its significance."

"Perhaps our unexpected presence prompted the assassins – if there were assassins – to act before their plot might be uncovered."

"That possibility cannot be ruled out," he agreed. "But one fact is certain: but for our arrival on the scene, Rudolf and Mary would both be safely in their graves with few questions asked. Instead, I intend to continue to ask questions and, I fear, disturbing facts are still to be uncovered."

He finished his thought and looked deeply pensive.

"Something else is on your mind, Holmes," I insisted.

He measured his words carefully.

"I must be straight with you, Watson. If my hypotheses are correct and our presence is causing considerable discomfort, there is the distinct possibility that the longer we remain in Vienna, the greater the danger to me – and to you, as well. I do not exaggerate! If we unwittingly have intervened in a nefarious plot, those who are responsible may very well determine that it is necessary to eliminate anyone who could expose the conspiracy.

"I fear, my friend, I may have dragged you into a far more sinister situation than I had anticipated, and on the eve of your wedding." He paused before continuing his thought. "I would not in any way think less of you should you decide to return to the security of London and the arms of your future wife rather than remain here at such risk to your personal safety."

Had I not known that Holmes was genuinely concerned for my physical wellbeing, I easily might have been offended at the suggestion of abandoning him at such a crucial moment in the case.

## Chapter 18: The Case Thus Far

"Well, it will not be the first time that we have faced considerable odds and substantial danger," I observed. "Certainly, we must continue our investigation -- *together*," I concluded, "and do so immediately!" I removed my service revolver from inside my waist coat and patted it carefully. "I am ready for whoever or whatever comes after us!"

"Bravo, Watson!" Holmes exclaimed. "I knew I could depend on your steadfastness!"

I was pleased at Holmes's reaction, but I was still reeling from the complexities of the case.

"Then on to our most difficult but critical interviews," said Holmes, "Albrecht and Taaffe. I would be very surprised if they cannot shed considerable light on what transpired in a locked room in Mayerling," he mused, "and why."

"But will they willingly cooperate with our inquiry?" I ventured.

"I cannot imagine why they would," replied Sherlock Holmes.

# Chapter 19: A Warning from President Taaffe

Few Austrians could match the stellar reputation of Count Edward Taaffe and none shared a closer relationship with Emperor Franz Joseph. Their friendship dated from childhood, and the count's sharp intellect had vaulted him into a succession of high governmental posts over a career that had lasted several decades. His reputation grew significantly following the signing of the Compromise that had cemented Austria and Hungary into a tight political alliance, one that he was deeply committed to maintain. Having earlier served as the Minister of the Interior, he was currently in his second term as Minister-President, a role comparable to that of our own Prime Minister.

His affection for many members of the royal family, however, most certainly did not extend to the Emperor's son, as he forthrightly demonstrated in his discussion with Holmes and me. Arrogant and aloof, he projected a sentiment of complete indifference to the Emperor and Empress' recent loss.

"You are not the first member of your illustrious family that it has been my honor to meet," Taaffe said as he shook hands with Holmes. Taaffe spoke in flawless English, the result of his membership in a dynastic Irish family. "My diplomatic responsibilities have taken me to London on numerous occasions where I had the occasional opportunity to converse with your brother, Mycroft, a most intelligent and thoughtful gentleman. I was deeply impressed with his sophisticated appreciation for the tribulations that we on the Continent confront both politically and militarily. It has been a pleasure to remain in close communication with him over the past several years. I would appreciate your conveying to him my very warmest regards."

"I shall certainly communicate your sentiments to my elder brother," Holmes replied, "but I am here to discuss the late Crown Prince."

## Chapter 19: A Warning from President Taaffe

Taaffe's expression changed immediately with the mention of Prince Rudolf.

"I cannot say anything as honorific about the late Crown Prince," he said with obvious disdain. "A most disreputable young man."

I felt it rather insensitive language to use in referring to the young man who had horrifically lost his life and had not even been laid to rest. But Taaffe was unrepentant.

"His personal behavior was disgraceful: flagrantly consorting with the most disreputable of women right here in the Hofburg while the Crown Princess and their young daughter remained but a few rooms away in their royal apartments."

"I must take exception to the use of such strong language against a Crown Prince!" I remonstrated, "let alone one who has recently been taken from his family!"

Taaffe flared back in response.

"I could say far worse," he vowed, "were I to comment upon his transgressions against the state."

"You have proof of the accuracy of that allegation?" Holmes pressed.

Taaffe glared harshly at Holmes, his eyes narrowing under a massive forehead and thick black hair.

"I am not prone to making accusations I cannot corroborate, Mr Sherlock Holmes," he said, carefully pronouncing each syllable of my friend's name with a clipped Irish accent. "One of the advantages of my position is command of the secret police under the very diligent leadership of Superintendent Krauss. They are a very efficient group of men who, on my instructions, have kept a close eye on the Crown Prince and those with whom he ... consorts."

"I had no doubt that was the case," Holmes replied blithely. "My question would be whether they were merely observing his movements and reporting them to you or whether they might have played a more consequential role."

## Chapter 19: A Warning from President Taaffe

Taaffe paused before selecting his response to Holmes's thinly veiled accusation.

"It is the nature of their job to conceal their presence from those who must be unaware they are nearby," he responded. "These special agents reported to me when Mary Vetsera arrived at Mayerling that fateful afternoon, and they remained there until the next morning when the great tragedy was revealed."

"You strongly disapproved of the Crown Prince's indiscretions, I would imagine," Holmes said.

Taaffe waved his hand in the air.

"I do not care with whom Rudolf went to bed!" he said. "We are all modern men, after all. It is *your* queen who extols the virtues of moral uprightness! My concern is the security of the state, which is vulnerable to the blackmailing of members of the royal family. We all were well aware of the Prince's perverse activities, but for the good of the Crown, we have remained silent for years. But when Rudolf's peccadillos risked creating pretenders to the throne, the dangers became far more grave."

"So, you believe the Baroness Vetsera was with child?" I asked.

"I had heard rumors to that effect," Taaffe vaguely conceded.

"But even if she were to make a claim about the paternity of the child, Rudolf surely could dispute any claim!" I protested.

"Undoubtedly he would," Taaffe responded. "She would hardly be the first strumpet to levy similar claims. Perhaps you have heard of actress Johanna Buska, a very beautiful woman and quite accomplished? She later married the Hungarian de Szendrö after Rudolf discarded her. Fortunately, she has remained discrete about her *affair de la coeur* with the Prince.

"But Mary Vetsera was different: an immature, inexperienced child, easily impressed by the titles and medals of the aristocracy. She had foolishly expressed a belief to friends that she would soon marry the Prince. If he refused to divorce Princess Stephanie, she may well

## Chapter 19: A Warning from President Taaffe

have chosen to publicise far more compromising material than had his earlier ... indiscretions."

"And are there questions about the line of succession in the wake of Rudolf's death?" Holmes asked. "Or does that role indisputably now fall to the Emperor's brother, Karl Ludwig?"

Taaffe could not conceal his unease at Holmes's comment.

"Karl Ludwig is *another* weak Hapsburg, although mercifully with little ambition to become Emperor," Taaffe said sharply. "At least he would be manipulable, you will pardon my speaking frankly, unlike the impulsive Rudolf. His son, Franz Ferdinand, is now likely to stand in line for the throne, which is also quite problematical. He considers himself a 'reformer' and like Rudolf, his naïve ideas would risk a war throughout Europe. Of course, there is always the chance that Rudolf's fate will influence Franz Ferdinand to proceed with greater caution where matters of national security are concerned."

He shook his head with resignation.

"I admit I had become increasingly anxious about Rudolf's activities," the president declared. "I doubt that he realized I was aware of his consorting with men like the traitor Johann Salvator, even writing letters whose contents, if released, would have the most humiliating impact on the Emperor. Indeed, if certain of those papers had become public, it is not beyond the realm of possibilities that the Crown Prince of Austria could have stood with his rebellious friends in the dock or even on the gallows or before a firing squad."

Holmes's stone face displayed no surprise by the mention of the Crown Prince's cousin but I less successfully attempted to stifle a reaction. Taaffe noticed my response and his expression turned scornful.

"Ah, I see you know of the traitor Salvator," he said, his mouth curling into a tight smile, "and of his little box of secrets, no doubt. I have heard that you are quite clever, Herr Holmes. But mark my words, we are looking for him and we will find him, I am quite confident." His eyes narrowed as he considered his next words carefully.

## Chapter 19: A Warning from President Taaffe

"Let me offer you some advice, Mr Holmes. Be very cautious about consorting with enemies of the Empire. Your notoriety and your English nationality offer you no protection in Austria."

"That is an outrageous insult!" I responded. "We are here at the request of the Emperor, not to undermine his authority. Please show us proper respect, Herr President. A detective like Mr Holmes does not sympathise with those he investigates or interrogates, as you must be aware. The facts we have gathered will be used to determine what happened at Mayerling lodge on the 30th of January, and we will not hesitate to lay culpability wherever it may belong."

"Bravo, Watson," said Holmes. "But since baseless accusations are being tossed about, Herr President, in the confines of this room, may I ask you a question? Given your lack of regard for the Crown Prince and your questions about his loyalty to his father, might not you and others with your perspective have looked sympathetically upon his removal from the line of succession, if not having facilitated it?"

It was Taaffe's turn to appear shocked.

"I must again advise you to be judicious, Mr Holmes. Surely you are not insinuating that I had a hand in the Prince's death."

"I have only posed a question as I might in any case to assess where a motive might exist," Holmes responded indifferently, removing his pipe and tobacco from his jacket and deliberately filling the bowl. "Your own words have revealed that you have several rationales for keeping Rudolf from the throne. And of course, as President, you possess the means of achieving just such a goal."

"I could have you thrown in prison for even intimating such treachery!"

Holmes's face grew grave, even menacing, as he responded to the President's effort at intimidation.

"Let me be equally frank with *you*, Herr President. You and your colleagues have done your best to cover up the true facts of the Prince's death. You knew he had been fatally shot and yet you publicly attributed his death to an aneurysm of the heart."

## Chapter 19: A Warning from President Taaffe

"I have no doubt the Emperor would have wished to keep the true cause confidential for as long as possible."

"That preposterous explanation of his death was designed to obstruct investigation into the possibility of a murder or conspiracy rather than a self-inflicted gunshot wound. You likely played a role in ensuring that a proper autopsy was averted, knowing that one might reveal pertinent facts about the Prince's cause of death. Indeed, even after the extent of his injury was well documented, you continued to promote the idea of death from natural causes and entrusted the superficial post-mortem to a pediatrician with no knowledge of mortuary or forensic science."

"The nation is in shock," he protested. "No one wants to make the situation any worse."

"You also arranged with Krauss for the clandestine removal of Mary Vetsera's body from Mayerling and her burial in an unconsecrated plot."

"We agreed that it is better to allow some facts to remain obscure, shall we say."

The two men looked harshly at each other.

"Those who advocate weakening the political bonds that hold our people together are traitors," Traafe intoned, "regardless of their pedigree. Failure to unify under benevolent leaders like Franz Joseph means that European peace will be replaced by nationalist fragmentation and war. I apologize to no one for devoting the last twenty years of my life to averting just such a conflagration."

"And Archduke Albrecht, the Emperor's uncle, shares your sentiments?" Holmes asked.

Taaffe tightened his jaw and gripped the back of a chair tightly.

"The Archduke is a great patriot," he observed. "I advise you to tread carefully, Mr. Holmes. Tread *very* carefully."

# Chapter 20: Albrecht, Duke of Teschen

"It appears that half the royal family and its functionaries had a reason for ridding the country of Crown Prince Rudolf!" I observed as we clambered through the streets of Vienna to our last meeting of the day. "I am frankly amazed that so many of them with obvious motives are so unapologetic about their low regard for the Crown Prince!"

"And I would not be surprised if Archduke Albrecht added yet another name to our growing list!" said Holmes. "However, the statements we have heard thus far are far from an admission of responsibility for Rudolf's death in any fashion. Far more specific evidence will be needed to establish guilt sufficient for a court, presuming the Emperor's judiciary would even consider prosecuting any of the august figures with whom we have spoken."

The office of the *Feldmarschall* was housed in a massive and elaborate building near the Parliament. Soldiers at the entry carefully examined our identification papers, including a message given to us by the Emperor's staff attesting that we were operating on his direct authority. Even so, the guards took several minutes to study the papers assiduously, conversing amongst themselves for at least a quarter of an hour. At last, a junior officer escorted us, with little geniality, to the Archduke's chambers on the third floor overlooking the central city.

"You will wait here," we were authoritatively instructed by the elaborately dressed guard. He directed us to the intricately carved and lavishly upholstered chairs that filled the garishly ornamental room before disappearing through a doorway. For the next half hour, we awaited the summons into the general's office, aware that any conversation between us might well be overheard. While Holmes sat with his eyes half-closed, I surveyed the walls, which were covered with portraits of men I presumed to be famed Austrian military leaders. Hanging near them were examples of the weaponry generations of

## Chapter 20: Albrecht, Duke of Teschen

soldiers had carried into combat: sabers, bayonets, knives, rifles and pistols. If the intention was to persuade visitors that the Austrian military was well armed and prepared to march into battle, the effect was achieved with great success.

At last, the door through which the guard had departed opened again and he emerged, walking briskly to where we sat.

"Now, you will come!" he ordered in a brusque and decidedly unwelcoming tone.

We rose and followed him into an even more ornate room that also was brimming with ostentatious displays of military art and battlefield memorabilia. Carved into the central panel of the massive desk was the double-headed eagle crest of the Hapsburgs, behind which stood the Archduke Albrecht. A veteran of decades of bloody military campaigns, the old soldier wore a heavily decorated military uniform that conveyed severity and authority. He maintained an erect posture despite the advanced years that had turned his short-cropped hair and full side-whiskers and mustache grey. On his nose was perched a pair of rimless eyeglasses.

Despite his long service to the Empire, he was not without critics who faulted his views of military organization and training as better suited to the threats of the century that was closing than the one looming on the horizon. For over three decades, they asserted, he had steadfastly refused to recognize the increasingly complicated political conditions and advancements in weaponry on the continent that presented a modern set of challenge to the traditional security afforded by borders. Austria under Albrecht's archaic leadership, these detractors insisted, had been perilously slow to acquire the armaments of modern warfare, believing that old alliances and tactics would prevail. (The criticism of this strategic analysis would, over the ensuing decades, prove well-founded indeed!)

"You are Holmes?" he barked as we approached his desk.

"I am," Holmes responded calmly, turning to me and gesturing. "And this is my able associate, Dr John Watson." I bowed slightly,

## Chapter 20: Albrecht, Duke of Teschen

which I thought appropriate given the old man's bearing although his curtness with Holmes rankled me. "I appreciate your making yourself available to discuss the late Crown Prince."

The Archduke snorted contemptuously at the mention of Rudolf's title.

"The Emperor is devastated," he said without an iota of sadness, "and I am therefore grieving." He dropped heavily into the chair behind his desk and motioned for us to sit on chairs facing him.

"I take it you do not view the Prince's untimely death as a grievous loss to the Empire?" Holmes questioned cynically.

"How is it a loss?" he demanded. "You obviously did not know Rudolf. I believe it was the intervention of the Divine Providence that led him to take his own life and spare his nation the grave conflagration that would invariably result from his accession to the throne."

Holmes grimaced at the mention of the handiwork of the Almighty.

"I question whether Divine intervention played much of a role in the unspeakable horror that occurred at Mayerling Lodge," he declared dismissively. "I rather see instead the hand of a very mortal man behind the death of Crown Prince Rudolf." He paused briefly to gage the elderly general's response. "Yes, a very mortal man," he slowly repeated, "or men."

Albrecht sniffed disrespectfully in response to Holmes's comment. He stood and turned his back to us, staring out the large window.

"His place in succession will be filled by someone far more qualified to wear the crown of the Hapsburgs," Albrecht responded, "someone less full of ideas that no one wants to hear!"

Clearly, the old man had no hesitation in expressing his unsentimental critiques.

"A harsh assessment of a young man your nation is mourning, it seems to me," I remarked.

## Chapter 20: Albrecht, Duke of Teschen

"Rudolf was a fool," Albrecht snarled, "a weak, womanizing buffoon: a self-centered libertine. He was a dreamer whose irresponsible 'reforms' would have meant disaster for our country." He rapped his knuckles hard on his desk and turned back to face us.

"Reforming what?" he demanded. "A government he did not understand? A military he knew nothing of commanding? And worse, he was a saboteur, a subversive, conspiring against his own father."

He must have seen the stunned look in our eyes; the use of such vitriol against a member of the royal family, not to mention the dead Crown Price, was scarcely believable.

"You think me disrespectful?" he queried. "*Ja*! I disrespected Rudolf and all he stood for. Better he is dead and a strong man will sit on the throne someday."

"A strong man like you, perhaps?" Holmes asked provocatively. "You are, after all, the grandson of an emperor yourself."

I looked to Holmes, impressed that he had uncovered the general's royal lineage, but Albrecht scowled at the suggestion.

"I am an old man, Herr Holmes," he said with a slight weariness, his eyes narrowing. "I have no claim to the throne of the Hapsburgs and no aspirations in that regard either. I have every hope that Emperor Franz Joseph will enjoy good health and long life. In time, he will determine who the new Crown Prince will be, and I will loyally embrace his decision."

"And I wonder who that might be?" asked Holmes.

"Karl Ludwig, I suppose, he is the next brother," he sniffed. Like Taaffe, he did not seem enthusiastic at the prospect. "He is preoccupied with matters of the arts and other frivolities, not affairs of state, but at least he has produced a male heir who can continue the Hapsburg line, albeit one with fanciful dreams of his own. That is something that the Emperor's other brother, Ludwig Viktor, is likely to do given his," here he paused, searching for the suitable English word,

## Chapter 20: Albrecht, Duke of Teschen

"predilections." There was no need to ask Albrecht to elaborate further on his low opinion of the banished brother.

"You knew of the Crown Prince's assignations with Baroness Vetsera, among others, did you not?" Holmes pressed, immediately encountering resistance from the old soldier.

"Am I to be subjected to interrogation by a foreigner?" Albrecht arrogantly responded.

Holmes shrugged his shoulders. "Obviously, I cannot compel you to respond. I only wish to learn as much as possible -- at the request of the Emperor -- about the events surrounding the tragedy," Holmes reminded him.

Albrecht grunted at the mention of the word "tragedy" and seated himself again behind his desk. He removed a large cigar from the drawer and cut off the end with a silver tool before taking several moments to light the end.

"Let me tell you something, Mr Holmes," he said, a thick cloud of acrid smoking filling the space between us. "Rudolf was not as clever in covering his tracks as he thought. I have a good many reliable sources of information. I had heard of his lechery and I have heard of his treachery, and I had concluded the Emperor must be informed of the irresponsible behavior of his son in hopes of persuading him to alter the line of succession."

"But the Emperor did not share that view, did he?" Holmes demanded. "Instead, he intended to assure Rudolf that he would be chosen as his successor in hopes that doing so would encourage him to end his flirtations with the Hungarians and other reformers."

Albrecht looked at Holmes coldly, realizing my friend possessed far more information about the relationship between the Emperor and Crown Prince than he might have imagined.

"If you say so," was all he remarked. "But Rudolf failed to come to the dinner where such a designation was expected to be made, or so I have been led to believe. Perhaps he feared talk of formally designating him heir was a deception and what actually awaited him

## Chapter 20: Albrecht, Duke of Teschen

was arrest and disgrace, which would have been more deserved. For whatever reason, he avoided his princely responsibilities and chose instead to remain in the arms of his child paramour."

He paused to take a long draw on his cigar, holding the smoke in his mouth for several seconds before again spewing the pungent smoke in our direction.

"How ironic! He likely would have been safer at the dinner in the Hofburg palace than in his bedroom at Mayerling!"

The President erupted in a brief but disrespectful guffaw at his own remark.

"I will tell you something you did not know, Mr Holmes," he continued, "because now, it does not matter and you will learn of it anyway. I was certain he believed I had acquired the evidence to condemn him. I do not believe he intended to return to Vienna from Mayerling. In fact, I believe his plan was to defect to Hungary and take up arms against his father!"

"And that, general, is likely why you dispatched your soldiers to Mayerling early the following morning," Holmes asked, "to meet the Minister-President's agents who had been watching the lodge throughout the night? The official military carriage parked near the stables was an unfortunate oversight that Loschek presumably was not intended to see."

Had Holmes poured the glass of water over the old man's head, I do not think Albrecht would have registered a greater shock. He sat up straight in his chair and gripped the armrests. His face grew red, his mouth opened and he seemed about to speak, but then he noticeably relaxed, his shoulders dropped and his eyes burned at Holmes.

"Do you come here to lock me up, Herr Holmes?" he growled. "Why do you question me like a pickpocket in the dock if you believe you already know the answers you seek?"

"Ah, but I did *not* know," Holmes answered, "until you very thoughtfully provided me with the confirmation just now. It was what you might call an 'educated guess,' something Watson will tell you I am loathe to make. In this case, however, such a speculation seemed likely to move this fascinating conversation along a little more rapidly. You see, I could not be certain the carriage Loschek observed was from the military as it had no obvious insignia on it. I offered what I might describe as an educated guess."

Albrecht's expression softened and his mouth curled into a slight but cruel smile.

"Perhaps I have underestimated you, Herr Holmes."

"I assure you, *Feldmarschall,* that you would not be the first."

"Yes, I sent a team of the commandos to Mayerling to arrest him before he fled to Budapest."

"Did you have the approval of the Emperor to apprehend his son?" Holmes probed.

Albrecht ignored the question.

"Taaffe agreed with me," he responded. "There was no alternative. The conspiracy against the Emperor had progressed too far. Once Rudolf had failed to appear at the dinner in response to his father's command, we knew what must be done. Our troops simply arrived too late. Rudolf was already dead when they arrived, by his own hand."

He paused to give Holmes an opportunity to respond to his version of what had transpired at the lodge, but my friend sat impassively.

"I will tell you Holmes, I was not surprised by this turn of events," Albrecht continued. "Rudolf was not sane. I was not alone in that belief. He had talked of killing himself many times, did you know that? How can a man like that sit on the Hapsburg throne? I thank God it will never happen."

"How on earth did you know he had sent troops to Mayerling?" I asked Holmes after we had departed the military headquarters.

"All in good time, Watson. I was reasonably certain I had reached the correct conclusion."

*Chapter 20: Albrecht, Duke of Teschen*

I knew it would do no good to press Holmes for information before he was ready to disclose it and so I shifted and raised a question that had occurred to me during Albrecht's recitation of his account.

"Doesn't it seem terribly ironic that on this particular occasion, with soldiers on their way or perhaps even at Mayerling to apprehend him, Rudolf would chose to commit suicide along with his mistress?"

"A coincidence, to be sure," Holmes agreed, "and perhaps too convenient. I rule out no possibility. As I have said many times, when you rule out the impossible..."

"Yes, yes, I know, Holmes, 'whatever remains.' But in this case, I am not sure what remains!"

"Nor am I, Watson," he said. "nor am I."

## Chapter 21: The Missing Witness

"I know that several of our recent interviews have highlighted motives for dispensing with the Crown Prince, but I cannot help but remain focused on the role of Archduke Johann Salvator," I opined as we walked back towards our hotel.

Holmes offered a smile that suggested tolerance rather than genuine interest in my speculation. I ventured to share my thoughts about the mysterious man who had secured the sealed box that might have contained incriminating information.

"Salvator was close to the Crown Price and had gained his confidence," I began. "They shared political beliefs and a sympathy for the Hungarian separatists. He possessed evidence of the Crown Prince's complicity in treasonous activities and the failed uprising that made him a potential danger to Rudolf. He also may have feared that the Prince, if captured or seized by political enemies, could reveal his involvement, which would mean a death sentence.

"He could easily have appeared at Mayerling, been welcomed by the unsuspecting Crown Prince and have delivered the fatal shot to end any chance of his betrayal. He then arranged to meet the Countess Larisch, to whom he knew Rudolf had entrusted compromising letters, secured the metal box and walked away with documents that would have sent Rudolf and himself to prison – or worse."

"Everything you have said about the Duke is true," Holmes replied, "but why would he believe Rudolf, his friend and companion in arms, would disown him?"

"Perhaps he had suffered a change of heart for the abortive uprising," I offered. "You recall the Countess Marie Larisch told us he considered Rudolf a 'contemptible coward.' If he could silence Rudolf and secure the box before Marie might open it herself, he might be spared any provable connection to the conspiracy."

## Chapter 21: The Missing Witness

"Why would Marie open the box?" Holmes replied.

"Perhaps she disliked Salvator and would suspect that he had killed Rudolf," I speculated, "or to regain the trust of Princess Elisabeth, who had banished her for bringing Rudolf and Mary Vetsera together. Or perhaps she had hopes of insinuating herself with whomever the new Crown Prince might be; her own financial resources, I understand, are rather paltry."

As we entered the Prater and passed by a large monument, a small piece of stone flew off the monument, followed by the sound of a sharp retort from somewhere behind us. Holmes grabbed my arm and pulled me downward and behind the monument.

"Was that a shot?" I asked breathlessly, looking up to where a piece of the monument had been broken off.

"Indubitably it was," Holmes said. When no further shots were fired, he stood cautiously and looked off to several official buildings from which the bullet might have come.

"It seems we have strayed too close to revelations that were not intended to be aired, my friend," Holmes said. "Someone obviously has decided to remedy our unwelcome presence by attempting to remove us from the case."

"Why, do you mean there was an effort to assassinate you?" I cried incredulously.

Holmes incongruously smiled. I must admit I saw little reason for such an expression.

"No, I think not. Had that been the goal, I very much doubt the shot would have missed, and there likely would have been more and from a closer distance. No, I suspect this was a rather pathetic effort to scare us off the case by encouraging our premature return to London. A futile act, but an instructive one. Well, we will certainly not be dissuaded by such a crude effort at intimidation!"

We hurried along through the park, taking care to blend in with crowds that would hopefully discourage any further attacks.

## Chapter 21: The Missing Witness

"Have you not been curious as to why Counts, Archdukes and Princesses have all complied with my request to be interviewed by an English detective," he noted as we walked briskly.

"Why, to find the answer to how Rudolf really died, of course!" I responded.

Holmes shook his head. "Each has offered a plausible rationale for disposing of the Crown Prince: a failed marriage, a refusal to secure a divorce, a habit of womanizing, fear of betrayal, involvement in the Hungarian conspiracy."

"Each of those explanations might well be true," I ruminated, "or all of them could be true, for that matter! If anything, we have too many possibilities! Thank goodness there isn't yet another person whom we have neglected to interview!"

"But, of course, there is!" Holmes cried. "There is one very crucial witness we have failed to interrogate!"

I ran the litany of names through my mind as quickly as possible, but it seemed to me that with the exception of the Emperor himself, who appeared above reproach, we had interviewed everyone related to the case.

"Who, Holmes?" I asked. "Who is it that we have overlooked?"

"The Crown Prince!" he said. "We have neglected to question Rudolf himself!"

I wondered if Holmes was playing a joke on me.

"But he is dead!" I sputtered.

Holmes had drawn up his collar against the brisk Viennese temperature and was racing to find an available carriage.

"Of course, he is dead!" he called back, as I struggled to catch up to him. "But that is no excuse for him to remain silent! And we have just enough time yet to interview him!"

# Chapter 22: Holmes Makes a Diagnosis

I caught up to Holmes as he hailed a passing carriage and we clambered into the seats.

"The Hofburg palace!" Holmes called out to the fiacre. "*Beeilen*! *Beeilen*! Hurry! Hurry!"

"What are you talking about?" I pressed. "Whatever do you mean that we must 'question Rudolf,' a man who has been dead for several days?"

"I noted that everyone has been willing to talk with us, whether they were admirers of Rudolf or loathed him," Holmes explained.

"But surely that is a positive development!" I insisted. "They have revealed much to us."

"True, but that long litany of conversations and meetings has also kept us quite preoccupied. Meanwhile, the plans for Rudolf's imminent entombment have been rushing forward towards tomorrow's funeral, after which certain essential answers will be impossible to ascertain. And to think I believed we were simply encountering good fortune that so many of the principal subjects were willing to indulge our inquiries! 'Pride cometh before the fall,' indeed, Watson! And all the while, the goal was to keep us from interviewing the victim himself!"

"I do not understand," I protested. "How will Rudolf respond to our questions?"

"By allowing us to gather evidence from his remains before they are committed to the tomb," said Holmes as we neared the palace. "Quick, to the palace's mortuary room where we will hopefully find Rudolf and one additional subject to interview, and this one will still be amongst the living."

We alighted from the cab at the large gate that surrounded the palace. Identifying ourselves at the guard station, we rushed into the

## Chapter 22: Holmes Makes a Diagnosis

palace and down several long corridors to the room that had been designated as the mortuary.

"Whom do you believe can provide us additional answers?" I pressed. "I mean, who amongst the living?"

"Dr von Widerhofer, if he will consent to do so!" he cried. "He has ministered to Rudolf and Mary since childhood. He may have disapproved of their misbehaviors, but he has a physician's desire to care for his patients, dead or alive. And like many others with whom we have met, I doubt he has told us everything he knows."

"What might he have concealed?" I questioned.

"Remember at Mayerling, he urged us to exercise extreme caution in handling the corpse, especially when I ventured to look inside Rudolf's skull? Do you recall that he was wearing those large rubber gloves that reached nearly to his elbows. What does all that suggest to you, Watson?"

"A perfectly understandable – and medically defensible – entreaty to avoid contamination from infectious disease," I responded. "As a medical man myself, I see nothing inappropriate about such cautionary advice. It makes good sense to take careful precautions, especially if a deceased patient might have suffered from a medical condition that could be communicable, even after death."

"And how might the sinister microorganism be transmitted from a dead person?"

"Any bodily excretions would be potentially dangerous," I acknowledged.

"Including tears, correct?"

"Why, yes, I agree," but I admit to being utterly confused by his remarks.

"Which perhaps explains the curious condition of the Prince's eyes."

"His eyes?" I questioned, trying to think back to the body on the slab. "His eyes were closed."

## Chapter 22: Holmes Makes a Diagnosis

"Not merely closed, Watson; I noted at Mayerling that Rudolf's eyes had already been sewn shut. Why stitch the eyes of a corpse so quickly after the patient has expired? During a funeral in which the casket remains open, as will be the case tomorrow, the undertaker certainly would glue or sew the eyelids to ensure they remained closed during the viewing by mourners. But von Widerhofer had sewn them shut even prior to performing the immediate post-mortem examination. Why?"

"To conceal the eyes?"

"Precisely!" he cried. "It might make little difference if the presumption of suicide was overwhelming. But upon reflection, is it not odd that the doctor, having learned that Sherlock Holmes was unexpectedly present, moved swiftly to preclude an examination of the Crown Prince's eyes and a thorough observation of the corpse?"

Holmes looked expectantly at me, but I admit I did not yet get the drift of where he was trying to lead me.

"Think, Watson!" he said with some growing exasperation. "You are the physician, after all! Put the clues together!"

I did not appreciate Holmes's admonition concerning my chosen profession and yet I admit I wracked my brain to draw the conclusion he had evidently already reached.

"A young man with a history of indiscriminate liaisons with women, many of them prostitutes," he recited. "Do you remember the newly emergent lesion on his nose that I mentioned to von Widerhofer who claimed not to have noticed it previously? Does not that strike you as peculiar?"

"Good Lord, Holmes, the man was lying there with half his head blown off. No, I do not think it odd that his doctor, a close personal friend for many years, failed to pay attention to a sore on Rudolf's nose!"

Holmes smiled at me in a way that I knew from past experience was intended to suggest I had once again failed to meet his standards of observation.

## Chapter 22: Holmes Makes a Diagnosis

"Holmes! Please do not disparage my observational skills further. Pray, what else have I missed?

"He also prevented me from removing the towel that afforded the Prince modesty, as you might recall. Do you recall the drug treatments von Widerhofer helpfully informed us that Rudolf had been taking – mercury chloride, zinc sulfate? Chemicals that unquestionably would show up in any forensic examination, which the Emperor might still demand. What conclusion would you, as a diagnostician, draw from such a set of medications?"

The answer, which now appeared so obvious, sprang into my head like a thunderbolt. I looked up into Holmes's expectant eyes.

"Advanced syphilis!" I exclaimed. "Von Widerhofer knew that the Prince was already dying."

# Chapter 23: An Unanticipated Arrival

"A diagnosis of advanced syphilis would also explain the Princess' inference that she and the Crown Prince would be unable to produce a male heir, even had he resumed his marital relationship with her," said Holmes as we rushed down the corridor. "But here is where we will find the person who can provide us the answers we are seeking!"

We brushed past the startled guard at the door of the mortuary expecting to find von Widerhofer making final preparations to the Crown Prince's body before the funeral. However, we found only an empty chamber in which a cleaning woman was busily tidying up.

"They have moved the body to hide him from us, Watson!" Holmes cried. "Where is the Crown Prince?" he demanded in an authoritative voice. "Where have they taken him?"

The woman was astonished by his emphatic tone but clearly had no idea what he was saying.

*"Der Kronprinz!"* I quickly translated. *"Wohin haben sie seine Leiche gebracht?"* ["Where did they take his body?"] Never before or since have I been so grateful to my German instructors.

*"Den Flur hinunter in den dritten Raum,"* the astonished woman replied, pointing out of the doorway.

"Third room down the hall," I cried to Holmes as I rushed out into the corridor.

We sprinted down a long, weakly lit passageway until we arrived at a heavy wooden door that was locked. Holmes threw aside any pretense of subtlety and banged forcefully on the door.

"Open the door!" he insisted. "Open the door!"

There was a noise from the other side of the door – a sliding bolt -- and the door creaked open revealing a stunned von Widerhofer. Holmes roughly pushed past the startled physician and rushed inside.

## Chapter 23: An Unanticipated Arrival

Rudolf's body lay within an elaborate wooden coffin dressed in his formal military uniform. A white turban had been tightly fitted just above his eyebrows and around the top of his head to conceal his fatal injury although a bloody residue had leaked through the bandage and onto the pillow. His gloved hands were folded on his chest, which was bedecked with various military medals. He was clean shaven except for his large moustache that had been carefully waxed into sharp, upward facing points. Garlands of flowers had been strewn about his torso.

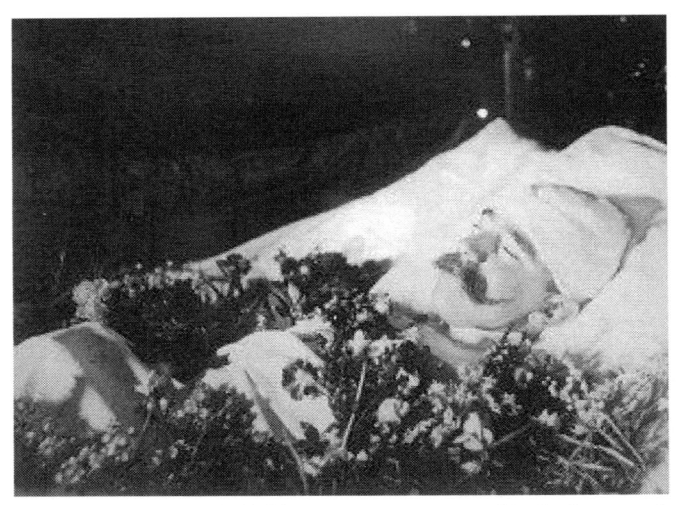

The body of Crown Prince Rudolf, his eyes sewn shut, with the large turban concealing his head wound.

"Holmes, what is the meaning of such an intrusion?" the doctor angrily demanded. His two assistants moved menacingly towards Holmes but the detective held up his hand to ward them off and they shrunk backwards. Sharply, von Widerhofer ordered them out of the room and the heavy door was tightly closed behind them.

"Cleverly done, doctor, cleverly done," Holmes said. "In a few more hours, the Prince's body would have been consigned to the family vault at the Capuchin Church with no chance for disinterment and examination."

## Chapter 23: An Unanticipated Arrival

He moved swiftly to the coffin and grasped one of the Prince's arms.

"I have warned you about handling the body, Mr Holmes," von Widerhofer advised.

"I have no doubt you would, doctor," Holmes replied. Holding up Rudolf's right arm, he pulled off the glove and turned the palm toward me. The telltale flat, dark spots on the palm removed any doubt about Holmes's theory.

"Syphilis," I said.

"Nonsense," replied von Widerhofer. "A common discoloration, perhaps connected with the manner of his death."

"Would you prefer me to remove the sutures with which you have sewn his eyelids shut so that the telltale redness can be seen?" he asked. I remembered Mizzi Caspar's comment about Rudolf's bloodshot eyes the night before he left for Mayerling lodge.

"Or shall I remove his trousers to reveal the chancroids that are doubtless present on his groin? I am quite sure Dr Watson would be quite capable of making a diagnosis if you continue to deny the obvious."

Fear had swiftly replaced anger in the doctor's eyes as he stared at Holmes and he seemed deflated by the sudden revelation.

"That will not be necessary," he said. "Yes, it is true what you have said. The Prince had a very serious case of syphilis."

"How could you have kept such information from us?" I demanded with considerable annoyance. "How long have you been treating the Prince for this malady?"

Von Widerhofer hesitated before answering my question.

"Three years. I have been treating him for three years. His case was quite serious and for some time he has not responded to the medications I have been using."

He walked to a chair next to the coffin and sat down heavily.

"What treatments have you applied?" I asked.

## Chapter 23: An Unanticipated Arrival

"I have given him mercury to address the disease as well as morphine and opium to relieve his discomfort." He shook his head sorrowfully. "Nothing worked. The illness was accelerating at a disturbing pace. His eyes had reddened; yes, you were right about that, Mr Holmes, and the skin abnormalities had become more prominent. Fortunately, most of these were in places on his body where they could easily be concealed. The last time I saw him, just before he left for Mayerling, the small sore you noticed had emerged on his nose. Such a condition is quite common amongst syphilitic patients, as you know, Dr Watson. If I could not control its growth, I warned him, his condition would soon become difficult to conceal."

"This explains several other changes people have mentioned," I pressed. "I presume you have heard of his tell-tale behavior changes associated with the disease: irrationality, even violent outbursts?"

"There were some, yes," he said. "Yelling, uncontrollable anger. Towards his wife, I understand, and others."

The doctor's admission helped explain the erratic behavior reported by the Crown Princess at the German Embassy, as well as the eruptions of sudden anger reported by Mizzi Kaspar and Marie Larisch.

"And despite this diagnosis, he continued his illicit liaisons?" I asked. "I do not mean to be indiscrete, but do you know if he took precautions against spreading the condition?"

"Of course, I urged that he refrain from intimacies that could infect others," the physician explained, "but I have little doubt that he ignored my admonitions. There is no question that he had infected the Baroness Mary Vetsera, who was also a patient of mine."

"Which is why her burial was conducted so swiftly and secretively," Holmes said, "without any opportunity for any other medical examination. Any post-mortem conducted on behalf of her family might have revealed some early signs of the disease, to the everlasting mortification of the royal family."

Von Widerhofer seemed to have aged years in just a few moments. He began to speak and then caught himself.

## Chapter 23: An Unanticipated Arrival

"There is more, is there not?" Holmes asked quietly.

The doctor's head sunk to his chest.

"There was a baby," he confirmed. "I do not know if Rudolf knew, but Mary had come to me worried about having contracted the disease. A baby would almost certainly would be born horribly affected. She did not want to bring that baby into the world, to have it face a life of illness and disfigurement, if it survived at all. She asked if I would perform an operation to end her pregnancy but I refused of course. I am a doctor! I do not take life! I cannot make such decisions!"

"So, Mary's decision to end her life may have been a consequence of her illness and pregnancy, you suspect?" I asked.

"I had no way of knowing that would be her response," he said. "But it seems this is what she preferred, to go to the Lord, diseased but with Rudolf's child." His voice broke and he sat silently. "And I failed to help her."

"Holmes! Remember Mary's note!" I exclaimed. "Do you recall what she wrote? *'In accordance with Him, I want to be buried next to Him in the Cemetery of Alland.'* Is it possible that 'him' referred to the child, not to Rudolf, who had given no intention of putting an end to his life that night? Might we have been misled by the assumption she was referring to Rudolf?"

"Certainly that is a possibility," Holmes replied. "If Rudolf had declined to participate in a joint suicide, then her reference to being buried 'together' might well have been a reference to the child who would perish along with her!"

"I presume there was no chance that someone other than Rudolf bore responsibility?" I asked.

"The Prince was the only possible source of both of her conditions, she assured me," the physician continued. "He had contracted the pestilence from his mistress, Mizzi Kaspar, the 'actress'!" He uttered a brief, hoarse laugh. "She was, you know, walking the streets when she was not treading the boards. I treated her, too, at the Prince's request. Another very serious case, I am afraid, and

## Chapter 23: An Unanticipated Arrival

not terribly responsive to mercury. She certainly will not live a long life."

"Could he have infected his wife, Princess Stephanie, as well?" I asked, recalling Holmes's speculation.

"He most certainly *did* infect her," von Widerhofer acknowledged, "Stephanie has been quite ill for some time. When I began to treat her, she had quite a harsh reaction to the medication and I was unsure that she could be cured of the disease. Then, fortunately, she proved remarkably responsive and I am convinced that she is now free of illness.

"However, she was left quite barren through Rudolf's unspeakable arrogance," the doctor continued. "After I first diagnosed his illness, he took the Princess to the island of Lokrum in the Adriatic, near Dubrovnik, to recuperate. I warned him against having any conjugal relations with her during treatment, but as usual, he was interested only in his own pleasure. I have blamed myself over and over again for not warning her myself. But he promised me he would behave responsibly."

"And you believed him?" I said incredulously.

"Who was I to question the solemn promise of the Crown Prince of Austria!" he insisted, with an exaggerated wave towards the body in the casket.

"When she complained of feeling ill several months later, she hesitated to come to me because of my closeness to the Prince. Instead, she saw another physician who stupidly diagnosed peritonitis."

"An inflammation in the abdomen," I advised Holmes.

The doctor nodded in agreement. "Eventually her physician realized the actual cause of her illness and, not knowing how she might have contracted the condition since she had illicit liaisons of her own. She hoped to conceal her illness from the Prince and the other court physicians. By the time she realized this physician's incompetence and sought my assistance, it was nearly too late. She was just 22 years old,

## Chapter 23: An Unanticipated Arrival

but I knew she would never bear another child, which meant Rudolf could produce no male heir to the throne."

"At least not with her," I added.

"Then the Prince's death did not change anything in this respect," Holmes concluded. "There would be no male heir from Rudolf and Stephanie. Perhaps that was why Rudolf was exploring a divorce or annulment – to be free to marry again and produce the heir Stephanie could not, although he certainly could not disclose the reason for her barrenness. Absent that concession from the Pope, the right of succession would eventually pass to another branch of the family, since the little girl Elisabeth cannot become Empress."

"Which is why you needed to conceal his illness," I said.

Von Widerhofer sadly nodded his head in the affirmative.

"Even in death, a syphilitic royal family in waiting is not something the Emperor and Empress could bear."

Holmes stood by silently as the old doctor's account came to an end.

"But surely, you did not make all these decisions alone," he said. "You were directed by someone in the royal family, someone loyal to the Emperor and yet willing to shield him from the appalling news you alone knew." He moved closer to where von Widerhofer sat slumped in his chair.

"Whom did you tell?" Holmes demanded. "Who knew of this pestiferous abomination tainting the House of the Hapsburgs?"

His voice rose in volume and anger as he spoke, and he drew nearer and nearer to the cowering doctor who was now visibly shaking in his chair.

"Who?" thundered Holmes one last time.

"It was I," came a voice from the doorway that was nearly dark due to the weak light and shadows. "I knew of Rudolf's debauchery and his affliction, Herr Sherlock Holmes."

We had not heard the door open but now we turned to the source of the voice. A regal looking man of perhaps sixty stepped into the

## Chapter 23: An Unanticipated Arrival

weak light of the room, his face largely obscured by a thick beard and mustache. His deep voice unmistakably conveyed an unequivocal sense of authority and gravity that compelled respect. At his entrance, the doctor leapt to his feet and bowed his head as the unfamiliar figure walked up to Holmes and me. He cast an apathetic look over to the turbaned head lying in the coffin and then focused intently on Holmes.

"I am Rudolf's uncle and the Emperor's brother" he said. "I am Karl Ludwig Joseph Maria, Archduke of Austria. As a result of the death of my nephew, I am now the Crown Prince of the Hapsburg Empire." He paused for effect, to allow his words to reverberate through the small room.

"You are surprised, Herr Holmes?" the Archduke inquired as he stepped past the doorway.

"Not particularly," Holmes replied archly. "I had narrowed the prospects to a very limited few and I acknowledge that your name, Your Grace, enjoyed a prominent place on my list."

"Really?" Karl Ludwig replied. "And why would you hypothesize my involvement?"

"I don't hypothesize," Holmes corrected, removing his pipe from his pocket. He looked into the bowl to confirm that some tobacco remained unburned and then scratched a match along the stone wall of the room. His eyes never left the Archduke as he sucked in the air and the orifice of the bowl of the full-bent glowed a bright orange.

"*Cui bono?*" he said. "It has always been a question of 'who benefits' by the Crown Prince's death. And you, sir, just answered that question most definitively, although you are just one of a substantial number of people had their own reasons for wishing Rudolf removed from the chain of succession."

"Yes, it is true I benefit. I have what you would call 'a motive' in your detective stories," the Archduke admitted. "But your hypothesis is flawed, Mr Holmes, because I will not benefit at all from Rudolf's death. I am well aware that I am ill-suited to be Emperor."

## Chapter 23: An Unanticipated Arrival

"But should you survive your brother, you would become Emperor," I interjected.

He shrugged his shoulders.

"Yes, although there is enough intrigue in the Empire to leave it an open question," he said. "There are rivals right here in Vienna and conspirators galore in Hungary, Serbia, Bosnia and who knows where else? One's nationality is not a determinant of who is chosen to rule. My Austrian uncle was dispatched by Napoleon to become Emperor of Mexico! Karl XIV of Sweden was a Frenchman. Who can say with certainty whose destiny it is to sit on the Hapsburg throne? Nor is this a matter of great urgency since my brother undoubtedly will continue to rule for decades to come!

"However, my nephew, Rudolf, was unworthy," he added with great seriousness. "He lacked the moral scruples needed to rule as Emperor. The liaisons, the scandals. His health was severely compromised, not only by syphilis but also by the epilepsy that has been another affliction of our family. And, of course, there is more than a little evidence of the insanity that has affected some of our members!"

"You refer to Ludwig, the so-called 'mad king' of nearby Bavaria?" Holmes asked.

The Archduke shook his head sadly.

"Just last year, his madness finally consumed him." He emitted a caustic laugh. "Do you know that his successor -- Otto -- is considerably more insane than was Ludwig! Yes, it was entirely possible that Rudolf was losing control of his mind. You have heard of his outbursts, his erratic behavior, his recklessness?"

"Rudolf's unpardonable behavior may well have created a motive for others to seek vengeance against him," Holmes continued.

"Vengeance? To whom do you refer?" Karl Ludwig insisted.

"Well, the Crown Princess certainly would have had a motive. He had given her a horrible and painful disease. He had left her barren,

## Chapter 23: An Unanticipated Arrival

unable to produce an heir, her singular responsibility as Empress. He had humiliated her before the entire court with his ceaseless carousing."

Karl Ludwig jumped to his feet.

"I will not let you accuse Stephanie," he insisted. "She could not have sanctioned such violence against her husband. In the end, he was her husband, however flawed, and the father of their daughter. I reject your implication. She could not have done this."

"I agree, Your Grace, she could not have acted against her husband," answered Holmes. "But *you* could have done so. Evidently the Crown Princess confided in you."

"Of course, she confided in me. We share many interests – in music, in art, the opera -- subjects Rudolf cared nothing for."

"And unlike Princess Stephanie, you *do* have the resources and motive to ensure that the Crown would pass not to Rudolf but to a responsible monarch who, unlike yourself, aspires to reign as Emperor. Your own son, Franz Ferdinand. *Cui bono*, Your Grace, *cui bono* indeed!"

We left the unexpected interview with more questions than answers, it seemed to me. New motives had emerged both for Mary Vetsera's suicide and as possible explanations for how Crown Prince Rudolf had met his death, and at whose hand if not his own. And yet in on a matter of hours, Holmes would either resolve the mystery or it would likely remain buried with Rudolf's shattered body.

# Chapter 24: A Summons is Issued

The following day was a somber one for the Austrian Empire. The funeral service itself was initially intended to be very private, in keeping with the bizarre circumstances surrounding the Prince's death. Even so, a state funeral requires certain formalities, and there would be a public procession replete with elaborately uniformed soldiers, horses outfitted with feathered plumes and a magnificent carriage bearing the coffin. All of the senior members of the Hapsburg family as well as their chief advisors and functionaries were expected to march in honor of the fallen Prince.

"Do you think they will all attend, given the very low regard in which they held Rudolf?" I asked Holmes.

"I have little doubt they will be there," said Holmes.

"How can you be sure?" I challenged.

"Because, Watson, I have invited them to attend a gathering with me before the service, without the Emperor and Empress being present. It is my intention to disclose certain indisputable conclusions I have reached. I took the liberty of advising each of them that it would be in their best interest to hear those findings before the funeral."

"Yes, but how can you be sure they will respond to your invitation?" I asked. "After all, you have no legal standing to compel their attendance."

"I have something they fear even more," Holmes said. "These are men who can manipulate and bend the law. They do not cower before the police or the courts. Indeed, they *are* the police and the courts.

"But they do fear something that they surely suspect that I may have in my possession: the truth. My invitation was not without some admonition behind it. I have advised that if they fail to attend my little conclave, I shall have no alternative than to lay the facts in their

## Chapter 24: A Summons is Issued

entirety, as I believe them to be, before Emperor Franz Joseph." He paused for a moment before slyly adding, "In fact, I may do so in any event. I am, after all, in his employ."

I stopped in my tracks and turned to Holmes.

"Are you saying you have solved the case?" I asked incredulously.

He allowed himself a slight smirk at my expense.

"Well!" I remonstrated. "You might have shared that information with me, don't you think?"

"My dear Watson, there remained several small matters that required contemplation after yesterday's interviews, but yes, I am reasonably certain I have unraveled this complicated matter. It was quite a three pipe problem, however, and I rather doubt you would have appreciated my waking you at four this morning when those last few pieces of the puzzle began to tumble into place in my mind.

"We shall soon have the opportunity to examine these theories with those who most certainly can attest to their accuracy. The denouement is upon us. Come, Watson! The players are all in their places and the curtain is about to rise."

The funeral procession of Crown Prince Rudolf

## Chapter 24: A Summons is Issued

The soldiers maintaining a guard before the entrance to the palace were wearing elaborate ceremonial uniforms to mark the melancholy ceremony. Their peaked caps were festooned with feathers, and they carried an assortment of swords, spears, and other weaponry of a bygone era. After several days of our regular appearance at the Hofburg, the guards recognized Holmes and myself and quickly allowed us to pass through the gate, escorting us up an elaborate stone staircase to the second floor of the palace. Before we entered through an impressively ornate wooden door, Holmes drew me aside.

"Take careful notes about what is said and by whom during this discussion," he said quietly. "I have no doubt that this meeting will be critical to resolving the mystery of Mayerling lodge. We cannot be certain the explanation will be revealed to history, and so I wish there to be an accurate account. Naturally you, Watson, are the perfect scribe."

I smiled in appreciation of his trust and assured him I would diligently perform the task he had assigned me. With an effort, the guard pushed open the door and we entered one of the most fabulously elaborate rooms I have ever seen.

On the walls were priceless works of art, tapestries of armies and hunters battling enemies both human and reptilian. There were detailed paintings of court scenes from the 17$^{th}$ and 18$^{th}$ centuries and two dozen portraits of Hapsburg ancestors in a vast array of uniforms, costumes, and every variation of facial hair. Numerous small sculptures adorned pedestals while colourful flags and pendants were arranged at various locations. Exquisite carvings and moldings, the product of some of the world's most skilled craftsmen, adorned the walls. The windows were framed by more ornate woodwork and the thick maroon drapes were folded back to allow the feeble winter sun to filter through the spotless glass. Massive sparkling chandeliers laden with crystal were suspended below ceiling frescoes and medallions, all rimmed with borders of gold leaf. On the floor, thick Persian rugs were laid over

### Chapter 24: A Summons is Issued

highly polished wood planks. An enormous stone fireplace, its chimney reaching all the way to the ceiling, roared with a fire that was consuming logs of a notable girth.

No room could more effectively have conveyed the sheer wealth and majesty of the Hapsburg dynasty. Seated in heavy wooden chairs, their faces turned impassively towards Holmes and me, were members of one of the most powerful royal families in the world. Also present was the police chief, Franz Freiherr von Krauss, a distinguished-looking man with an aristocratic moustache and beard. Behind this formidable array of powerful men stood a small cluster of the most trusted members of the royal household including Rudolf's valet Loschek, Dr von Wiederhorn and the fiacre Bratfisch. The lone woman in the room, the Countess Marie Larisch, was barely recognizable in the heavy black dress and hat that enveloped her, a lace veil covering her face. At Holmes's request, he later informed me, she had been admitted to the palace this one last time notwithstanding the Empress' banishment order.

Archduke Karl Ludwig, stood as we entered the room and bade Holmes be seated in a chair that faced the Archduke Albrecht, the Minister-President Taaffe, Count Joseph Hoyos, and Prince Philipp of Saxe-Coburg and Gotha. I recognized the much younger man with thick black hair and an impressive pair of moustaches seated next to Karl Ludwig as his son, the Archduke Franz Ferdinand, who was likely to become second in line to the throne.

In keeping with Holmes's admonition, I found a chair in an inconspicuous part of the room, close enough to overhear the conversation so that I might fulfill my role as official recorder. Holmes and Karl Ludwig sat down as the others looked suspiciously at the detective with great anticipation.

"I need not inform you, Herr Holmes," Albrecht began in a voice dripping with contempt and impatience, "that the men before you

## Chapter 24: A Summons is Issued

are not used to be summoned like servants to a meeting with a commoner, let alone a foreigner like yourself."

"I am well aware of the uniqueness of this meeting, Your Grace, I assure you," Holmes replied in a remarkably restrained tone.

"This is, as you well know, a day of the most profound sadness for all of us," Hoyos added in a less confrontational tone. He spread his arms to encompass the assembly of seated noblemen.

"I have no doubt," replied Holmes with a hint of disapprobation that might well have been missed by the august gathering.

"Well, let's move along, then," Philipp urged. "Share with us whatever observations compelled you to seek our attendance, and do so as quickly and succinctly as possible. We must join the Emperor and Empress in the ceremony to honour the Crown Prince."

Several of the others muttered and nodded their agreement with that sentiment and a low murmur circulated around the room. A look of annoyance was evident on most of their faces.

"Yes, Holmes, why don't you get on with it?" Taaffe echoed petulantly. "We are busy men and duty calls."

"Well said, Your Grace," Holmes began. "Let us 'get on with it,' as you have requested." He looked into the face of each of the powerful men seated before him. "I have no doubt you are anxious to offer comfort to the Emperor and Empress at this grievous moment, and I thank each of you for your frank conversation with me over the past three days. Those discussions have greatly helped me to reveal the role that each of you played in the series of events that has brought us to this solemn occasion.

"I imagine it was quite disconcerting to learn that Sherlock Holmes had arrived in Vienna at the request of the Emperor at such an auspicious moment, since you were all planning to attend the dinner at which he likely would was designate Rudolf his formal successor. I now know that was a decision that many of you regarded as extraordinarily imprudent. Had I only been on holiday when my own Prime Minister Lord Salisbury came calling, that ghastly scene at

## Chapter 24: A Summons is Issued

Mayerling lodge likely would have been quickly cleaned up with few questions asked. Crown Prince Rudolf would have been given a speedy funeral to spare the royal family any embarrassment, and the details of his death would have been securely entombed along with his remains in the royal vault forever. Countess Mary Vetsera, whose presence at Mayerling lodge was an unexpected complication, would surely have been consigned to historical anonymity with no one the wiser. And no one would have been compelled to waste a perfectly good bullet yesterday in the Prater in a futile attempt to intimidate me to abandon the case."

He paused to study the faces of the men. None betrayed the slightest indication of surprise or chagrin.

"But as it happens, I was in Vienna, although Rudolf's unanticipated death quite transformed the reason for my mission. Rather than examining possible threats to the security of the Austrian state, I was thrust into something more akin to my normal line of work: an investigation of how two young people came to lie dead, side by side, in a locked room at the Mayerling hunting lodge."

"And I suppose you can explain all these events, Herr Holmes?" Taaffe interrupted, a note of impatience and skepticism in his voice. I recognized the arrogance as a common response when ingenious plotters – particularly those of the upper class – realize that their meticulous planning had been foiled by Holmes' consummate skill.

"Oh, I do not think it is too difficult to paint the complete picture," Holmes replied. He paused for dramatic effect, reaching into his pocket and withdrawing a Meerschaum pipe with an impressive carved ivory bowl, a gift from a Turkish sultan. The edge of the white bone rimming the bowl was deeply stained amber by years of smoking. I was surprised that he had brought the expensive item with him to Austria as I had never seen him smoke it outside our Baker Street rooms. He took a small bag of tobacco from the same pocket and filled the pipe, thoughtfully tapping down the tobacco with a long, bony finger. He withdrew a wooden match from his trouser pocket and

## Chapter 24: A Summons is Issued

scratched it on the hearth stone to light it before tossing the burnt stick into the fireplace.

"I hope you will not begrudge me a bowlful of shag as I outline for you what the facts – and the use of my deductive skills – incontrovertibly reveal about the Prince's death. Of course, any of you should feel free to fill in any missing details."

"Or correct your mistaken insinuations," Albrecht said menacingly.

"Oh, I rather doubt that will be necessary," Holmes smiled as he sucked in the smoke.

There was a stirring from one or two of the titled men as they shifted uneasily in their chairs.

"There were three questions that needed to be answered concerning the death of Crown Prince Rudolf," he said, and then added "as well as the death of Baroness Mary Vetsera. When did they die? At whose hand did they die? And for what reason did they die?

"The two deaths are, of course, inextricably linked despite the determined efforts to conceal Miss Vetsera's presence at Mayerling and to bury her in an anonymous grave. I can certainly understand why, given the superficial physical evidence, those who discovered their bodies initially might have believed that each had died by their own hand. The wounds appeared to have been self-administered; a pistol that was owned by the Prince evidently had been used to shoot both of them and was most conveniently discovered still in his hand; the lovers were found together," he looked apologetically towards Marie Larisch before adding, "on the bed they evidently had shared on numerous occasions."

The countess shifted uncomfortably in her chair at the reference to the intimacy between Rudolf and Mary.

"And the suicide notes!" Albrecht interrupted. "Do not forget the suicide notes. They were incontrovertibly genuine, in their own handwriting!"

## Chapter 24: A Summons is Issued

"And so they were," agreed Holmes, "including Mary's note to her sister Hanna, which declared that 'Just a few hours before my death, I want to say adieu. I am happier in death than in life.'"

"Well, that seems to settle your ridiculous speculations," insisted Karl Ludwig as he stood up abruptly.

Holmes held up his hand, a signal to pause the premature effort to adjourn the meeting, and the Emperor's brother resumed his seat.

"I will grant you that Mary Vetsera seemed to welcome the opportunity to pass into the hereafter. The Crown Prince almost certainly had informed her there would be no divorce or annulment from the Princess Stephanie. Her expectation – however fanciful -- of a life with him, perhaps as Empress, appeared utterly phantastic."

"Of course, it was!" boomed out Karl Ludwig, looking towards commissioner Krauss. "Had she not been a baroness, she might well have found herself in serious trouble with the police for her recklessness!" The police chief stiffly nodded his head in agreement.

Holmes considered the comment before continuing.

"I think Baroness Vetsera had far more immediate and grave problems than legal prosecution, Archduke. For this child – and she was little more than a child – the future seemed to be filled with only disappointment, disapproval and unhappiness."

Karl Ludwig sniffed loudly at the rebuke.

"Mary Vetsera was with child," Holmes disclosed, looking to von Widerhofer for confirmation. The assemblage turned, as if on cue, to face the somber physician who stood behind them.

He solemnly affirmed the statement, adding, "*Ja*, and almost certainly, Rudolf was the father."

"Well, at least he proved he could produce a child," responded Albrecht cruelly, "something he had failed to do with his wife for several years!" The tasteless remark drew sniggers from several men near Albrecht.

"That unfortunate situation was doubtless the result of another circumstance I have no doubt the royal family would wish not be

## Chapter 24: A Summons is Issued

bandied about the capitals of Europe," Holmes continued. "As at least some of you are aware, that Rudolf has long suffered from syphilis, very likely acquired from one of his mistresses, Mizzi Kaspar, the actress."

There were more sniggers at the mention of her name and her purported profession.

"Despite treatments by his physicians," he cast another look to von Widerhofer for confirmation, "Rudolf was unable to prevent the worsening effects of the disease. The irritable behavior to which many of you have doubtless been subjected in recent months is symptomatic of advanced cases of syphilis, as are spots on the hands and sores on the cartilage of the nose, all of which I observed on the Prince's body during my hurried examinations.

"It should come as no surprise that Rudolf transmitted the pestilence to Princess Stephanie several years ago, despite warnings to use extreme caution in his marital relations. At the age of just 22, she was rendered completely sterile. The Prince, however, had recently transmitted the same noxious infection to Baroness Vetsera. Again, doctor, you can confirm my diagnosis."

The royal heads turned as one again to stare. The doctor grimly shook his head in the affirmative.

"I gave her the diagnosis myself just days ago," he confirmed. "Syphilis would be a danger to her and to the child she was carrying. She was nearly inconsolable and admitted she must have acquired it from Rudolf, the only man with whom she had ..." He looked to Countess Larisch and decided against finishing the thought. "In any event, she intended to confront Rudolf as quickly as she could."

"Which turned out to be in Mayerling, where she traveled, doubtless uninvited and unannounced," Holmes declared, "setting in motion some of the events that followed. Of course, syphilis would likely have been quickly identified had a formal post-mortem been conducted on her body, which is one reason Dr von Widerhofer refused to permit an examination. Instead, the poor girl's body was stuffed into

## Chapter 24: A Summons is Issued

a basket in an outbuilding for several days while her death went unreported in the newspapers and her mother remained distraught over her disappearance. Then followed the clandestine removal of her body from Mayerling by her uncles and her unceremonious burial in the *Heiligenkreuz* monastery's graveyard," Holmes declared.

Holmes looked about the room seeking any reaction but received only silence.

"I would be pleased to seek a disinterment if anyone insists upon a confirmation of my suspicion," he offered provocatively.

No one in the room made a sound.

"That will not be necessary," von Widerhofer declared.

"It does not take much of an imagination to contemplate the utter helplessness poor Mary must have faced that last night of her life," mused Holmes, pacing before the fireplace and warming to his narrative. "She must have realized the grim options awaiting her and accepted that, in all likelihood, she faced them utterly alone.

"A baby would be born out of wedlock, very likely severely ill from the disease inherited from both infected parents. Either she would be forced to give up the child, a grievous option for any mother, or she would raise it alone in shame, undesirable for marriage and mothering a permanent reminder of her obsession with Rudolf."

"She had decided to confront Rudolf but he spent the evening before leaving for Mayerling in Vienna with his mistress, Miss Kaspar, rather than with her. And so Mary hired a carriage to take her to the lodge, where she was admitted by servants who knew her from her earlier visits. There is no point in challenging this part of my narrative, gentlemen. The servants have thoroughly corroborated this account.

"She waited for her lover's arrival in the room they had previously shared. Rudolf was undoubtedly surprised to find her at Mayerling given his own plans, which evidently involved surreptitiously leaving Austria for Hungary the following day to take up leadership of the faltering independence movement. Distracted by such concerns and pressured by her unrealistic demands, he was

## Chapter 24: A Summons is Issued

unlikely to have offered her much in the way of compassion. Before he departed the room for his scheduled dinner with Count Hoyos, he likely informed her that there was no prospect for marriage, a further blow to her romantic and immature nature."

Even in that room of cold Hapsburgians, I was convinced there must have been some measure of compassion for the confused and troubled girl whose life had been tragically abbreviated by her futile involvement with the Crown Prince. Yet no one spoke up on her behalf.

"Left alone while Rudolf dined with Count Hoyos, she became increasingly desperate. She must have found the pistol that Rudolf carried with him for security – the same one, I would expect, with which he had threatened Marie Larisch just days earlier. Perhaps Rudolf had left it in open view with some anticipation it might prompt the very outcome that occurred. In any event, she was consumed by an extreme melancholy. Perhaps in her delusion, she believed that the Prince would join her in eternity since she had been told of his earlier flirtation with suicide.

"With Rudolf preoccupied with his supper with Count Hoyos, she used the lodge stationery to write farewell notes to her mother and sister explaining her preference for death over the grim future that appeared to await her.

"'Just a few hours before my death, I want to say *adieu*,' she wrote to her sister Hanna. 'We are both going blissfully into the uncertain beyond. I am happier in death than in life.' Those who have seen the note mistakenly assumed he reference 'we' was to Rudolf and herself. I think it more likely she was referencing her baby than her lover.

"Having completed the note, she waited for the Crown Prince to return to the room."

"There you are," insisted Karl Ludwig as he stood up abruptly. "Her death was a suicide as has been evident all along. Who cares how misguided were her motivations or how fanciful her expectations? After all, she is hardly the first young girl to find herself with child after

## Chapter 24: A Summons is Issued

a dalliance with a member of a royal family, even, I should hasten to suggest, your own royal family in England!"

A thin ripple of laughter passed amongst a few members of the group but most remained hesitant, awaiting Holmes's next disclosure.

"I do not dispute that Mary's note was composed at Mayerling," he agreed. "The evidence is quite incontrovertible."

Albrecht issued a grunt of satisfaction. "And Rudolf's suicide note to Princess Stephanie, found at the very same time, surely ends all speculation about his intentions as well, Holmes!"

Holmes turned to face the aging military leader, extending his long, sinewy hand in the Archduke's direction.

"That surely is the conclusion it was hoped we would draw from Rudolf's suicide note," he responded. "Rudolf was unquestionably in an agitated frame of mind, estranged from his wife, pulled in multiple directions by other women, at odds with his father, perhaps recognizing his own failing health and at risk of exposure as a collaborator in treasonous acts. But did he also seriously contemplate suicide?"

"The note proves he did!" insisted Taaffe loudly.

"No, sir, it does not: at least not that evening at Mayerling. Indeed, much of this intricate plot began to unravel once I recognized one singular feature of those seemingly conclusive notes."

The Archdukes and other nobles murmured amongst themselves.

"You see, Mary's suicide note was written on stationery that included the Mayerling letterhead. Several sheets of that stationery were on the desk when I examined the room. She obviously utilised whatever paper was available to compose the note. Moreover, the ink bottle on the writing table matched a small spot of ink I found on her right index finger where she had held the pen, which also helped remove any question that she was right-handed, an important element in considering the shot that killed her.

"I am quite certain everyone else who examined her body overlooked that bit of evidence; I did not. Therefore, Mary's note was

## Chapter 24: A Summons is Issued

an improvisation, which suggests she came to Mayerling for a meeting or assignation with Rudolf, not to kill herself. The idea of a dual suicide doubtless arose only after he informed her that there was no hope for a divorce from Stephanie.

"Now, Rudolf's note, in contrast, was almost certainly not written that evening," Holmes declared.

A louder murmur moved through the assembled company.

"How can you possibly know that?" asked Albrecht defiantly.

Holmes smiled. "My friend Watson would here have me exclaim 'elementary,' wouldn't you?" he asked, looking in my direction. He reached into his pocket and removed a rectangle of thick ivory-coloured paper, which he displayed to the assembled people in the room's dim winter light. Like a single organism, they craned forward in their seats to inspect the small card that Holmes held in his hand.

"This is a very singular piece of blotting paper that I picked up from the writing table at Mayerling. I took the liberty of placing it in my pocket when I examined the desk – just to make sure it was not misplaced, of course," he said with a chilly grin toward Krauss.

"If, as we are supposed to believe, this tragic couple simultaneously wrote those farewell messages with the pen and ink found on the desk, might one not expect that they both would have used this very blotter to ensure the ink would not be smudged? There is no question that Mary Vetsera used it for precisely that purpose that evening."

He held up the blotter and pointed to the lines of dried ink on one side. Taking a step closer to the aristocrats, he pointed to faint writing on the blotter.

"Let me read to you from this most extraordinary piece of evidence," he said. He pulled a small mirror from his pocket and held up the square of paper so he was able to read the writing in reverse on the glass.

## Chapter 24: A Summons is Issued

"Quite distinctly I can make out the faint words 'could not resist love' as well as the signature, 'Mary,'" he read. "Would anyone care to examine the writing?"

No one stirred from his seat.

"That evidence establishes beyond question that the note was written in the bedroom at Mayerling, in the hours before the evening's dreadful events unfolded."

He held up the card again and turned it so the officials could see both sides.

"And where is the blotting from the Prince's note?" Hoyos asked.

"That is the curious thing," Holmes said. "There *is* no evidence of blotting from the Prince's note."

"Perhaps the Prince did not need to blot his writing," Hoyos suggested.

Holmes shook his head.

"This was a farewell note to his wife," he countered. "I am quite sure he would want to ensure there were no smudges on the paper. Besides, my close examination of the Prince's note established incontrovertibly that it had indeed been blotted. One could tell by the way the thicker portions of the ink's flow had dried. There does not appear to be any other place in the room suitable for writing, so it is more than reasonable to conclude that if he also sat at the table to compose his last letter, he would have availed himself of the blotter as had Miss Vetsera, especially since it was in front of him on the writing table, where I found it."

"And since he evidently did not do so, your conclusion is what?" Karl Ludwig asked.

"The Prince's note was not composed that night!" Holmes declared. "It was written on a blank sheet of paper, not the Mayerling stationery used by Mary Vetsera. I hardly think the Crown Prince was carrying around blank sheets of paper so he might scratch off a suicide note if the circumstances moved him.

## Chapter 24: A Summons is Issued

"Rudolf had become an increasingly moody and unhappy man, and during one of his increasingly frequent fits of depression some weeks earlier, he had written that note when in the company of Miss Kaspar, his mistress. She had been shocked when he proposed they enter into a suicide agreement. He attempted to prove his sincerity in the proposition by drafting the note for her to read and neglected to take it with him upon his departure. I also assume that, if I summoned her, she would identify that note as the exact one Rudolf had composed months earlier!"

"Surely you aren't suggesting Mizzi Kaspar is behind all of this carnage!" exclaimed Philipp.

"Certainly not!" Holmes responded. "But she did know of Rudolf's flirtation with suicide, and even more important, she had retained the undated suicide note he had written. Undoubtedly, in keeping with her arrangement as a police informer, she gave that note to you, Commissioner Krauss," he said, turning to the police official, "and you shared it with Archduke Albrecht as a matter of national security."

The bald, bearded Krauss sat impassively during this recitation. None of the others turned to look in his direction.

"If the note was not written that evening, how came it to be on the desk in a locked bedroom at the Mayerling lodge?" he challenged Holmes. "Did it walk on its own from my desk to Mayerling?"

"It would but be a small matter for you to arrange for the note to be placed on the writing table by one of the guards who had access to the room," Holmes said accusingly. "Its discovery would help establish incontrovertible proof that the Prince killed himself."

"That is preposterous!" fumed Albrecht as he rose almost menacingly, although Krauss remained impassive.

"Not at all, Your Grace," Holmes responded, "and please be seated. You see, the appearance of this note at Mayerling established two inescapable facts about this case in my mind even before I interviewed any of you.

## Chapter 24: A Summons is Issued

"First, the appearance of the note on the desk at Mayerling proved that there had been a conspiracy at work. Notes do not just fly on their own from Mizzi Kaspar's home to the office of the police commissioner and thence, as if by magic, to a writing table in the Crown Prince's bedroom. Someone had helped it along its way, arranging for this note to be in that room, at that moment, for the specific purpose of misleading investigators." Again, he looked deliberately at each of the powerful men in the room.

"And secondly, since Rudolf most assuredly did not kill himself, despite a very clumsy effort to make that appear to be the case, then someone else most certainly did.

"Who murdered the crown price Rudolf Franz Karl Josef," Holmes demanded, "and why?"

"If you do not mind," said Krauss, "you seem to be drawing many sweeping conclusions from a series of random clues, Herr Holmes."

Holmes smiled patiently at the police chief.

"Well, that is what we detectives do, isn't it, Baron Krauss?" he said, looking towards the stone-faced official, "whether police or private consulting detectives. We assemble clues, test out various hypotheses and draw conclusions. As to the facts being 'random,' no, not at all. To the trained mind, these clues lead as clearly to the culpable parties as if I had a signed confession in my pocket, I assure you."

Several of those in the room coughed at this remark while others again shifted uneasily in their chairs.

"You see, I never found plausible the assertion that Rudolf intended to commit suicide on the night of 30 January," Holmes observed. "He had asked Philipp to return from the dinner at the Hofburg palace so that they and Count Hoyos could reschedule their hunt. He had enjoyed a substantial dinner with Hoyos despite his complaints earlier in the day about feeling unwell, which he used as a rationale for missing the dinner at the Hofburg palace. He might have intended to conduct a hunt the next day, or return to Vienna or abscond

## Chapter 24: A Summons is Issued

to Hungary. But he most assuredly did not intend to die that evening at Mayerling.

"Having discovered that the Baroness Vetsera had arrived uninvited and engaged in a distressing conversation with her, he doubtless sought a way to soothe her nerves and summoned whistling entertainment by Herr Bratfisch after dinner. He asked Herr Loschek to prepare his breakfast by 7:00 o'clock and reminded him to arrange for a carriage for the next morning. None of these actions seem conducive to a man on the verge of turning a pistol on himself."

"But Mary Vetsera clearly intended to kill herself, Holmes!" insisted Philipp. "Even you do not deny that she wrote that note in the room at Mayerling, and it clearly anticipates that both of them were going to do away with themselves."

"Yes, that may well have been *her* expectation, but there is no evidence that Rudolf intended to take *his* life. Herr Bratfisch, can you explain what happened when you finished your musical presentation? You were, quite probably, the last person to see Mary Vetsera alive."

Bratfisch stepped forward and looked to me to translate the question, which I readily did.

"As I prepared to leave, the Baroness took me by the arm," he said. "She thanked me for entertaining them, and then she said something very strange. She told me it would be the last time we would see each other. I thought it meant she was going away for a long trip, perhaps with the Prince. It never occurred to me what she actually meant, or I would never have left the poor girl."

"Why didn't you ask what she meant?" Holmes pressed.

"A carriage driver does not interrogate a Baroness," Bratfisch insisted. "My business for the evening was finished. I retired to my cottage near the stable and heard nothing further until Loschek came to fetch me the next morning."

"After Herr Bratfisch's departure," Holmes continued, "Mary likely told Rudolf of her plans and pleaded unsuccessfully with him to join her in death. Their heated discussion, I suspect, that was the

## Chapter 24: A Summons is Issued

conversation that Herr Loschek heard indistinctly through the adjacent wall."

I looked across the room to Loschek who was almost imperceptively nodding his head in the affirmative.

"Perhaps Rudolf had promised the young lady he would join her and take his own life or perhaps he refused; perhaps he changed his mind; perhaps he did not believe she would take such a destructive act. We shall never know," Holmes continued. "But it is evident that for the impressionable Mary, there was no turning back. She found the gun that Rudolf always carried with him for self-defence and, as he prepared for bed, she lay down, held the pistol to her right temple, where a right-handed person like Mary would naturally aim such a shot, and fired. Now here is where, upon examining her body, I noticed something quite curious.

"The force of that shot incontrovertibly would have jerked her head towards her left shoulder. But when I examined her, her head was turned in the opposite direction, towards her right shoulder. How to explain such a discrepancy?

"The evidence led to the inescapable conclusion that Mary Vetsera's last act upon this Earth was an incompetent one."

"A harsh conclusion, Holmes," said Hoyos. "The poor girl did kill herself, after all."

"Did she?" Holmes responded. "The placement of her head was the clue. You will remember, Dr von Widerhofer, that I demonstrated to you with the probe that the bullet Baroness Mary fired did not traverse her brain, which certainly would have killed her instantly. But her aim was poor, perhaps because her hand shook uncontrollably. Rather, her shot passed through her nasal cavity and out through her left occipital bone, pushing her left eye out of its socket. That bullet then continued through the curtain on the far side of the room and broke the window that faced the garden."

It was now becoming apparent to me that the men who sat facing Holmes realised the formidable nature of their adversary.

## Chapter 24: A Summons is Issued

Certainly, whoever was responsible for these terrible crimes had never anticipated someone with Holmes' observational and deductive skills would review the evidence in so detailed a manner, if it were investigated at all.

"Rudolf must have been horrified by the impetuous action of the foolish girl. He rushed to her side only to discover that Mary had failed at her attempt to end her life. Instead, she lay gravely wounded from her bungled shot and was likely in unimaginable agony."

"But if her shot did not kill her, what did?" Hoyos asked.

"That is the explanation I was about to share with all of you in the bedroom at Mayerling when Captain Brüder burst in and disrupted the investigation. Yet everything I have deduced since that moment has reenforced my conviction as to what actually transpired, and that conclusion, I am afraid, makes this story even more tragic.

"Rudolf discovered that Mary's injuries were likely to be fatal, although not immediately so; yet she was in horrific agony. What is he to do? Out here in the royal forest, many miles away from any physician, there is little chance of securing medical care for perhaps several hours. Even with such care, it was highly unlikely Mary will survive, wouldn't you agree, Watson?"

I declared that to be the very likely outcome given the grave injury Holmes had described.

"Rudolf understood that a scandal of unimagined proportions would reverberate should Mary be discovered mortally wounded in his bed, and so, he made a dreadful decision to spare her pointless agony," Holmes continues. "As she writhed on the bed in anguish, he took the pistol from her hand and fired a *second* shot into her temple closest to him, the left temple. He administered a *coup de grace* if you will, to end her suffering. But he overlooked the fact that the second shot jerked her head towards her *right* shoulder, as it was positioned the next morning when I examined the scene."

"How did you know to look for this second shot?" asked Hoyos.

## Chapter 24: A Summons is Issued

"My cursory examination revealed that a gun had been fired close to Mary's left temple; the burned hair and powder residue on her scalp established that fact beyond any question," Holmes answered. "Clearly the second and fatal shot had been to her left temple, since her head was facing to the right when it was found, an impossibility had a bullet been fired into the right temple. It was a small caliber gun, and it is highly likely that this second shot, which traversed her skull, never exited. Were there a proper post-mortem, the spent bullet would almost certainly be found lodged inside her brain.

"Clearly someone other than she had fired the second shot. That could only have been Rudolf because we know that Mary died about midnight, and no one else had access to their room at that hour.

"Herr Loschek reported hearing two shots around midnight," he continued.

"That is correct!" Loschek called out.

"Perhaps the second shot was the Prince shooting himself," suggested Taaffe.

"That would have been quite impossible if, as Loschek told us, he saw the Crown Prince quite alive the following morning." said Holmes. "I believe that portion of Loschek's account."

The valet bowed to Holmes, who turned to confront him.

"But you lied about hearing the second shot sometime later while in your room."

"I did not lie!" Loschek protested.

"Oh, but you most certainly did, and I can explain why I am so certain!"

"If you say so, Herr Holmes," Loschek mumbled from where he stood.

"You surely could identify a gunshot, Loschek, and more than perhaps anyone else at Mayerling, you knew there was reason to fear for the Prince's safety. A gunshot most certainly would have caused you to do something more than sit up in bed and wonder from where the sound might have come."

## Chapter 24: A Summons is Issued

"It could have been poachers in the forest," suggested Albrecht. "It *is* a hunting lodge, after all."

"Rather a dangerous business to hunt in the middle of the night, wouldn't you say?" Holmes replied. "No, that is a poor explanation. I suspect, Loschek, that it was when you heard the *first* shot that you quickly rushed to the Crown Prince's room to check that he was alright," Holmes said.

Loschek had hung his head low.

"*Ja*, that is true. Just as you say. The door was not locked and I entered." He took a deep breath and looked at the Archdukes and then back to Holmes. He closed his eyes, as if attempting to recreate the horrible image in his mind. "I do not understand how you know these things.

"It was a terrible sight. She was lying on the bed, Baroness Vetsera, and there was blood all over her face and her pillow. She was gurgling deep in her chest and thrashing about on the bed in pain! It was horrible!" he cried, looking around the room in desperation.

"Where was Rudolf?" asked Hoyos.

"The Crown Prince was standing next to her. He was staring at the Baroness and then he turned to look at me and then back again to her.

"'Look what she has done to herself, Loschek!' he shrieked. '*She* did it. She is dead! Oh, dear God, she has actually killed herself!'

"'She is not dead!' I told him as I saw her move. 'We must call a doctor at once!'

"'Are you mad?' he hissed at me. 'She is 17 years old! She is pregnant with my baby!' I was stunned by his revelation. She continued to squirm on the bed, her cries becoming frantic. Both the Prince and I were transfixed by the sheer horror of it. The she began to choke and blood was coming from her mouth."

"The shot had caused massive bleeding into the nasal cavity and throat," I diagnosed. "I have seen more than my share of such injuries in Afghanistan. She was undoubtedly suffocating on her own blood."

## Chapter 24: A Summons is Issued

"*Ja*," Loschek agreed. "Choking, blood everywhere. Suddenly, the Prince reached across her to the gun in her right hand.

"'I will not let her suffer so,' he insisted. "Before I could take a step, he had fired another shot into her head."

"Into her *left* temple," Holmes clarified, "causing her head to snap to the right, as we found it."

Loschek glumly nodded in the affirmative.

"Now, she *was* dead," he said quietly. "We stood there together. We said nothing." He looked about the room for sympathy. "What was there to say?

"After a few minutes, I asked, 'Your Grace, what shall I do now?' He looked at me without expression and waved his hand in the direction of the door.

"'Go back to your room,' he told me, pulling the bedclothes up to conceal the Baroness' body. 'We are far from the other bedrooms and it appears that no one has heard the shots. Come back at 6 o'clock and we will dispose of her body before the others arise. Now go back to your room, and forget this terrible scene ever occurred.'

"'I cannot leave you here like this, Your Grace,' I implored. 'We must move her now.' But he would not hear of it.

"'Leave me with her until morning. I will figure out what must be done. But now, go, and say nothing to anyone of what has happened here tonight.'

"So, I went back to my room, but I did not sleep.

"In the morning just before 6 o'clock, I dressed and went into the corridor where I encountered the Prince as we had agreed hours before. He instructed me to bring blankets to wrap the baroness' body and I went off to find some of them. About twenty minutes later, I returned and knocked on his door. There was no answer, so I knocked harder and when there still was no response, I called out to him.

"'Your Highness, it is Loschek,' I said, but again, there was only silence. I became quite concerned and I turned the doorknob but

## Chapter 24: A Summons is Issued

it would not open. The door was locked."

"And that was very unusual?" asked Holmes.

Loschek nodded his head. "It is never locked while the Prince is inside!" he said. "Never! Now I banged even harder on the door and called out to the Crown Prince again."

"And that is when you heard that unfamiliar gruff voice you mentioned from inside the room ordering you to leave?"

"Yes, I thought he must have become distraught over what he had done, and I feared for what he might still do," Loschek said excitedly. Now I was worried that something might have happened to the Prince and despite my dread at revealing the Baroness Vetsera in the room, I decided to alert Hoyos and the Zwerger, the game warden. They were both in small cottages beyond the stables and I ran over to summon them."

"Did you see or hear anything unusual as you made your way to their quarters?" Holmes pressed.

"Nothing other than the military carriage waiting near the stables. It was just on the other side of the stables, out of view from the lodge."

"Did that not strike you as irregular?" Holmes queried.

Loschek hunched his shoulders in response.

"I assumed it was the carriage that was to transport the Prince back to Vienna after the hunt."

"Was there anyone in the carriage?" Holmes asked.

"There was a driver. I went to him and asked for his help. I explained the Crown Prince was not responding to my calls but he told me he was under instructions not to leave his post. I knocked first at Count Hoyos' door and while he dressed, I went to rouse Zwerger. Then, together, we walked back to the lodge, stopping to pick up the hammer from the stable."

"Did you mention what had transpired with Countess Mary Vetsera during the night?" Holmes asked.

## Chapter 24: A Summons is Issued

"No, I thought perhaps the Prince had already removed her body already and I did not want to disclose any information before I was certain what had transpired."

"Did you stop to talk with anyone else?" asked Holmes. "Did you speak with the carriage driver again?"

"No! The carriage had departed. The three of us went quickly to the house."

"How long would you say it took for you to run to the two cottages, rouse the men, and hurry back to the lodge?" Holmes pressed.

"Perhaps fifteen minutes," Loschek replied.

"And you saw nothing else out of the ordinary?"

"Nothing! I was interested only in gaining access to the Prince's room to ensure that he was alright."

"How were you going to explain Mary Vetsera's body to Hoyos and Zwerger, should it still be in the Prince's bed?"

Loschek looked confused.

"I wasn't thinking of the Baroness," he wailed. "I was concerned only with the Prince's safety. As we approached the front door, we saw that Prince Philipp had just arrived back from Vienna and I realized that it was he who had, in all likelihood, arrived in the carriage that I had seen near the stables."

"Yes, that it exactly right," Philipp affirmed. "I had departed Vienna quite early to be here in time for the hunt. When I disembarked from my carriage, I saw the three men rushing back to the lodge.

"We entered the lodge together," Loschek continued, "and as we rushed to the room, I explained my concerns about the Prince's security."

"And when you arrived, you tried again to open the door?" Holmes asked.

"We all did," answered Hoyos. Prince Philipp added his agreement that the door was incontrovertibly locked.

"We called out to Rudolf to open the door and assure us that he was alright." Philipp agreed, "but there was no response."

## Chapter 24: A Summons is Issued

"The Count and Prince ordered me to use the hammer to force our way into the room," the valet continued. "I began to bang away furiously. In only a few minutes, I was able to break through and open the lock from the inside."

"And what did you see?" Holmes asked.

"The bedclothes were still pulled up concealing the Baroness Vetsera, but on the other side of the bed lay the Prince, although he was hardly recognizable because of all the blood.

"'It is the Prince,' I announced to the others. 'We must find the police!'"

# Chapter 25: Holmes Explains

Holmes turned to the Archdukes who had sat silently as Loschek related his revised story, studying their impassive faces. Despite his stare, they remained stoic. Holmes walked around to the fireplace and pensively contemplated the remnants of tobacco in his Meerschaum before turning back to the silent group.

"Now let me tell you what happened to the Prince in that room, although I have no doubt that little of what I say will come as a revelation.

"In my considerable experience, those who commit crimes, particularly the more intelligent and practised amongst them, often believe they have concocted a plan so flawless as to defy detection," he began. "I have seen such misplaced self-confidence a great deal in my career. There was the case of Dr Bordwell and the arsenic-infused pork bangers, and the matter of Ron Tsu Ni, the blind Chinese knife-thrower and his porcupine with its poisoned quills. Their crimes were brilliantly conceived and, but for my involvement, almost certainly would have avoided detection. Each of those gentlemen met the hangman at Newgate."

I thought the mention of the gallows might provoke an outburst from the distinguished assembly, but no one made a sound.

"Those involved in the plot against Crown Prince Rudolf also expected to escape detection and might well have done so but for my unanticipated arrival in Vienna. As a result, they carelessly left a plethora of clues strewn about that make the solution of the case mere child's play."

"You have mentioned the shattered window and the blotter that revealed when the suicide notes were written," Hoyos noted. "Are you telling us there are still more clues?"

## Chapter 25: Holmes Explains

"Most certainly," replied Holmes, "clues that surely would have escaped detection by the local police, especially since they were certainly operating under the direction of some of those in this room."

"You have me in complete suspense, Herr Holmes," declared Taaffe, stifling a yawn.

Holmes ignored the sarcastic remark.

"In the Prince's bedroom, for example, there were traces of mud that incontrovertibly came from square-toed military boots."

"I did not see them!" Loschek objected.

"You were not looking for them," responded Holmes. "I was."

"They could have been made at any time," Albrecht interrupted. "There are military men in and out of this lodge every day."

"Not with fresh mud on their shoes. You declared no one had entered the bedchamber to examine the Prince's body other than yourself, Prince Philipp and Hoyos," he said to Loschek, who affirmed this fact. "But the moistness of the mud indicated the deposits had been made within an hour or two at the most. I am well aware that the Austrian military boot has a very distinctive print. Indeed, I have published a short monograph on the unique designs of different footwear issued to military men in Europe. There was clear evidence of at least two men in the floor of the room, each wearing boots issued by the Austrian military.

"Second, I found six flecks of fresh blood on the wooden floor and four more on the carpeting near the door. Other might well have missed them because they were nearly hidden underneath the shattered wood caused by Loschek's handiwork with the hammer. The difficulty of finding such evidence," he said, withdrawing his convex lens from his coat pocket, "is why I make it a habit of carrying this glass with me at all times."

"But there was blood spattered widely because of the gunshots," Hoyos protested.

"Around the bed where the shootings took place, yes," Holmes agreed. "But the entry is several yards from the bed. How came there

## Chapter 25: Holmes Explains

to be bloodstains so far away from where the shootings occurred? Obviously, some other act of violence had taken place near the entry, and I immediately suspected the Prince had been violently assaulted near the entry way. He likely opened the door thinking a knock was from Loschek, as arranged, and was instead set upon by the men who wore those military boots, undoubtedly soldiers operating under the command of a very high-ranking official. They seized him and struck him on the head, causing these blood drops near the door and rendering him unconscious. It was then quite a simple task of carrying him to the bed where they deposited him. The small drops of blood and the bit of mud that fell from the boots create a virtual trail of clues."

"We are all aware of your little games, Herr Holmes," Taaffe snarled. "Your theories, your deductions! Dr Watson has done a very entertaining job of describing your unconventional methods to the world. But these bits of what you call 'evidence' hardly add up to what you are suggesting: a monstrous plot to murder the Crown Prince! The fact remains," he said, somewhat triumphantly, "that you have offered no unimpeachable evidence that the Prince did not enter into a pact with Baroness Vetsera, write a suicide note with her, and shoot himself after she had killed herself. Stories! Fiction! The stuff of your dime novels is all you offer us, as well as the most heinous of charges again the leaders of a great Empire!"

"Quite the contrary, Your Grace," Holmes replied with complete coolness. "I have yet to describe the most irrefutable piece of evidence establishing that this was murder: the very shot that killed the Crown Prince."

"But *he* must have fired that shot himself!" insisted Loschek. "He was still holding the gun in his hand!"

Holmes looked dismissively at the valet.

"Of course, that is what we are *supposed* to believe. Does it not strike you as terribly convenient for the pistol to be found in his hand? But that explanation will simply not do. Had Rudolf fired the shot that killed him, the chance of the gun remaining with his finger on the

## Chapter 25: Holmes Explains

trigger, is preposterously negligible, as I am sure you would agree, Dr von Widerhofer."

The doctor continued to look at Holmes impassively and offered no affirmation of the detective's conclusion.

"Well, the fact is easily enough established. Surely, after firing a shot fired to the head, Rudolf's arm would have been flung involuntarily to his side and the gun would have fallen onto the floor rather than remain nestled in his hand." He shook his head in disbelief. "An amateurish effort to stage a suicide scenario."

"It is difficult to account for the reflex after such a trauma," Dr von Widerhofer declared, looking around to the Archdukes. "His arm could possibly have been thrown onto the bed where it was found rather than away from the body."

My friend involuntarily was shaking his head negatively.

"I would beg to differ, *Herr doktor*," Holmes insisted. "Perhaps you are familiar with Dr Slocum Davis's study of involuntary movement following traumatic death? No? Well, you might find time to peruse it: a most instructive monograph.

"In any event, the position of the Prince's arm is a minor matter. There are two other indubitable facts that establish this murder was clumsily staged to appear to be a suicide.

"We can acknowledge that the small pistol found in the Prince's hand almost certainly is the one that killed the Baroness Mary Vetsera. The relatively mild damage that was done to her head, along with the small hole in the window caused by the first shot she fired establish incontrovertibly that a small caliber pistol was used. I would be delighted to exhume her body and locate the second bullet lodged in her skull, if that would end any speculation on this point.

"But the cause of the Prince's injury is a very different matter. Indeed, I knew for certain the moment I saw the Crown Prince's head that the injury had not been caused by his own hand and that it must have been murder."

## Chapter 25: Holmes Explains

"How could you know that without even examining his injury?" insisted Albrecht.

"Surely you know, Her Albrecht, that a single shot from that tiny pistol could not possibly have been powerful enough to remove the entire upper portion of his skull. That damage could only have been caused by a much larger bullet than those that fit the gun found in Rudolf's hand. Now, how came a pistol with a smaller caliber to be in the Prince's hand if not placed there as part of an elaborate ruse? This was the question I asked myself the moment I saw the discrepancy between the damage done to Mary Vetsera and to Rudolf.

"If there had been two guns used, I thought, then where was the second one – the one that had most assuredly caused the damage to Crown Prince Rudolf's head? Why was it not found in the room? And even more obviously, why was a gun that most definitely did not cause the injury to Rudolf found in his hand? The conclusion is, indeed, elementary: someone else had staged the Crown Prince's death so as to appear to have been a suicide. And moreover, the assassin who shot the Crown Prince then placed the outdated suicide note, which he had brought with him, on the table so as to confirm he had taken his own life. I presume he did not even notice the other notes on the table that had been written by the young woman whose corpse still remained hidden beneath the bedclothes, where Loschek found her."

Here Holmes paused and looked around the room.

"Does any of you wish to offer a speculation?"

None of the people in the room uttered a sound.

" I thought not," Holmes continued. He looked hard at Archduke Albrecht. "Surely you are aware that the weapon that killed Crown Prince Rudolf must have been the sort of pistol issued to the military."

"Perhaps, but Rudolf certainly would have had access to such a pistol," Albrecht said, adding dismissively, "he was, after all, the newly designated Inspector-General of the army."

## Chapter 25: Holmes Explains

"Undoubtedly," Holmes replied. "But then why was it not found in the Prince's hand or elsewhere in the room? No, that is not an adequate response, Field Marshall."

"But of course, the last piece of testimony is the most incontrovertible and was provided by none other than Rudolf himself," Holmes continued.

"Preposterous!" cried Taaffe. "Rudolf is dead. You never even had an opportunity to interview him. How can he possibly provide testimony to you?"

Holmes smiled in a way I have seen before when he believes he has cornered him prey.

"To the contrary, the Prince was most forthcoming with information, Herr President!" Holmes declared. "Indeed, he was among the most obliging witnesses I had the opportunity to interrogate in this case. And, I might add, he certainly uttered the fewest falsehoods.

"Rudolf was right-handed, as you are all undoubtedly aware," he began. "Whoever placed the pistol in his right hand was surely aware of that. But the essential piece of evidence is not his hand, but his head!

"The fatal shot entered the Prince's left mastoid bone, behind his left ear, and traveled upward through the top of his skull. Even though you are no trained anatomist, von Widerhofer, you can confirm the site of the entry wound that I showed to you."

Holmes turned his back to his audience, raised his right hand and attempted to reach behind his head to a spot below his left ear.

"Observe the difficulty of a right-handed person reaching behind his head to fire a large pistol into his left mastoid bone. I invite you to attempt such a contortion. And remember that you must also aim the shot upward, so that it emerges from the top of the skull."

A glimmer of recognition entered the doctor's eyes. He involuntarily lifted his own right hand and attempted to position it behind his head, pretending to hold a pistol to the spot where the bullet entered Rudolf's skull. Recognizing he could not maneuver his hand

## Chapter 25: Holmes Explains

into such a contorted position, he lowered it again to his side and nodded his head slowly.

"*Impossible!*" he muttered. "I did not even consider it!"

"Neither did the assassin," Holmes said. "In your case, *doktor*, I am not surprised by the oversight. Your training is in the curative arts, not the detection of crime. Of course, any competent police inspector would draw the same conclusion as did I. But police inspectors were not summoned to Maylering, were they, Herr Krauss?" He turned to confront the commissioner.

The police chief was barely able to contain his discomfort but still sat silently.

"Even if such a shot were feasible, which it is not, why would the Prince shoot himself in such a contorted fashion?" Holmes continued, shaking his head. "Indubitably, he would not! And he certainly would not be found with a small caliber pistol clutched in his hand afterward!

"Therefore," Holmes cried exultantly, "someone else shot and killed Crown Prince Rudolf!"

The room fairly exploded with shouts and cries, mostly in German that I was barely able to comprehend. But the clear message of the portions I could translate expressed outrage and thinly veiled threats directed towards Holmes.

My friend seemed undeterred by the commotion and continued his description. Quickly the room calmed down and the men sat transfixed by his analysis.

"The assassin could not have been the only other person we know to have been in that room, Mary Vetsera, because she was already dead. The state of rigor mortis in the bodies that morning incontrovertibly establishes that she died hours earlier than the Prince, as Loschek has confirmed. So, who fired the shot that ended the life of Archduke Rudolf?

"Loschek, you could have become outraged when you watched him fire the fatal bullet into Mary's head," he said, confronting the

## Chapter 25: Holmes Explains

valet. "You might have struck him unconscious and then carried the Prince to his bed and fired the fatal wound."

The servant stared at the detective with wide eyes and mumbled incoherently.

Holmes waved his hand. "But you could not possibly have overpowered the Prince, and your loyalty to him was unshakable. I think it a fair conclusion that you were not the perpetrator of this terrible murder."

Loschek closed his eyes and murmured an appreciative word of thanks.

"Besides, Loschek's feet are considerably smaller than the muddy prints I found inside the bed chamber. Therefore, someone else had entered the room, someone wearing military boots who had recently been outdoors. Someone physically capable of subduing the Prince once he opened the door expecting to find Loschek ready to help him dispose of the body of Mary Vetsera. Someone who quickly inflicted a blow that splattered blood on the floor near the door. Someone who carried an unconscious Rudolph to the bed, laid him on the pillow and, without considering the implausibility of the wound, fired a bullet into his head, killing Rudolf and destroying the evidence of the earlier injury to the head."

"And when did the conspirators hatch this grand conspiracy you have described?" Taaffe challenged, his voice dripping with disdain.

"Here, of course, I must hazard a guess, Herr President, but I would venture a plan for disposing of Rudolf had already been devised and the ringleaders were waiting for an opportunity to set the plot in motion. The Emperor's scheduled dinner at which he might proclaim Rudolf his successor, the trip to Budapest the next day, combined with suspicions of Rudolf's intention to join the Hungarian revolt, may well have triggered the plot into action. His decision to spend the evening in the relative isolation of Mayerling, far from the palace, certainly would make the execution of the plan less complicated.

## Chapter 25: Holmes Explains

"After it became known that Rudolf had defied his father and remained at the lodge, soldiers were dispatched to Mayerling, probably in the very early morning hours before sunrise. Archduke Albrecht admitted as much when I questioned him yesterday, although you suggested they were sent only to apprehend the Prince. You made that decision without the approval of the Emperor but in conjunction with police chief Krauss, who had provided you Rudolf's suicide note, and President Taaffe who had posted agents at Mayerling to signal the assassins when it was safe to enter the lodge. It is no good to deny it; the facts are as clear to me as if you had each signed confessions to your guilt.

"These soldiers arrived early in the morning by military carriage, which was parked discretely away from the lodge. Little did you suspect that Loschek would notice it when he went out to summon Hoyos and Zenger, and indeed, Philipp reported that it was the carriage he had used to return that morning to Mayerling from Vienna. And so he had – together with the assassins – to help them gain access to the lodge and secure entry to Rudolf's room!"

Upon hearing this remark, Prince Philipp bolted to his feet and took a menacing step towards Holmes.

"How *dare* you sir!" he exclaimed. "Rudolf was my friend, my hunting partner, my own brother-in-law! Your innuendo is beyond insulting! Rescind it now, or face me in a contest of honour – and I assure you, it would not be my first duel!"

Holmes seemed completely unfazed by the Prince's livid eruption.

"Your protest is noted, Your Grace, but unpersuasive," Holmes responded. "Your role in the matter is incontrovertible. You are the one who returned to the palace for the dinner with the news that Rudolf would not be attending. Given your close ties to the Hungarians – I believe you are an officer in that country's army – you undoubtedly had learned of Rudolf's conspiring against his father in support of the independence movement and, very likely, his plan to flee to Budapest

## Chapter 25: Holmes Explains

rather than return from Mayerling. You alerted Rudolf's enemies at the dinner and the plot to eliminate the Crown Prince was launched that very evening to assure he would never reach Hungary.

"How else can you account for your own return early in the morning, the precision of the assassination plot, which required detailed knowledge of the lodge and those attending to the Prince, and the convenient appearance of the military who carried out the crime?

"They had hidden near the Prince's room and saw leave the lodge to find the blankets, as requested by Loschek at about 6:00. They realized the Crown Prince would be alone after receiving signals from the watching agents sent by the Minister-President that it was safe to enter the lodge."

"And I suppose the Prince just opened his door and invited these soldiers in so they could assault him and discover the dead girl in his bed?" Taaffe blustered.

Holmes thought for a moment before responding.

"I suspect Philipp called out to him to open the door. He would likely have responded to such an entreaty from a friend. Or perhaps he thought Loschek had returned with blankets to help dispose of Mary's body. When he opened the door, he was overpowered by the soldiers – the boot prints establish that unequivocally -- one of whom grabbed the Prince while another likely knocked him unconscious with a blow to the head. Then they carried him to the bed, where Mary Vetsera's body lay still undisclosed under the blankets. One of the soldiers took out his standard issue military pistol and fired a shot into Rudolf's head, its large bullet causing the devastating injury with which we are familiar. As instructed, they then placed Rudolf's suicide note on the writing table, ironically next to Mary's own farewell note they overlooked!

"As they prepared to leave, they likely noticed the small pistol Rudolf had used to shoot Mary and hit upon the idea of placing it in his hand to make his death appear a suicide. In their haste, they obviously did not consider the consider the illogic of such a small weapon having

249

caused such a grievous injury any more than they considered the illogic of shooting him on the left side of his head when he was right-handed. Another oversight, but one they had no reason to believe would be disclosed by the police charged with investigating the Prince's 'suicide.'"

"But I spoke with the Crown Prince when he refused my entreaties to open his door," recalled Loschek.

"Yes, you reported the voice sounded unfamiliar and gruff," recalled Holmes. "It was undoubtedly that of one of the conspirators pretending to be the Crown Prince, waiting for your departure so they could escape from the death chamber."

"And how did these purported assassins depart the locked room undetected?" challenged Taaffe. "Loschek, Philipp and Hoyos all agree the door was locked. We all are aware there is but one key, and the Prince alone had it. You, Mr Holmes! You found the key *inside* the room after the door was broken down."

Holmes smiled at the Minister-President.

"It is true that I found the key inside the room," Holmes agreed. "But why was it not in the keyhole if the Prince had locked it before shooting himself? If you will recall, I found it on the floor, under the chips of wood caused by the damage to the door."

"Undoubtedly Loschek had knocked it out of the keyhole when he banged on the door with the axe," Taaffe insisted.

Holmes slowly shook his head in disagreement.

"That is what I presumed would be offered as the explanation," he responded looking at Loschek. "But there was no wood underneath the key at all, which suggests it was placed there before the pounding on the door began. Once I found it, I inserted it into the keyhole, as those who were with me will recall. I had Watson hold the door fast whilst I pounded on it with great effort to simulate Loschek's blows with the hammer, but the key was not dislodged from the keyhole despite my best efforts.

## Chapter 25: Holmes Explains

"No, it was extremely unlikely that the key had been left in that keyhole. Nor would it have made much sense for the Prince to have locked himself in the room had he intended to commit suicide. After all, what would have been the point? There was no one to rush in and stop him; he would simply have walked to the bed, laid down and shot himself. It is clear the door was locked to delay the entry of the rescuers to allow the assassins time to escape."

"But then how came the key to be inside the room?" asked Loschek.

Holmes again withdrew his lens from his pocket and held it up to his right eye.

"When I examined the entry way with my lens, I not only found the blood spatters but one other very interesting discovery," he continued. "There is a space under the door into the Prince's bedchamber – a slight one, but large enough to push the key through if some pressure were exerted from the outside. The soldiers had made the same observation and had hit upon a way to confuse those investigating the Prince's death.

"After shooting him, they took the key – which was probably on the writing table or in the Prince's pocket – and locked the door from the outside as they left. Then using a knife or bayonet, they pushed the key back under the door so that it would be found on the floor, onto which it would be presumed to have fallen when the door was forced open."

"Pure speculation!" cried Albrecht, "A clever theory for which you have not a shred of proof."

"Oh, but I do," said Holmes. "You see, what I found on that floor, under the shards of wood from Loschek's chopping, was a very fresh scratch made when the key was forced through the crack under the door. It will be a simple matter of putting the key (which I have retained) under a microscope, which will reveal some wood fibers that adhered to it from being pushed along the floor. This evidence is not something an ordinary investigator might have looked for, but it is

## Chapter 25: Holmes Explains

dispositive! By the time Loschek gained entry to the Crown Prince's chamber with Hoyos, the game warden, and Philipp, who had positioned himself at the front door to make it appear he had just arrived, the assassins and their carriage were on their way back to Vienna to report on the success of their clandestine mission."

Holmes used a long finger to clear the burnt tobacco ash from the bowl of his pipe, tossing the detritus into the fireplace. He then withdrew his tobacco pouch from his pocket and tapped a new plug of tobacco into the bowl while his words were absorbed by the most powerful men in Vienna. Lighting a match, he puffed as the bowl grew a brilliant orange, and then returned to the hearth to dispose of the match.

The silence in the room was almost painful as the gravity of Holmes's remarks was digested. Finally, Karl Ludwig stood and broke the silence.

"What you are implying, Herr Holmes, is a most serious accusation," he said gravely, "one that might well be punishable by arrest and imprisonment if uttered outside these four walls." He motioned to the thick stones that encapsulated the room. "Do you offer anything but conjecture? Do you have evidence that would be admissible in a court? Or is this just what Dr Watson, in his little stories, describes as an example of your creative deductive skills?"

"Oh, I think I have offered a good deal more than conjecture. And a quick examination of the Prince's wound will remove any question of doubt as to the accuracy of my analysis, which is why we are having this discussion today rather than after the Prince's body is entombed in the royal vault."

He sat in a chair and took a long draw from his pipe.

"As to arrest and imprisonment," he uttered a guffaw, "I would remind you I am here at the behest of your Emperor, with whom I have not yet shared this analysis of the crime that cost him his son and heir." He took several long pulls on the pipe and blew out a thick stream of

## Chapter 25: Holmes Explains

smoke that dissipated as it curled up in the air. "That is, however, exactly what I intend to do.

"I might add that I am rather confident my own Queen and Lord Salisbury would look most unfavourably at any hostile action against a British subject, even were I to stand on a soap box and reveal my conclusions in the heart of the Prater."

"I don't think that would be a very good idea," said a deep voice arising from the darkened far corner of the room furthest from the windows. The speaker's identity was concealed from our view by the high back of the leather chair in which he had been sitting, but the accent-free enunciation was vaguely familiar, if quite out of context.

"Monumental forces are at work here," the voice continued as Holmes slowly stood and turned to face the speaker, his face suddenly a mask of disbelief and his arms hanging helplessly at his side. "I congratulate you, of course. Your deductive skills have never been more formidable. But from this point forward, the conduct of diplomacy is better reserved for those who possess skill and authority in such matters."

The voice trailed off as a formidable figure rose from his chair and stepped forward to face us. Even in the faint light from the fireplace, it was not difficult to discern the familiar form of Mycroft Holmes.

## Chapter 26: A Shocking Appearance

"Upon my word!" I cried, leaping to my feet upon recognizing the face and considerable bulk of Holmes's reclusive older brother. It was all but unprecedented for the elder Holmes to venture very far from the walls of the Diogenes Club let alone a journey halfway across Europe to Vienna. A quick glance at my friend revealed he was no less thunderstruck by the appearance of his sibling.

Mycroft Holmes walked around the large chair into which he had been slumped and walked towards his incredulous brother.

"I must confess that your appearance is something of an unanticipated turn," Sherlock Holmes admitted, quickly regaining his aplomb. "I had no doubt that your hand was behind Salisbury's visit to Baker Street that enlisted me in this matter. I presume," he said, looking at Taaffe, "that your camaraderie with the Minister-President explains your presence?"

"My arrival serves as an indication of the significance with which our own Prime Minister views this very delicate situation," Mycroft said, giving a slight bow towards the assembled members of the Austrian hierarchy. "It is my pleasure to serve Crown and country," he declared, "especially in a matter upon which may well rest the security of the continent itself."

"My work here is not authorised solely by the wishes of the Prime Minister," Holmes challenged his brother. "Perhaps you are unaware of a telegram I have received from Her Majesty on this matter."

Mycroft Holmes's eyebrows raised slightly at his brother's statement. The younger Holmes dug his hand into his pocket and fished out the note Salisbury had given him in London.

"'Secure all details you can gather,' he read, 'however distressing they may be." He looked up and handed the note to Mycroft.

## Chapter 26: A Shocking Appearance

"I would direct your attention to the august name that follows this instruction." Mycroft cursorily read the telegram before balling it up and throwing it into the fire where it burst into a momentary ball of flame. My friend's eyes followed its trajectory into the hearth and betrayed a mild consternation as it was consumed.

"New instructions have arrived, Sherlock," the elder Holmes proclaimed. "Had we been aware of how tangled matters would become, I assure you would not have been drawn into this matter in the first instance. However, with these new developments, I am here to ask – indeed, to insist -- that you now withdraw entirely. I need not tell you how oppressive it was for me to undertake this pilgrimage, but Salisbury understood that you would accede to no one's entreaties but my own, delivered in person." He spread his large arms in front of his enormous bulk and moved them to his sides, taking a small bow as he did so.

"My inquiries here have raised some very disturbing facts about the intentions and actions of many of those gathered here in this room," Holmes declared. "May I add that I have my doubts about your motives as well, brother?"

Mycroft ignored the comment.

"You have described, I suspect these gentlemen agree, a remarkably clear account of the events at Mayerling," Mycroft Holmes acknowledged. "I must tell you that I reached somewhat similar conclusions based upon reports delivered to me in my chair at the Diogenes Club. Oh, there are a few trifling details – nothing to be concerned about – but also nothing that requires further involvement on your part."

"And this is the official determination of the Emperor?" Holmes asked.

"It is the official determination of our Sovereign," Mycroft intoned. "You are officially relieved from all further engagement in this case, Sherlock. I have come to Vienna to direct you and Dr Watson to return to England forthwith."

255

## Chapter 26: A Shocking Appearance

I had never before witnessed my friend rendered speechless. This abrupt dismissal from the case by his own brother, and in the presence of those he had unequivocally demonstrated to have been implicated in the conspiracy, seemed to disable him in a way I have never seen before or since. As the assembled group waited for his response, I walked to his side and spoke up.

"Well, I for one am not satisfied we have the entire matter laid out on the table," I insisted. "Even if the explanation goes no further than the people in this room, I, for one, demand to know not only what transpired at Mayerling lodge, but also why."

Mycroft looked towards me with undiluted approbation, but Sherlock Holmes seemed revived by my bold comment.

"Before I am sent packing for London, I am hoping you will indulge my response to Dr Watson's thoughtful comment," he said defiantly. "Just a matter of tying up some loose ends, with which you are all of course already familiar. After all, I did journey here at considerable cost to my schedule and purse and I have conducted a rather lengthy inquiry into the case."

"Your expenses will all be covered, naturally," said Mycroft, "and a comfortable honorarium will be provided as well."

"If you wish to lay out your theories, Herr Holmes, I raise no objection," vowed Taaffe. "But your explanation must go no further than this room. Your words could well have severe diplomatic implications that would reverberate across the European continent. No one else – and certainly not the Emperor or Empress – must ever know of the conversation in which we are now engaged."

He sat back down in his chair and crossed his legs. The others followed suit, and after several had lit their cigarettes and warily regarded the detective, he began his summation of the case.

"I understand that none of you will acknowledge or apologize for any of what I relate," he said. "I assure your contrition is of no importance to me whatsoever. This is not my country nor my laws, and my own government," he nodded disapprovingly towards Mycroft,

## Chapter 26: A Shocking Appearance

"seems singularly uninterested in any public accounting of the matter. So be it. Ultimately, your consciences will judge what use to make of the conclusions I am prepared to share with you."

It was Holmes' turn to take out a cigarette. He strode to the section of the room before the hearth, almost as though he had become a performer on stage. The flame from the match eerily illuminated his long face that, I could discern, was tinged with a degree of fatigue and even sadness as he realized every effort would be made to conceal his findings for all time.

"It was abundantly clear to me from the outset that virtually everyone in this room had a reason for wishing Rudolf removed from the line of succession. Any one of you might easily explain how these events came to pass.

"First was his chronic philandering with women including the unfortunate Baroness Mary Vetsera, who had been both impregnated and infected with syphilis by the Crown Prince. When Rudolf rejected her proposal for a dual suicide, she botched the effort to kill herself, resulting in a horrific wound. Rudolf, distraught at her agony and fearing the impact of publicity about the shooting and her pregnancy, lead him to put the poor girl out of her misery with Loschek looking on. He then placed her body beneath the bedclothes until the two of them could dispose of it in the morning. Of these basic facts I was aware even before Loschek acknowledged them to be the case.

"Of course, Rudolf never has the chance to dispose of Mary's body because he was killed by assassins who were unaware she was in the bed when they intruded into the Prince's bedroom. The deplorable decision to leave Mary's body in a laundry basket for several days, as well as her clandestine burial in an unmarked grave all suggest her presence, let alone her suicide at Mayerling, came as a surprise to those behind the Prince's assassination. Of course, once she was discovered, her body could not be examined by any physician other than Dr von Widerhofer who already knew not only that she was pregnant but also

## Chapter 26: A Shocking Appearance

that Rudolf had likely infected her with syphilis, as he had long ago infected his wife."

There was an uncomfortable grumble from the collection of men listening to Holmes's account.

"Some of you already knew that the Prince suffered from syphilis and were distressed by his increasingly violent temper and outbursts. With good reason, you feared this erratic behaviour connoted a swift descent into the insanity that ran rampant through the family.

"The dinner on 30 January – the dinner Rudolf missed when he decided to remain at Mayerling – was crucial. The Emperor was leaving the next day for Hungary to confront those plotting against the alliance with Austria. There had been 'violent scenes and altercations between the Emperor and Rudolf' on this topic, according to our own Queen's daughter, the Empress of Germany. The Emperor was anxious to end Rudolf's involvement with the Hungarian insurrectionists and hoped to achieve that objective by declaring his support for his son as his designated successor. But that formal announcement, you gentlemen knew, would greatly complicate your plot to ensure the disease-addled Crown Prince never sat on the throne of Austria-Hungary.

"Removing Rudolf from the line of succession had a political impact as well," he said, turning to face the Emperor's younger brother, "especially for you, Archduke Karl Ludwig. Rudolf's elimination elevated you, and then your son Franz Ferdinand, to the probable status of Crown Prince. You were also deeply offended by the Prince's promiscuity and immorality, qualities quite at odds with your own strict ethical standards. And so, you fell in with a plot to ensure he would never wear the crown."

Karl Ludwig said nothing, but his son, Franz Ferdinand, came over to place a supporting hand on his father's shoulder.

"If my father did anything, he did it for me and for Austria-Hungary," the young Archduke declared.

Karl Ludwig stood indignantly to confront Holmes.

## Chapter 26: A Shocking Appearance

"If all you say is true – and I do not admit for a moment that it is – there is a flaw in your argument," he replied. "If Rudolf were so ill, it is unlikely he would survive to become Emperor and I would assume the crown anyway. Why would I involve myself in such a dangerous plot for something that was very likely to be mine in any event?"

"To eliminate the risk," Holmes insisted. "Despite the limited effect of von Widerhofer's treatments to date, it was certainly well within the realm of possibility that Rudolf might be successfully treated and live well beyond your own lifetime. Even if he never had a male child, there was always the prospect that he would designate someone other than Franz Ferdinand as his successor.

"Better to leave nothing to chance, I can imagine you concluded. I need not remind you that your own namesake, Ludwig, was declared insane and deposed just three years ago. The following day, he and his doctor were found dead. A perfunctory examination concluded that these deaths were convenient 'suicides.' Perhaps that event planted the seeds of just such a plot in the case of Rudolf?

"I think you came to believe – or were perhaps persuaded – that it was essential to eliminate the licentious, diseased and potentially mad Crown Prince and restore to the order of succession to a reasoned and respected senior statesman -- like yourself."

The Archduke glared at Holmes but did not again offer a rebuttal. Instead, he exchanged glances with Archduke Albrecht, who remained silent and stony-faced.

"But that is only one reason behind the murder of the Crown Prince," Holmes added. "I do not believe for a moment that Archduke Franz Ludwig could have orchestrated such a complicated plot on his own. There is another, equally compelling motive," Holmes said, looking at the elderly *Feldmarschall*, "one that one throws greater suspicion onto you."

"Onto *me*?" Albrecht said, springing to his feet with an agility I would not have thought possible from the older man. He squinted at Holmes through his spectacles, an indignant expression twisting his

## Chapter 26: A Shocking Appearance

face. "How dare you issue such an accusation against a Duke and general!"

Holmes waved his hand dismissively at the old soldier.

"I have made many accusations against those who had attained significantly *higher* rank, Your Grace, and with unfailing accuracy," Holmes rejoined, "and with grave consequences to their life and liberty. You had just as many reasons as your cousin here to wish Rudolf permanently removed from the line of succession. Together with Herr Krauss, who made little secret of his contempt for the Crown Prince on whom he set spies, it would have been child's play to achieve this objective with little risk of exposure."

Holmes turned away from the men and stood facing the fire in the hearth. He remained there thoughtfully for a moment before spinning about to face the former head of the army.

"You were utterly contemptuous of his father's appointment of his son as your successor as Inspector General of the army, a decision that would be publicly revealed at the Hofburg dinner," Holmes accused.

"He was not competent to serve in such a capacity," Albrecht brusquely interrupted. "It is true I had nothing but contempt for his military judgment, and that is an opinion that I do not possess alone. No one, especially not an English detective, need lecture me on the question of Austria's military security!"

It was clear that Holmes had hit a sensitive nerve and Albrecht's storied discipline was dissembling.

" I have been an officer for decades," he reminded the group. "I led the defence of the city in 1848. My leadership at Custoza was decisive when Rudolf was barely out of his short pants. And he dared to challenge my leadership! An impudent, spoiled ..."

He caught himself, realizing he was condemning not only the Crown Prince, but contradicting the Emperor's declaration of national mourning. Albrecht was clearly a man of rigid thought and an explosive

## Chapter 26: A Shocking Appearance

temper. He sat down and resumed glaring at Sherlock Holmes in a most threatening manner.

"Yes, I can certainly see his views of reform offended you," Holmes said. "Had he become Emperor rather than a crown price, such sentiments they surely would have represented a grave threat to the Empire to which you have devoted your life.

"Even more than reform in Austria, you were appalled by his sympathies for the Hungarians' independence movement, a sentiment he shared with his mother. As you gathered evidence of his consorting with the Hungarians, you became convinced that in his role as Prince Royal of that country and Bohemia, he was plotting an imminent challenge to his father's authority as Emperor."

"Yes, and I very nearly had the evidence in my hand," Albrecht defiantly said, standing to confront Holmes. "Evidence that I could show to the Emperor, evidence that could most definitely alter Rudolf's future, perhaps even result in a charge of treason against him!"

"And where, pray, is that evidence?" Holmes pressed.

Albrecht's face grew deep red as he considered his response.

"The Prince and his co-conspirator discovered I was on to them."

"You refer, of course, to Archduke Johann Salvator of Tuscany."

"Yes, that dam'd Italian!" he spat out. "I had acquired papers showing incontrovertible evidence of their treachery and I warned Rudolf that he was about to be exposed as a traitor to the Emperor. What a fool I was! My office was burgled and the papers stolen."

"Undoubtedly by his agents, who turned the papers over to Rudolf," Holmes deduced. "And Rudolf, in turn, fearful that you would stop at nothing to secure them back, hid them in a sealed metal box that he entrusted to Salvator, his loyal friend."

Holmes half-turned to look at Marie Larisch, to whom the Prince had given the sealed box. The countess remained silent and

## Chapter 26: A Shocking Appearance

Holmes did not relate her role in turning over the box to Salvator. A slight nod of her head expressed her gratitude to Holmes.

"Those materials, I have no doubt, are now safely out of Vienna and far from your reach," said Holmes.

"Do you think so?" the Archduke sneered. "You may be very clever, Herr Holmes, but it is possible that you underestimate my capabilities."

"That may be the case, Herr Albrecht. The arm of the Austrian army is indeed a long one. In any event, regardless of whoever possesses this evidence, the danger presented by Rudolf's Hungarian sympathies was undeniable. Despite your threat, revealing this disloyalty to the Emperor would have crushed the old man as much as did his son's death."

There was no sound in the room as Holmes fished in his coat and removed a match and a cigar the Emperor had given him two days earlier. The match scratched against the stone of the fireplace and exploded into flame and Holmes drew it towards the cigar.

"So, we have two unimpeachable motives for removing Rudolf from the line of succession: his moral and medical unfitness (that was your greatest concern, Archduke Karl Ludwig) and the danger to the Empire (concerns particularly shared by Archduke Albrecht and your colleague, Minister-President Taaffe). Doubtless you agreed upon the necessity of eliminating him in a manner that would ensure the least scrutiny into his demise: an apparent suicide that might be attributed to his growing madness, a family trait.

"His presumed intention to defect to the Hungarian cause after an evening isolated at the Mayerling lodge provided the opportunity for your plot to be executed."

The Archdukes leapt to their feet and began shouting simultaneously in German using unmistakably angry words that required no translation to convey their outrage. They gesticulated angrily, turned crimson and hurled threats of retribution at Holmes who looked on unperturbed, making no effort to silence their tantrums. After

## Chapter 26: A Shocking Appearance

several minutes, the old men seemed to have exhausted themselves and again fell quiet.

"It will do you no good to deny the facts or to threaten me," Holmes said. "There is no other possible explanation for the events that followed."

He puffed calmly on his cigar as the crackling from the burning logs filled the small room.

"You saw the prospect of an increasingly distraught, indiscrete, syphilitic Crown Prince flirting with treason against his own father by fomenting uprisings in Hungary," he declared. "And you did what men of power do with their power. You acted."

# Chapter 27: The Confession

The silence from the accused conspirators lasted for painful moments before the Emperor's brother Karl Ludwig finally responded to Holmes' indictment of their actions.

"We do not expect you to understand the crisis that faced we Austrians, Mr Holmes," he began. "You did not know Crown Price Rudolf and you do not know our country or the challenges facing those who govern the Empire. I do not mean to be disrespectful to you, but coming here and dispassionately assembling the facts, as you call them, neither describes the depth of the problem we faced nor the urgency that it be addressed by those with the power and the authority to do so.

"You do not know my brother, the Emperor, or his wife, Empress Elisabeth. We do, and we know they could not endure the shame as a son who conspired against his own father, who betrayed his wife and daughter through his immoral behavior, or who inevitably, despite his growing disease and madness, laid claim to the crown of the Hapsburgs. It is far from the first time in our history that such decisive action was taken to ensure the continuity of the family's rule. I urge you not to be too critical, Herr Holmes; you English have experienced more than a few cases of intervention by the nobility to rescue the state from incompetent leadership."

"Yes, it was a terrible thing that had to be done," Taaffe declared. "But be clear: no one here had any role in the death of the Baroness Vetsera. That was by her own hand and, if Loschek's account is to be believed, Rudolf's."

"And that is how you explain your treachery?" I sneered at them. "As a result of your actions, Mary Vetsera lies in an anonymous grave, unvisited even by her mother!"

Holmes was even less sparing in his condemnation.

## Chapter 27: The Confession

"These are not the first efforts I have encountered to rationalize the inexcusable," he declared. "Do you imagine your actions are somehow less condemnable because you recite to me Cromwell's insurrection of some 250 years ago in my own country? Your actions are not just criminal, they could alter the very history of the Austro-Hungarian Empire and perhaps even the history of Europe! You have defied rather than defended your Emperor. Who knows what conspiracies, rivalries and vendettas your actions have loosed for the years ahead?"

"We have prevented a far more imminent threat!" insisted Karl Ludwig.

Holmes spun around to face him.

"And in doing so, Your Grace, you have elevated yourself to be Crown Prince, haven't you?"

Karl Ludwig became indignant.

"How dare you, an Englishman, speak to me in such a contemptuous manner!" he fumed. "I seek no grandeur or title. I seek only a secure monarchy, a safe transfer of power from the Emperor to his successor, whenever that may occur, and continued peace on the European continent. I have no personal ambition whatsoever.

"When the day dawns for a new Emperor to preside over a united Austria, Hungary, Bosnia and the remainder of our Empire, it is my hope that the crown will sit on the head of my own son who, I am certain, will rule in peace and with wisdom for many years. My son, Franz Ferdinand, will be the new Crown Prince of Austria."

The young Archduke stood and surveyed the gathering in an act designed to impose his expectations of loyalty on the assemblage.

"And that is where this account must end, Sherlock," Mycroft again solemnly intervened. "Revealing all of this sordid information would do inestimable damage to the delicate diplomatic arrangements that preserve the peace of Europe. Disorder – even disloyalty – amongst the Hapsburgs could not only undermine this venerable dynasty, but provoke the most serious challenges to European order. Hungary might

## Chapter 27: The Confession

well be motivated to seek full independence; the nationalists in Germany, Bosnia and elsewhere may well seek to fill this political vacuum with unimaginable results. The dominos, should they begin to tumble, could well reach across the Channel to our own shores.

"Had we known how these events were to unravel, you must believe that Salisbury and I would never have implored you to come to Austria in the first place. And given the involvement of many of her children, grandchildren, nephews and nieces and their families on the Continent, I have no doubt the Queen will agree that there is no need for your further intervention. I had thought that purposefully errant warning shot in the Prater might have discouraged you from continuing in the matter, but I suppose I should have known better.

"However, now, in the name of the government, I must direct you to allow those with formal political and diplomatic portfolios to determine how the facts that you have uncovered are addressed. This information goes no further than those in this room, Sherlock. That is not a request; it is a command from the Prime Minister himself."

Holmes looked with disgust at the men who now stood defiant, glaring back at him. He also cast an unmistakable look of disenchantment towards his brother as well.

"*Die Geschichte wird mit eurem Verrat nicht freundlich umgehen!*" he hissed at them. Then he turned abruptly on his heels and walked out of the room. I followed in close pursuit, amazed at Holmes's admonition, "History will not deal kindly with your treachery!"

"Holmes!" I called after him as he hastened down the hallway. "Do you mean to tell me that all this time, you have been able to speak German?"

"What purportedly cultured man of Europe cannot command some of the language of Goethe?" he blithely asked as he vigorously strode from the palace.

"Then why have you pretended not to comprehend it throughout our stay?" I asked.

*Chapter 27: The Confession*

"Sometimes," he explained, "one can learn much more if presumed to be incapable of understanding what is being said. People often make the most incriminating admissions when they believe their words are falling on deaf ears."

# Chapter 28: The Aftermath

The funeral of Rudolf Franz Karl Josef, Crown Prince of Austria-Hungary, took place just two hours after Holmes' bitter confrontation with the Austrian leadership. Despite initial plans for a somber and private ceremony, the procession was elaborate and very public. The coffin, set on a catafalque, was covered with a heavy black drape edged with tassels that formed an elaborate fringe along the bottom. Perched on top of the casket were bouquets of flowers and ribbons from "Stephanie," "Mama" and others. The bier was surrounded by soldiers in full military regalia, their hats topped by tall plumes of white feathers.

Holmes and I had arranged to attend the funeral service before beginning the long journey back to England, but I could find no trace of him in the chaotic moments after departing the raucous meeting in the palace. Frustrated and somewhat concerned about his unexplained absence, I nevertheless set off alone for the *Kapuzinergruft,* the Capuchin Church of St. Mary of the Angels where the archbishop made an exception to the prohibition on burying a victim of suicide in hallowed grounds as a result of von Widerhofer's testimony that a "mental unbalance" was to blame for the Crown Price's having taken his own life. As a result, he would be entombed with his ancestors in the Imperial Crypt of the Hapsburgs. As I nervously settled into my seat and was admiring the enormous rose stained glass window, Holmes silently slid in beside me.

"Where have you been?" I asked with great relief. "A great many powerful men in Vienna are extremely displeased with you! For all I knew, another assassin was on the prowl. I certainly hope you were exercising great caution!"

Holmes smiled warmly at me.

## Chapter 28: The Aftermath

"I appreciate your concern, old friend," he said. "I assure you I could not have been in a safer place."

Speeches by several powerful Archdukes and other officials, bedecked in their finest uniforms and medals, unsurprisingly averted any mention of the sensitive issues swirling around the late Crown Prince. No mention was made of suicide, of Hungarian rebels, of mental illness or of the poor, forgotten Baroness Mary Vetsera. From time to time, during lulls in the speeches, the mournful weeping of the Empress Elisabeth and others was clearly discernible.

The following day, utterly exhausted and considerably demoralised by our experience, we were again speeding across Austria and Germany on a train toward Belgium, where we would spend an evening before taking a short boat ride across the Channel. Holmes professed he had neither slept nor eaten since the confrontation with the Archdukes in the Hofburg palace and by the time we approached Ostend, he was grey and drawn.

His mood was as low as I had ever seen it, and I was overjoyed that he lacked access to the cocaine to which he often turned during periods of such emotional stress. I certainly shared his sense of outrage and helplessness over the events of the past week, but I knew better than to offer bromides or platitudes about the vexing machinations of the world of politics. That evening, he merely picked at the excellent steak and chips we were served at a quiet bistro in the Hazegras neighborhood not far from the waterfront. I decided to focus on my dinner and not intrude into his thoughts, at least for the evening.

Once on board the ship the next morning, however, I could no longer restrain myself. As we sat on the deck, wrapped up in thick blankets to ward off the chill, with steaming cups of coffee to warm our insides, I turned to him. He lay still with his eyes closed and his hands folded above the blanket, but I knew he was not asleep and ventured to engage him in conversation.

"Would you care to discuss the case?" I tentatively asked.

## Chapter 28: The Aftermath

Nothing but utter silence followed my inquiry, and I was determined to leave the next move in Holmes's hand. For fifteen minutes, he lay as still as an Egyptian mummy in an undiscovered tomb in Thebes as the ship cut through a thick Channel fog towards the Dover coast. Then, without any acknowledgement of my earlier query, he spoke for the first time in more than a day.

"A tragedy for nearly everyone," he pronounced, "and one whose impacts will surely be felt for years to come. These foolish people think they have removed a cancer that threatened their rotting and doomed Empire but they are quite wrong, you know. The decay goes far deeper than they might imagine. Whatever were Rudolf's shortcomings, and they certainly were plentiful, the actions of the conspirators has only hastened the spread of a contagion that, I anticipate, will consume them, their children and much of Europe."

"Perhaps they will be chastised by this experience and redouble their efforts to find political stability on the continent," I suggested hopefully, but Holmes was in a much darker mood.

"Good old Watson! Always aspiring for the optimistic conclusion! Well, I hope that your prediction is fulfilled, but I gravely fear a far more tumultuous outcome, one that Mycroft and these Austrians are desperate to avert. I see little prospect that the tensions between the Austrians and the Hungarians will be lessened by the removal of Rudolf," he insisted. "The disagreements between those who support and who oppose the great compromise that binds the two nations together will continue to rage. The nationalists in Serbia, Bosnia, Croatia and other states will grow in influence and resentment. Those who have endured acts of violence against their supporters doubtless will not hesitate to employ a similar viciousness against the Hapsburgs and their myrmidons. To think that this familial rivalry among competing nations can be assuaged by removing one mediocre Crown Prince is the sheerest of folly."

He paused and then leaned in closer to me to ensure that no one passing us on the deck might overhear his confession.

## Chapter 28: The Aftermath

"It is a somber message, Watson, and yet it is the one I conveyed to the Emperor and Empress!"

I was stunned; so *that* was where he had been in the hours before Rudolf's funeral -- in open defiance of the explicit instructions he had been given.

"Did not Mycroft advise you against relating your conclusions to the Emperor or to anyone else for that matter?" I asked.

"There are greater imperatives than following the advice of my older brother," declared Holmes. "And besides, I was no longer employed by the British government. My only employer was the Emperor himself, and my obligation was to provide him with the information he sought."

"Against the expressed wishes of Lord Salisbury?" I challenged.

"Do you not agree that His Majesty deserved to know the kinds of men in whom he has placed his trust and with whom he has entrusted his life? Of course, with the investigation abruptly terminated as it was, I could not provide him the level of proof that I fully expected he would demand."

"And what did you advise him, if I may ask?"

"To keep a firm grip on power and to refuse to yield it to any pretender for as long as he is physically capable of ruling."

"And did he indicate his intentions with respect to his advisors and family members who conspired against the Crown Prince?" I asked.

"He appeared both saddened and angered, but as a monarch, he knew better than to display open emotions to a commoner," Holmes said, "and I certainly did not expect him to share with me how he might respond to the revelations."

"And did your findings provide him any measure of comfort concerning Rudolf?" I inquired.

"The Emperor was hardly unaware of his son's many shortcomings – as a husband, a father or a statesman. And yet, he was

## Chapter 28: The Aftermath

genuinely distraught by the Crown Prince's death. In the end, Rudolf was his only son, and he was brutally taken from him. I suspect he shares my outlook that many more misfortunes will doubtless flow as a result of this skirmish with a new world order!"

\*     \*     \*

As was so often the case, Holmes's prophetic words, even in a field as alien to his expertise as international diplomacy, proved prescient. Many of the central figures in the Mayerling tragedy would live curiously brief or unhappy lives -- or both -- in the immediate aftermath of the affair. Some lost the prestigious careers that had elevated them to great power in the Austrian Empire. I cannot offer any proof, but it does seem that their fates may have been ascribed to the intervening hand of an avenging Emperor who, as a result of Holmes' revelations, understood the truth of what had occurred that grim night in January, 1889. A select few would reap rewards from their unmitigated loyalty to the royal family and especially to Rudolf, but the grim predictions Sherlock Holmes and Emperor Franz Joseph shared were proven all too accurate in the years ahead.

**Karl Ludwig**, the 56-year old younger brother of the Emperor never followed through on his private pledge to disclaim publicly all aspirations to the crown, although he immersed himself in the arts and sciences rather than statecraft. He was never designated Crown Prince by the Emperor, which proved irrelevant since he did not survive long enough to succeed his brother. During a visit to Palestine and Egypt in 1896, he mysteriously contracted typhoid and died after drinking from the purportedly restorative waters of the Jordan River. To be sure, there were rumors of his having been poisoned with arsenic, and after the experiences of Mayerling, neither Holmes nor I was prepared to dismiss the possibility. He was buried swiftly in the family crypt without benefit of an autopsy that might have ruled out foul play.

The **Archduke Albrecht**, whose iron-fisted control of the military had provided him with both a motive and means for disposing of Rudolf, aged rapidly in the aftermath of Mayerling. Perhaps the

## Chapter 28: The Aftermath

elderly general was haunted by guilt for his role in the plot. It was speculated that his unwillingness to yield his military authority -- even when he had grown virtually blind – was attributable to his fear that a successor might expose classified materials that revealed the old man's complicity in Rudolf's murder. Early in 1895, Albrecht died and was granted a state funeral and burial in the Imperial crypt, not far from where his victim, Rudolf, lay entombed.

The Minister-President **Viscount Eduard Taaffe** was abruptly dismissed from office by the Emperor in 1893 amid increased agitation between the German and Czech communities in Bohemia. Like Albrecht, Taaffe had seemed a diminished man following the death of the Crown Prince he had so clearly disdained. Like Albrecht, he curiously died just six years later.

Although **Franz von Krauss** remains alive as of this writing, he was soon removed from his position as Vienna's police president. A commoner who was more vulnerable than members of the aristocracy to prosecution for his role in the affair, he reportedly escaped punishment by claiming to possess a "secret file" containing explosive revelations about Mayerling that would deeply embarrass the conspirators. Von Krauss was effectively banished from Vienna by an appointment as the president of the Duchy of Bukovina, a distant and insignificant outpost of the Hapsburg Empire.[6]

"One must be struck by the rather rapid fall of so many of those implicated in the Mayerling tragedy," I said to Holmes after reading of Karl Ludwig's death in May of 1896.

He shrugged his shoulders. "Who is to say?" he speculated, tamping down the tobacco in his pipe. "In such an explosive scandal, one can never be sure that an incriminating detail or two will not find a fissure and bubble to the surface. Eliminating those who share the

---

[6] Editor's note: Krauss' "secret file" was given to his successor as police chief and did not surface publicly until 1955. While containing valuable information about the Mayerling case, materials containing important details about the true nature of what occurred at the hunting lodge had clearly been destroyed.

## Chapter 28: The Aftermath

secret is the only sure way to guarantee silence. Perhaps we should keep a careful eye cast over our own shoulders!" he said with a thin smile.

Not all those involved in the events of 30 January 1889 suffered such a loss of life, power or prestige; as is often the case in such political matters, loyalty has its rewards. Later in 1889, **Dr von Widerhofer**, who had concealed the Crown Prince's underlying health medical condition and spared the royal family much embarrassment by remaining silent on the fate of Baroness Mary Vetsera, was awarded the Order of the Iron Crown, 1st Class, an honour unheard of for a children's physician. One year later, he was elevated to the position of Freiherr, or Baron, granting him access to high society.

**Loschek**, the diminutive valet who had faithfully attended his Crown Prince to the end and remained silent on the fate of Baroness Vetsera, retired shortly after the tragedy and received a substantial grant of money from the Emperor in gratitude for his continued silence. Unsurprisingly, some of the wagging tongues in Vienna speculated that the silence of the former valet to the Crown Prince had been purchased. He spent the remainder of his life in the small town of Kleinwolkersdorf, where he renovated an abandoned brewery into a splendid residence, a remarkable achievement on the pension of a retired valet!

**Mizzi Kaspar**, the actress whose association with Rudolf did little to enhance her reputation or social standing, received a windfall of 30,000 guilders in the Crown Prince's will, a testament to the high regard in which he held the mistress to whom he had once proposed a suicide pact.[7] The money did her little good. The contagion that she had transmitted to Rudolf, who then passed it to Princess Stephanie, Mary Vetsera and perhaps many others, could not be effectively treated and grew steadily worse. She died in agony in 1901 at the age of just 43.

**Josef Bratfisch**, the carriage driver and whistler extraordinaire, refused all entreaties to reveal what really took place in the bedchamber

---

[7] Editor's note: Worth about $550,000 in 2023.

where he entertained the Crown Prince and Mary Vetsera just hours before they both were found dead. Soon after the tragedy, he appeared like Loschek to profit from a financial windfall. He acquired a private cab license and a house in the city's fashionable Lackergasse district that was far beyond the means of even the finest cab driver. Holmes suspected he used incriminating information to demand blackmail payments from one or more of the wealthy figures implicated in the assassination. Yet if that were the case, fate intervened, paying him back dearly for his manipulative behavior. Just three years after the Mayerling tragedy, at the age of just 45, he took his secrets to the grave.

The powerful influence of the royal family successfully repressed the details of **Mary Vetsera**'s presence at Mayerling for a very long period of time. A short note in the newspaper several days after Rudolph's funeral referred only to an "unknown female body" that had been found at the lodge, mentioning nothing about a suicide or any connection to the Crown Prince. The notes written that last evening by Mary to her family members have disappeared, although some believe them to be in the possession of her grieving mother, the **Baroness Helene**, whose pitiful pleas had been icily ignored by the Empress.[8] Distraught and embittered at the royal family, Helene Vetsera was nevertheless quietly paid a fantastic sum – 800,000 florins – in compensation for her loss, enough to purchase a sizeable estate where she continues to live as of this writing, mourning for her forgotten child whom some insist was the product of Helene's own illicit affair with the Emperor.[9] If true, the ramifications of a liaison between Rudolf and Mary Vetsera, not to mention the possible child of the half-siblings,

---

[8] Editor's note: As noted earlier, Mary's letters were discovered in a bank vault in the Schoeller Bank in Vienna 126 years after her death. The Austrian National Library reported that in 1926, "an unknown person deposited a leather-bound folder ... including the farewell letters of Mary Vetsera." It seems likely that Helene Vetsera is the person who deposited the family papers in the vault.

[9] Editor's note: Worth many millions of dollars in 2023.

## Chapter 28: The Aftermath

would add additional layers of intrigue and tragedy to the Mayerling story.

Mysteries continued to affect those involved with Rudolf and Mayerling. The Crown Prince's cousin, friend and likely co-conspirator in the Hungarian independence movement, **Archduke Johann Salvator**, apparently made good on his escape from Vienna. But Salvator must have known that he was not safe from Krauss, Albrecht and the others who knew he possessed the incriminating documents in the sealed metal box. He soon changed his name to John Orth and married his mistress, the opera dancer Milli Stubel. Together, they fled to South America on a ship he had acquired and spent a year sailing along the coast of that distant continent, only rarely coming ashore and then with the greatest of caution. Even with all these precautions, the ship, the Archduke and his wife disappeared in a terrible storm off Cape Horn in July, 1890. When reports reached Vienna of Salvator's loss at sea without a trace, rumors circulated that agents of Franz Joseph, who had detested him, or one or more of the Mayerling conspirators were behind his unexplained vanishing. In any event, the box has never reappeared and like Salvator himself, is presumed lost to the deep.

**Prince Philipp**, Rudolf's hunting companion who had brought the assassins to Mayerling (perhaps believing they were only under orders to apprehend him) suffered a different but no less envious fate. Trapped in his troubled marriage to Louise, the Empress Elisabeth's sister, he clashed frequently with his father-in-law, Belgium's Leopold II, over the savage abuse of the natives in the Congo, the King's private holding. The bitter disagreement destroyed whatever remained of the marriage and Philipp obtained a divorce in 1906, but his family troubles were far from over. A decade later, his son Prince Leopold Clement offered his mistress a substantial bribe to end their affair. She responded by shooting the young Prince five times and then throwing a bottle of sulfuric acid in his face before fatally shooting herself. Six months later, horribly disfigured and in unspeakable pain, Prince

## Chapter 28: The Aftermath

Philipp's son died an agonizing death. The Prince himself continues to live hermit-like in his palace in Coburg, devoting himself to his obsession with numismatics.

The **Countess Marie Larisch** was permanently banished from royal events by Elisabeth for facilitating the liaisons between the Rudolf and Mary Vetsera. After attending the momentous conclave with Holmes on the day of Rudolf's funeral, she never again set eyes on the interior of the Hofburg palace or upon the Emperor or Empress. Our communications with the Countess were not yet ended, however. Just one month after returning to England, Holmes received a letter in which she included a copy of a message that had arrived at her home shortly after the Prince's funeral. Suspiciously, the envelope had already been opened and resealed before being presented to the Countess.

"Forgive me all the trouble I have caused," read the note. "I thank you so much for everything you have done for me. If life becomes hard for you, and I fear it will after what we have done, follow us. It is the best thing you can do." The strange missive had been signed, "Mary."

How came the letter to the Countess weeks after the tragedy at Mayerling, and who had opened it prior to its delivery? Had Mary sought to entice the Countess from her grave to follow her in committing suicide? The Countess implored Holmes to investigate the curious missive, but my friend declared that while intrigued, his patience for the intrigues of the Austrian court was exhausted and he sent a response politely declining the request.

Trapped in the unhappy marriage that Empress Elisabeth had arranged, the Countess Marie finally secured a divorce from her elderly husband, fled to Bavaria and married an opera singer. But Mayerling followed her and due to her tainted reputation, her new husband's career faltered and he took to drink. Desperate for money, she contacted Emperor Franz Joseph and threatened to disclose licentious information about Rudolf unless she was given a generous financial settlement. Although he acquiesced in the demand, as the Empire hurtled towards fragmentation in the early years of the new century, she published her scandalous memoirs anyway.[10] At last report, she has been serving anonymously as a nurse in the current Great War.

The **Emperor Franz Joseph**, alerted by Holmes of the machinations of his family and closest advisors, spared no effort to confiscate (and likely destroy) as much of the evidence surrounding Mayerling and his son as he could locate. He even demolished most of the hunting lodge itself in hopes of obliterating the memory of the scandal, replacing it with a Carmelite monastery. Remarkably, he outlived virtually every other key participant in the Mayerling drama. Still, his own marriage suffered grievously in the aftermath of Mayerling and the related political intrigue. Relations with the Empress, never especially strong, rapidly deteriorated following their son's death, with some insisting that he blamed her for encouraging Rudolf's embrace of Hungarian independence. He continued a longstanding dalliance with Katharina Schratt, an actress, even building her an extravagant villa located in the same hideaway village as the Empress' own retreat.

For her part, **Empress Elisabeth** sought escape through extravagant travel to exotic locales, often in the company of the Hungarian Count Gyula Andrássy, whom she treasured as her "last and only friend." Her grief over the loss of her son was compounded by the deaths of her own sister and her mother in quick succession. Beset by death, she chose, like her close confident and our own Queen Victoria, to wear black mourning gowns for the remainder of her life. Always unconventional, she became increasingly eccentric, obsessed with her health, spending hours bathing daily in olive oil and wearing a night-

---

[10] Editor's note: Subsequent to Watson's authorship of this story, Marie Larisch moved to America (a newspaper claimed she offered to marry anyone who would pay her fare!) where she lived with yet another husband before returning to Germany in 1929. The one-time Countess, confidante to the Empress of Austria-Hungary and the Crown Prince, died impoverished in a nursing home in 1940.

## Chapter 28: The Aftermath

time mask of raw veal to preserve her skin's appearance. For months at a time, she subsisted on broth, oranges, eggs and raw milk.

The Emperor largely overlooked her undisputed adultery (he was hardly in a position to object) and her bizarre dietary regimen (for a time, she traveled with her own cow). But nearly a decade after the Mayerling tragedy, he became alarmed by the Empress' intention to publish her memoirs to correct the unfavourable portrayals of Rudolf, who had become the subject of wild rumors and ridicule.

I mentioned reading of her threat to Holmes just after he solved the case involving the curious "dancing men" in the summer of 1898.

A dark look crossed his face.

"I would advise the Empress to be cautious in offering a strident defense of her son or in venturing to disclose aspects of the Mayerling mystery that have long remained hidden," he said. "It is true many who were implicated in the plot escaped earthly justice, but others remain poised to exact a price against anyone who might reveal the details of the conspiracy."

"But the Empress of Austria!" I protested.

"These are the associates of men who thought nothing of killing the future *Emperor* of Austria," Holmes reminded me. "In light of the grave unrest churning across the continent, I doubt they would look favourably on attempts to dredge up Rudolf's ghost, let alone level new accusations about the conspiracy."

"Might you not raise these concerns with Mycroft?" I asked. "Perhaps he might find a way the Foreign Office could help deter publication of such revelations."

Holmes's jaw set firmly at my words.

"Mycroft's advice was quite clear a decade ago when we last immersed ourselves in the affairs of the Hapsburgs," he said sourly through tightly clenched teeth. He waved away the thought as though it were a pesky gnat. "I have no interest in elbowing my way into the maelstrom of international politics again. If Mycroft or the government determines it is in the nation's interest to intervene – and I presume they read the newspapers as well as you and I – they are free to do so without any effort on my part."

I knew Holmes well enough to know his mind was irrevocably set against playing any role whatsoever and I allowed the topic to drop. I began instead to ramble on about the new racing season and some Derby prospects that seemed very promising.

Soon enough, however, calamity again visited once of those involved in the Mayerling affair. Just three weeks later, all of Europe was stunned by the murder of the Empress Elisabeth in Geneva. Out for a walk with her lady-in-waiting, the Empress was assaulted by an Italian anarchist, Luigi Lucheni, who buried a metal file deep in her chest. No clear connection was ever made between the assassin and the Empress, although the speculation ran rampant that he was engaged to prevent her from revealing details of the Mayerling affair. A decade later, despite unsuccessful efforts to pry answers from him, Lucheni was found hanged -- in a locked prison cell!

The assassination of the Empress Elisabeth of Austria by Lucheni

## Chapter 28: The Aftermath

With the turn of the twentieth century, it seemed that the spate of deaths associated with the Mayerling case finally had come to an end, but one more victim was still to meet his fate, and with dreadful consequences.

**Franz Ferdinand**, who had been officially designated Crown Prince after his father's death, was a "reformer," sharing many of the late Crown Prince's ideas for modernizing the Empire. The Emperor was frustrated not only by his nephew's political views but also by his adamant refusal to marry Rudolf's widow, Princess Stephanie. Instead, he wed the Countess Sophie Chotek, a marriage so vigorously opposed by Franz Joseph that he declared it a morganatic union, which rendered any children of the union ineligible to inherit the throne. The Emperor underscored his disapproval by truculently refusing to attend the wedding ceremony, as did the new Crown Prince's own brothers.

"The royal house of Hapsburg appears to have learned nothing from the turmoil and tragedy of the last decade," said Holmes as we read a particularly lurid account of the 1900 nuptials. "Between their palace intrigues and petty jealousies, the conspiracies and secret agreements, they and the other inter-related rulers of the European states have spun so flammable a web that it will require only a small spark to set off the entire continent like a barrel of dynamite."

"I should say so!" I agreed wholeheartedly. "Counts and Baronesses, assassins and anarchists. Why, it is impossible to know who the statesmen are and who is bent on destroying the established order so they may profit from its collapse! I thank goodness we have the trusty Channel between us that ensures England our continued security whenever that spark ignites in Europe."

"Ah, Watson, as I warned at the outset of this adventure, I fear you put undue faith in the security of the Channel," he responded. "There are new artillery guns with awesome range, bombs of unimaginable destructive capacity, even military vehicles made from amoured motorcars," he declared. "For all we know, men will someday be dropping bombs on London from hot-air balloons! The most

## Chapter 28: The Aftermath

creative inventions of man are soon converted into weapons of destruction." The prospect of our island enduring such vulnerability left me speechless.

"We are inextricably linked to the continent, I fear," Holmes continued. "Not only do we share trade and colonial relationships, but its leaders are inextricably related to our own. Victoria's uncle became king of the Belgians, while her grandson Wilhem, is the Kaiser of Germany. Many fear he may be the one to take up arms against us. One might hope these relationships would bind us together but I fear they will prove useless in preventing a conflagration."

Of course, as we now know, that dreaded spark was ignited a decade and a half later in 1914. Not surprisingly, it originated with the star-crossed Hapsburgs. As with Hungary in the days of Rudolf, once again a part of the Empire seeking greater independence from Austria was connected to the tragedy. As Crown Prince Franz Ferdinand and Sophie visited Sarajevo in June of that year, a Bosnian-Serb demanding independence assassinated the royal couple. The Emperor, who seemed to have learned little from his family turmoil of the prior 30 years, expressed little sorrow at the murder of his nephew and even less appreciation for the implications of the catastrophe.

"For me," he told his daughter following Franz Ferdinand's brutal death, "it is a relief from a great worry." Within a month, however, Austria-Hungary had declared war against Serbia, a response that rapidly metastasized into the Great War that continues to rage across Europe even as I write this account.

"I wonder how this might have been had Franz Joseph embraced the reforms and diplomatic alliances sought by Rudolf all those years ago," Holmes wondered one evening during his visit to my home in London. "How strange to think that the visit from Lord Salisbury to consult with the Austrian Emperor should have started us down this tragic path."

"Do you fancy events may have turned out differently had you challenged Mycroft's admonition to leave the matter in the hands of the

*Chapter 28: The Aftermath*

Austrians?" I wondered. "Perhaps Britain might have played a more constructive role in tempering the internecine passions of the Hapsburgian court."

Holmes smiled and drew on his pipe. It was nearly thirty years since the affair at Mayerling lodge, and he surely had long ago dispensed with speculation about how different the world might be had Rudolf survived or his killers had been officially brought to justice, if he had ever considered the subject at all.

"No, Watson, it is 1916 and there is no benefit to playing the game of second-guessing history," he advised. "We could not have known in 1889 that Mayerling would represent the seed from which such a deadly and destructive weed would spring. But I do hope the world is paying closer attention today so that we never again will witness so tragic and misguided a chapter in history."

# For Further Reference: A Selected Bibliography

Earlier accounts of the events at Mayerling lodge obviously lack the vital additional information made available in this newly uncovered eyewitness report authored in 1916 by Dr John H. Watson, which remained unpublished for over a century. Nevertheless, numerous examinations of the case might be of interest to readers seeking additional information.

Among the valuable source material on the subject are Greg King and Penny Wilson, *Twilight of Empire: The Tragedy at Mayerling and the End of the Hapsburgs* (St. Martin, 2017), Ann Dukthas, *Time of Murder at Mayerling* (St. Martins, 1996), Countess Mary Larisch, *My Life* (Putnam, 1913), Georg Markus, *Crime at Mayerling: The Life and Death of Mary Vetsera, With New Expert Opinions Following the Desecration of Her Grave* (Ariadne, 1994), Count Egon Corti and Catherine Alison Phillips *Elizabeth, Empress of Austria* (1934, reprinted Kessinger Publishing, 2008); Brigette Hamann, *Rudolf: Crown Prince and Rebel* (Peter Lang, 2017 reprint); and Alan Palmer, *Twilight of the Hapsburgs: The Life and Times of Emperor Francis Joseph* (Monthly Press, 1994).

Articles of interest include "Memoirs Give Light on Mayerling Deaths," *New York Times* (August 6, 1930); "*Mayerling Remains A Mystery" New York Times (January 26, 1964)*; Lucy Coatman, "Love Is Dead" *History Today* (vol. 72, #2 (February 2, 2022); Serge Schmemann, "Mayerling Journal; Lurid Truth and Lurid Legend: A Hapsburg Tale, *New York Times* (March 10, 1989). In 1929, a French author wrote an article bemoaning the fact that Holmes had missed the opportunity to investigate the Mayerling mystery. Joseph Quintin, "De Sherlock Holmes à Mayerling" *Les Maîtres de la Plume* (v. 5 No. 3) (February, 1929).

There are also numerous highly dramatised and largely (often preposterously) inaccurate film version of these events including " "Mayerling" (1936), "Le Secret de Mayerling" (1949) and the cringingly terrible "Mayerling" with Omar Shariff as Rudolf and the supremely ill-cast Catherine Deneuve as Mary Vetsera (1968). The Empress," a multi-episode German series released on Netflix in 2022, focuses on the Empress Elisabeth's early life as does "Sisi," a series broadcast in 2021 on PBS Masterpiece.

An exhaustive list of books, plays and other literature written about the Mayerling case may be found at
https://en.wikipedia.org/wiki/Mayerling_incident#cite_note-21.

BELANGER BOOKS

BELANGERBOOKS.COM